The Stepping Match
and Other Stories from Rural Kerry

Martin Mulvihill

RED HEN PUBLISHING

The Stepping Match and Other Stories from Rural Kerry
First published in 2007
by Red Hen Publishing, Duagh, Listowel, Co Kerry, Ireland
www.redhen-publishing.com
Email: redhen1@eircom.net

Cover painting 'The Blacksmith' by Jane Hilliard.
Gallery and Studio, The Mall, Tralee, Co Kerry, Ireland
Tel: +00353 (0) 66 718 0055.
www.janehilliard.com
Email: info@janehilliard.com

Cover photography by Dillon Boyer, Listowel, Co Kerry

Copyright Martin Mulvihill 2007

All rights reserved.
No part of this publication may be reproduced or used in any form or by any means – photographic, electronic or mechanical, including photocopying, recording, taping or information storage and retrieval systems – without the prior permission of the publisher in writing.

ISBN 0-9552920-4-2
ISBN 978-0-9552920-4-0

Printed in England by JH Haynes & Co Ltd, Sparkford, Somerset

The Stepping Match
and Other Stories from Rural Kerry

*To my wife, Peggie,
to my family,
and in memory of my late sister, Mai*

Contents

Foreword 6
Introducing Ballymachad, County Kerry................................ 8
The Mighty Spadesmen.. 15
The Redden Farm 20
The Pig in the Tub 27
The Fair and the Gamble 34
Turkeys 51
The Stepping Match 59
The Handball and the Goat 83
Poaching and Toaching 88
A Day in Bog and a Day in Court 107
Wakes 118
Evictions and Emigration 126
A Memorable Match 132
Wedding Bells 153
The McGurks 182
Postscript 223

Foreword

My life has spanned the best part of a century and I have seen extraordinary changes in Ireland throughout that time. With the arrival of each successive generation, I see traditions and lifestyles changing and as we move and progress and develop, I often think of the people who came before us and who survived in a harsh Ireland most of us would not recognize today.

I met some of those people when I was a boy and they were in the last years of their lives. I also heard stories of their lives from my parents, grandparents and neighbours. I have written their stories as I recall them in an attempt to honour the history of our ancestors who lived through one of the harshest periods in Irish history, from the late 1800s through the early decades of the 20th century. Many of these people had survived famine, as had their forebears. They continued to endure lives of great poverty as peasant farmers who had to rent land from landlords, paying exorbitant rents and striving just to survive and feed their families.

This was the era of Penal Laws, a time of great persecution and hardship. Yet, in spite of their living conditions, the people remained resilient, sharing with each other what little they had and helping out in times of desperation. They sowed and reaped, sang and danced, loved and married and raised large families. Hard work was the norm but people also made time for enjoying themselves. They would enjoy crossroads dancing on summer evenings and sparks were knocked off the road as they danced sets and hornpipes with their hob-nailed boots.

They also enjoyed the odd football match between townlands and during the long winter nights there were visits to rambling houses to play cards and maybe dance sets if someone arrived with a fiddle or concertina. The card game would continue until the early hours, even though the stakes weren't high, only a few pence per man. It wasn't the money they were playing for, but the sheer love of the game and, of course, relaxation from the harsh existence of the times. Women had their own ways of relaxing, including sewing and knitting. Many houses boasted a spinning wheel and operating it was a form of relaxation. From the cloth they spun, the women made beautiful clothes for themselves and their children, as well as bawneens for the men.

Although they were mostly uneducated, these people were a proud race whose Christian faith meant a lot to them and whose dependence on their neighbours forged bonds of community no longer seen in Ireland. These people are our ancestors and their determination to survive and live helped form the basis for the Ireland we have today.

Ní bheidh a leithéid ann arís.

Martin Mulvihill

Introducing Ballymachad, County Kerry

Back in the distant and, indeed, not so distant past, each parish community in Ireland had the autonomy to be, more or less, economically viable. Visits outside the parish were few and far between. Those that took place were generally to cattle fairs or markets for agricultural produce such as potatoes, oats, mangolds, turnips and butter. The make-up of the parish included the parish priest and usually a curate, the carpenter, the stonemason and the shoemaker supported by a few cobblers. There would also be a tailor, and two in some parishes. The dressmaker was an important and busy person. The teacher was a highly respected person in the community as were the doctor and the midwife who attended at all the parish births. A very important person in the community was the woman who would 'lay-out' the dead. Then there was the plasterer and the blacksmith and, as the poem says, "A mighty man was he".

Every parish would have its thatcher, or maybe two or three, as most houses and outhouses of that period were thatched. Each community boasted about its mowers and spadesmen. There used to be fierce competition and jealousies between parishes concerning the 'deeds', that is, the output of work and the style and taste of their mowers and spadesmen. The cooper ran a very important business, making barrels and firkins for the butter trade. There was also the travelling tinsmith who would make various items from discarded tin, such as cups and pannies and tin plates. The good thing about those utensils was that they were unbreakable.

There was the traveling dancing master and music teacher as well as horse trainers and the odd amateur jockey. The amateur butchers were usually farmers and they would oblige a neighbour who needed to kill a pig for their own consumption. There would be a variety of handymen, often despised by the professionals who would describe them as the 'Jack of all trades and master of none'. The village constable was the most unpopular person in the place, both hated and feared. The bulk of the parish community comprised farmers and farm workers, who laboured hard for poor reward. Also present in the parish was every kind of a character – tricksters and pranksters, bluffers and gamblers, patriots and spies, trainee soldiers, armed and otherwise, anxious for a 'crack at the Crown'. There were quacks of various disciplines. There were dancers and singers who enjoyed the crossroad dances on summer evenings and the rambling house on winter nights. Though sounding like a motley crew, there was a wonderful spirit of co-existence and, as everyone knew each other and almost everything about each other, there was great camaraderie.

The Thatcher Brady and Mickey Joe Dan never spoke to each other. They didn't know why, it was just that their fathers were never on speaking terms, it was just handed down. One day a cow of Mickey Joe Dan's fell into a dyke and he and his son, Mickey Óg, were trying to lift her out. As the Thatcher Brady walked down the road he spotted them and, without hesitation, knowing that a cow on the flat of her back in a dyke wouldn't live long, he jumped over the ditch and ran across the field to help them. The operation successfully completed and the cow saved, the Thatcher Brady walked back across the field again and continued his journey and not one word passed between the men. As the saying goes, 'actions sometimes speak louder than words'. That was standard behaviour in rural communities at that period.

The Farmer

Back in the days after the three Fs were achieved, that is Fair Rent, Fixity of Tenure and Freedom of Sale, rural communities in Ireland became more or less self-sufficient. Farmers produced their own food, for example, every farmer in that period grew potatoes, turnips and cabbage. They also grew wheat, oats and barley – the oats and barley were fed to the cattle, horses and pigs, while the wheat was ground into flour for human consumption. In many parts of the country there were water-powered mills to which farmers took their grain to be crushed into flour or animal feed. Many farmers also had hand-operated crushing stones on which they could crush the wheat and produce their own flour. At that period every farmer, big or small, would have at least one sow which would produce about two litters of banbhs each year, or possibly five litters in two years. Most farmers would sell the banbhs at ten to twelve weeks of age, while others would fatten them to slaughter weight, but all farmers would fatten at least one 'for the tub' – this meant a pig for their own consumption which would be slaughtered on the farm and cured by salting. It would then be stored in a barrel in pickle. Money might be scarce and the work might be hard, but the family that would have a pit of spuds, a pit of turnips, a haggard of cabbage and a pig in the tub as winter approached would be as 'happy as Larry'.

The 'strength' of a farmer was judged by the number of cows his farm was able to carry. Ten cows was considered a big herd, but a herd of seven or eight was more the norm. As there were no creameries at the time, the milk, which had to be hand-milked, would be set in big basins and kept in them for several hours until the cream came to the top. It would then be skimmed off and made into butter by various means, depending on the amount of cream available. This was usually done in a churn with a handle fitted with a flat, circular board at its base and the cream would be pounded until the butter was made. It would then be collected, squeezed of the buttermilk and weighed into one pound units for sale to local shops. Bigger quantities would be stored in firkins and would be sold to butter buyers for the export market. Some farmers would come together when they had what they considered a horse-load of butter and one of them would drive his horse to Cork to sell the load. This journey would take at least two and sometimes three days depending on a number of factors, such as waiting their turn to unload, as farmers from a large hinterland would be supplying that market. There were certain farmhouses along the way where they could feed, water and rest the horse and have a meal and a rest themselves. The next time there was a load ready for the market, another farmer would take his horse and make the journey. That system continued for many years until creameries were established.

The Priest

The priest was considered the most important person in the community, not alone because of his ministry, but also for the fact that people could go to him for advice and help with any problems they might have, especially if it entailed letter writing. It must be remembered that, at this period in Irish history, the vast majority of the population were semi-literate or illiterate. Consequently the priest was the obvious person to go to when parishioners had any correspondence which demanded confidentiality. The priest was also called upon to settle disputes between neighbours, including those involving rights of way, marriage settlements and various other incidents that arose in the parish. His arbitration was usually accepted by all parties concerned. Nowadays people go to a solicitor to deal with similar issues. The priest was, perhaps, the one person in the parish who understood the value and indeed the necessity of education for the local children.

Pondering this in his mind for some time, the parish priest of Ballmachad decided to go public on the matter, so one Sunday, after the homily, he mentioned the subject. He felt it was well received and was thrilled that there was a positive response to his views on education. Just as soon as he had his vestments off, two men and one woman came into the sacristy to talk to him about it. Delighted that the parents were interested, he said, "Ye can put the wheels rolling right away if ye let me know of any old buildings that could be converted to a school". They promised him that they would make inquiries and would come back to him. Within the week, the priest got an offer of a large, semi-derelict house situated about two hundred yards up a boreen. Of course, it needed some repairs but all the tradesmen and handy men of the parish came together and, suffice it to say, within a month it was a school. And it must be recorded that the interest of that priest in the education of the youth changed the lives of those children forever.

The Tailor

The tailor, sitting in his unique way on a big, specially designed table, made the clothes for the men. The customer bought the cloth complete with the 'trimmings' and would take it to the tailor. For the suit to keep its shape, the quality of the trimmings was most important, the tailor would stress. The biggest part of his business though, would be the making of bawneens, a white, cardigan-like garment made of a homespun, flannel cloth which was very popular with the menfolk of the time, both for everyday working use and for Sunday wear. Even though many women were capable of making their own clothes, there were also dressmakers in every parish. These too were kept busy as there were no clothes shops as we know them nowadays and anyhow the town was too far away. There was one particular tailor whose table was in the kitchen, up against a big wide window facing the public road. It was the proper place for it as it gave the tailor plenty of light to do his sewing and it also gave him a view of all the comings and goings in the village. If someone wanted to know if a particular person had gone up or down the road, 'twas just a case of ask the tailor and all would be revealed.

Ballymachad's tailor was very interested in football and, as it happened, just across the road from his house was a football field where all the young boys of the parish would meet every evening to play football. It transpired that two boys, Jack and Joe, became very accurate place kickers and every evening they would hone their skill by taking shots at an old door standing in the middle of the field. One fateful summer evening they noticed the tailor watching them from his window, which he had opened as he carried on sewing. Of course, temptation is always lurking in the background and the thought came to Joe that it would be great sport to take a shot at the tailor across the road sitting on his table, sewing. No sooner said than done! The two boys tossed a coin to see which would take the kick and it fell to Joe to take it. Joe, the instigator of the idea, wasn't too happy now when the chips were down. But Jack urged him on, saying, "I'll place the ball on a nice spot for you, so take your time and wait until he has his back turned you and then give it a lash".

By now, a big crowd of players and spectators had gathered and were watching events in awe. After trying a few spots, Jack placed the ball where he thought was dead straight in front of the tailor's window. Joe stood a good distance back and, after a few minutes, walked to the ball and moved it slightly to the south and then moved back again. "Come on, give it a lash – you can do it no bother to you," urged Jack. Joe made no reply, but moved back a big distance and, with hands on hips and taking big breaths, he suddenly ran forward at terrific speed, gave the ball a lash and it hit the tailor between the shoulders and nearly knocked him off the table. What was going to happen now? That was the next problem. The tailor settled that. He appeared at his front door with the ball in his hand and he shouted at the boys, "One of yer balls went astray. I'll kick it back to ye" – which he did and the episode was never mentioned again.

The Carpenter

Carpenters made horses' and asses' cars. They were also adept at making the wheels for those cars, which was a great art. They roofed houses and made the doors and windows and all the furniture, including tables, chairs and beds. They floored the lofts and made the ladder to get up to them. They made wooden troughs for feeding pigs and calves and poultry. In short, they made everything wooden that was needed in the house and farm. The local carpenter also made the coffins for the dead. The family of the deceased would ask a neighbour to go to town with a horse and car for the timber, the 'mountings' and the 'padding' and deliver them to the carpenter's workshop. The carpenter would have given him a list of what was required. The following day the coffin would be ready and would be collected by the same neighbour. A very decent type of man, the carpenter of Ballymachad was reputed to have made coffins for many poor people who couldn't afford to pay him. He would know well in advance of some deaths that a particular family would not be able to pay him, but he would always make it a point to have a coffin ready for them.

He would be called upon to make three types of cars – a horse's car, a pony's car and donkey's car. To keep the required stocks of timber, he would go to town to the 'dale' yard on a day every two or three weeks and his orders would be delivered to him by horse in due course. He would also have to order nails and paint and all the requisites for his business. If he was called upon to roof a house and make the windows for it, he would have to take measurements of the proposed roof and windows and would order the timber accordingly from the dale yard. The merchants of that era had big horses for delivering orders of that size, although such large orders were relatively few as the ordinary people could not afford large houses. Landlords were the only people who could afford the luxury of a big house, providing work for the stonemason and the carpenter in their construction.

The Blacksmith

The blacksmith was a very important man in the community and his forge was a great focal point and a hive of activity. It was unique for two reasons – the sound and the smell. The sound came from the 'ring' of the anvil and the smell from the burning hoof of the horse, as the blacksmith pressed the shoe against it to ascertain size and fit. The forge was the place where farmers took their horses and ponies and asses to be shod and on a wet day it would be very busy as no work could be done on the land. As there would generally be a long wait to get an animal shod, in order to pass the time, customers would swap yarns, many of them tall stories. It was a well-known fact that anyone who had the reputation of been inquisitive would get an earful and it would take him some time to sift the lies from the truth. But the curious thing about such a character was that, although he'd find out in time that he'd been lied to, he'd still come back for more. The precision measurements needed for shoeing animals were ascertained by using a tool called a 'traveler'. The traveler consisted of a timber wheel, probably six or seven inches in diameter, with a wooden handle. With this the smith would measure the circumference of the wheel by the number of rotations and match it to the internal circumference of the band.

The real precision test was to have the internal circumference of the band smaller by the exact amount so as to have the perfect fit when the band 'cooled' after 'shoeing'. The farmer might also have to supply a load of turf to redden the band. The band was reddened to expand so that it would fit easily over the wheel and, when cooled immediately with plenty of cold water, it would contract and settle at the correct pressure and give many years of service. The smith would usually arrange to have a number of wheels to shoe at any one time as the one fire would be capable of reddening several bands together, thus saving the considerable length of time it took to get a fire started and up to the required heat to redden the bands. Before the introduction of the mowing machine, the smith was adept at tackling scythes for the haymaking season. Tackling a scythe was a great art and the men that worked them were very critical if they weren't set to their liking. Hard to blame them as a badly set scythe was very hard on the mower and the men's output would be reduced accordingly. Some of the blacksmiths were very witty and jocular characters, presumably because there were some great characters among their clientele and they had to be able to hold their own. Their humour brightened up an otherwise difficult existence and, even though someone had to be the scapegoat, everyone tried to get their own back and this in turn added to the craic.

The Mighty Spadesmen

Nowadays they are referred to as the 'bad old days', the times when money was a scarce commodity, when work on the land was hard and strenuous, when the farmer and farm worker really earned their bread by the sweat of their brow. Those were the times before the advent of the sliced pan or bottled milk, or dance halls, or, more importantly, social welfare payments. How useful the cheque in the post would have been then! Those were the times when the pattern of work separated the men from the boys, when the spadesman and the mower were held in high regard. Men like Jimeen Hynes, nicknamed 'Jimeen the Man', and Peter McAdoo, known as 'Small Peter' (not that he was small by any means but he happened to be somewhat smaller than his very large father who was also named Peter) – these men could go down in history as the first agricultural contractors. These were two mighty men with the spade or the scythe who few men could follow. To 'follow' meant to be able to keep up with them turning a 'tiobh-oid' or mowing a field of hay. The tiobh-oid was 'turning bawn' with the spade, which was a great art and hard work. It consisted of preparing the ground for the planting of the potatoes and it had to be done as 'straight as a rule' otherwise it would be considered shabby and unworkmanlike and any farmer or spadesman with pride in their work wouldn't tolerate it.

And it was a fact of life at the time, even though incomes were bad, that farmers had great pride in their farming and it was as a consequence of this that the services of Jimeen the Man and Small Peter were in such great demand. Their work was always first class and they always gave an honest day's work for a good day's pay. And they had the sign of it – their hands were calloused as hard as iron from the spadetree and the dourneens of the scythe. They were lean and fit with muscles in their arms as big as small turnips. For dinner they would eat bacon and cabbage and a handy pot of spuds washed down with mugs of buttermilk. It was reckoned that during the warm weather of the mowing season they would each drink a gallon of porter a day. The porter was part of the contract and it was a common sight on those hot summer days to see a farmer's wife with her donkey and cart driving to the public house with the gallon jar lying flat in the cart in a bed of hay and then coming home with the jar standing erect full of porter for the mowers.

Most farmers in that period hired a 'servant boy' and some would have a 'servant girl' as well. The hired boy or girl would live in with the farm family and would not go home again until the period they were hired for, usually from mid-January to Christmas, had expired. They would make the trek home, perhaps on the day before Christmas Eve, and would be welcomed by their families, who expected them to have spared a bit of money over the year to help with the Christmas buying. The amount spared would have been small as the wages paid to a servant boy would have been, perhaps, two pounds per month, and many farmers couldn't afford to pay even that much.

One such farmer was Mickeen Hendron – he was nicknamed the 'Briar' because of his abrasive manner and quick temper. Mickeen was a powerfully built man, over six feet tall, and a great spadesman. He and his wife worked their small farm on their own as they could not afford the luxury of a servant boy. However, in the springtime, Mickeen would hire a man for a week or two to help him 'set' the garden and, believe it, that man would earn his money. Mickeen would call him at five o'clock in the morning and, after a quick breakfast, would start turning bawn without stopping, except for dinner in the middle of the day and tea taken out to the garden to them by the wife at four o'clock, until around seven o'clock in the evening. Mickeen would work so hard that in time no man who ever had the misfortune of 'giving' him a week would ever want to have anything to do with him again. That included all the local labouring men who normally would be anxious for a few weeks' work in the springtime. So the Briar had to go further afield to get help. One Sunday afternoon he tackled the jennet and drove across the hill to an area where he was unknown. He arrived home at some hour that night with a tall, lanky, hungry-looking young fellow, a poor misfortune who had no idea of what he was facing – or so it seemed.

On Monday morning the Briar started with the usual routine – up at five o'clock and himself and his man went to the garden. On the way they met Patsy Crowley who was driving in his cows to be milked and, as they exchanged a few pleasantries, Patsy was sizing up the stranger with the Briar, wondering who he was and where he got him. Patsy was quick to convey the news to the neighbours about meeting the Briar and this 'gorsoon' with him – who was a complete stranger – and their spades over their shoulders, heading for the garden.

"What kind of a bloke is he?" asked Paddy the Lad. Now Paddy the Lad's proper name was Patrick Connelly but he was such a character for cod-acting and playing tricks on people that he was nicknamed 'Paddy the Lad'.

"To tell you the truth and I won't tell you a lie," said Patsy, "but I must say that I never saw a spade on the shoulder of a weaker, thinner, more miserable looking human being in my life. He's tall and rawney with nothing there but skin and bone."

"Where did he get him?" asked the Lad.

"I haven't an idea," said Patsy, "but wherever he found him or wherever he came from he must be starved."

"Do you think that he'll be able to follow the Briar?" asked the Lad.

"Follow him is it? Not at all, he was hardly able to follow him up the passage," said Patsy.

So the news spread about this 'poor misfortune', who, it was widely thought, the Briar would have killed before the week was out. It must be said that there was great sympathy for this boy and from none more so than the Lad who himself suffered, as he often said, a week's penance at the hands of the Briar.

Would he survive the day? That was the question on everyone's mind.

In the meantime, the Briar and his man were working away. In fairness to the Briar, he took it nice and handy for the start, just to see how Tommy – that was his name, Tommy Burns – was faring. As the day wore on he'd step up a gear now and again, and if he would, so would Tommy. Day two arrived and Patsy met them again, their spades over their shoulders, as he drove in his cows. They passed a few words about the weather and moved on. An hour later Patsy met the Lad.

"Any news?" asked the Lad.

"Well," said Patsy, "wonders will never cease. I met the Briar and his man again this morning."

"And how's the young fellow?" asked the Lad.

"The same way, miserable looking, but no better or worse. Today will be the real test," Patsy said.

Having arrived at the garden, the Briar started turning tiobh-oids at a lively pace and, if he did, Tommy kept with him. Soon he was at his best and still Tommy stayed the pace with him. The Briar was beginning to get frustrated, no one had ever pushed him to the limit before and now this slip of a young fellow was doing just that.

"I can't get away from him," the Briar thought to himself, "and I only hired him so as not to give it to say to the neighbours that I couldn't get a man. It never dawned on me that he'd be able to turn bawn like a man."

Thinking these thoughts and getting slightly worried about himself, Mickeen wondered if there was something wrong with him, if he was slowing down. However, when they finished for the night, he looked long and hard at the length of tiobh-oids the two of them had turned that day and he felt happy. With a smirk on his face he said to himself, "I'm a good man all the time, but that young fellow is no bad man either," and they turned towards the house and supper. The Lad made it his business to meet them as they came towards the house, just to get a look at this poor fellow and see if he was able to stagger home. His comment to Patsy afterwards was, "He's mighty thin but, fair play to him, he's still walking!"

And so the Briar and his gorsoon worked every day with great tempo, the young fellow really pushing the Briar to the limit. Saturday arrived, Tommy's last day as he had been hired just for the week, and at around three o'clock curiosity got the better of Patsy, the Lad and a few others.

"Wouldn't it be great craic to ramble up to the Briar's garden and see for ourselves how the young fellow is faring," said the Lad, "he'll surely be fagged out by now. How did he stick it at all?"

With such thoughts they walked leisurely to the garden. There, to their amazement, they found the Briar and Tommy neck and neck turning bawn at a furious pace. Neither even bothered to look at their visitors, so engrossed were they in their work. And then it happened. Tommy gave a shout – "Come on Mickeen, let's show them how 'tis done". And then, like a man inspired, he started slowly but surely to pull away from Mickeen the Briar. The Lad and company couldn't believe their eyes and were rooted to the ground at the sight of this slip of a gorsoon ever so easily moving away from the feared Briar.

They could sense, too, that the Briar was feeling the ignominy of it, especially in front of such a critical audience. They waited to see the finish to headland and saw Tommy finishing six spades ahead. They waited on until the Briar finished his tiobh-oid and, when he did, he stuck his spade in the ground, took off his cap and, wiping the sweat from his face with it, he turned to Tommy, shook his hand and said, "Tommy, will you give me another week?"

"No," said Tommy, "you're a good man Mickeen and if you do as much work every week as you did this week you wouldn't need me at all. Anyway I have to defend my title next week and I must say that this week was a great practice run."

"What title?" asked the Briar.

"What title is it?" said Tommy. "I'm the champion tiobh-oid turner of Kerry for the past two years and next week I hope to win it again."

The Lad and his friends were flabbergasted and the Briar, looking in awe at Tommy, said, "Say that again boy. I want to be sure I heard you right". When he had repeated that he was indeed the Kerry champion, the Briar shook Tommy's hand again and said, "I wish you the best of luck and I hope you will win it again".

"And we all wish you the same," said the Lad, still in a bit of a trance.

The Briar looked at his garden and then looked at his neighbours and, with a smirk of a triumphant smile said, "I thought I was slipping but now I feel great – to be able to stick the pace for a full week with the Champ". His honour as a spadesman was restored in the presence of his neighbours and that meant a lot to him. When Patsy got his speech back, he exclaimed, "God rest my Mother. She always used to say 'never judge the book by the cover and always be cautious of strangers'". They all went home and after supper the Briar tackled the jennet and took Tommy home across the hill and to this day the story is told of the day the Briar met his match. But the Briar was happy – he was now ready to set his spuds.

The Redden Farm

In terms of scale Tom Redden's farming operation was unique around Ballymachad. It must be remembered that, at that period, the average size of cattle herds on the vast majority of farms was eight to ten dairy cows and was often as low as four or five. With a herd of some forty cows, Tom Redden's farm was indeed unique. How he built up such a herd nobody knew or questioned. Rumour had it that, at one stage, he had received a big legacy from an old aunt in America. A legacy considered big in those days wouldn't, in today's terms, be considered big at all. But at that time two or three hundred pounds would do wonders for the average farmer, it would set him up for life. Whether or not Tom Redden got a legacy is irrelevant. What is relevant is his farming practice and the scale of it. Forty cows to be hand-milked every morning and evening was a lot of work and required a lot of help.

This help came in the form of dairymaids, mostly young girls – and Tom Redden would probably have six, or possibly eight, employed. Their wages would be small, as all wages were at that time, but they would be 'fed and found', which meant that they would get their wages, their grub and their lodgings. At that time dairymaids would consider themselves lucky. Their job was to milk the cows twice a day and set the milk in large pans in the dairy. The dairy was a building close to the cow byre, or cow stall as it was sometimes known, and it was always kept spotlessly clean and rodent-proof. It was fitted with tables the full length of the building and on those tables the pans to hold the milk would be laid out in rows. The dairymaids would deposit the milk as they milked it into these pans or containers. Here it would be left to set for several hours until all the cream came to the top and then the dairymaids would skim off the cream and store it, usually in white enamelled buckets, for transfer to the churn to be made into butter. Then the containers would have to be washed perfectly clean in preparation for the evening milking.

As there was no such thing as running water at the time, all the water required had to be drawn in buckets from the well. The evening's milk would be let set for the night and on some farms the dairymaids had to be up very early in the morning to have the cream skimmed off and the pans washed and ready for the morning milking. Some farms, including Reddens, had the capacity to store the two milkings, morning and evening, which made the work that much easier. The churning, that is the making of the butter, was done on a daily basis at Reddens. A man with a modern outlook, Tom Redden equipped his farm with a rotary churn, considered state-of-the-art at the time and which was much faster in the production of butter. With handles at each end, two girls would keep revolving it until the butter was produced. The butter was then collected and placed in trays in preparation for sale. The resulting buttermilk would be fed to calves and pigs. As all this work was the responsibility of the dairymaids, they had a very busy schedule indeed.

There were a lot of tillage crops sown on all farms at that period and, because of all the work the maintenance of the cattle herd entailed, Tom Redden also permanently employed two servant boys and some casual labour at busy periods. The meitheal of local men would come to his aid for certain jobs such as wynding hay, cutting corn and cutting the turf as these were very labour-intensive operations. Tom would also get help at peak periods from 'bull men'. These were neighbouring small farmers who would not have a bull running with their small herds of cows and who would have taken their cows to be served by Redden's bull. This was the usual practice at that time, a practice that continued until the introduction of artificial insemination. The saving of the hay for such a big herd entailed a lot of work. Jimeen the Man and Small Peter would be hired in to mow the hay, usually starting in mid-June or thereabouts.

Extremely weather-dependent, it was a chore that could be accomplished in a short space of time in good weather conditions but, if the weather was mixed, it could be very prolonged. In this latter type of weather, the workforce would usually be put weeding turnips and mangolds. With meal bags tied around their knees to protect their pants and also to protect them from the dampness of the ground, they would crawl along the furrow pulling weeds that would ultimately choke the crop if left unhindered. If the sun shone out again they would immediately return to the hay-field. Mowed with a scythe, the hay would then have to be shook out to dry, and in mixed weather it would be made into 'grass cocks' – these were a small amount of hay neatly piled to throw off the rainwater in showery weather conditions and farmers used to say, "It would save in the grass cocks".

On one occasion Tom Redden had a big field of grass cocks and one sunny morning, after a few bad days weather-wise, he was wondering whether he should shake it out. Pensively looking up at the sky, he asked Tom Seán, a man reputed to be a great judge of the weather who lived down near the sea and who used to help him at the hay, what he thought of the day. Tom Seán scanned the horizon and, clearing his throat, he exclaimed, "The day will be good".

"Are you sure?" Redden questioned.

"Certain," replied Tom Seán, "because I saw the sea-pigs going out the mouth of the Shannon this morning and that is a sure sign of a fine day."

"So, it would be safe to shake out the hay, you'd say?" persevered Tom Redden.

"Shake away, man, and get all the help you can, it might be fit for wynds in the evening," advised Tom Seán.

On this advice, Redden decided to shake out the hay and in half an hour there was a meitheal gathered to help with the work. They came across the fields and the shortcut and some arrived by ass and car. The meitheal was made up of comhar men, bull men and neighbours. The 'comhar' men were neighbouring farmers who Tom Redden used to comhar with – that is a situation where two farmers would have an understanding of helping each other at certain jobs and saving hay was one of them. Tom Redden would be expected to repay the comhar when the need arose.

Rebecca Redden, helped by one of the dairymaids, arrived with lunch for the meitheal just as they finished the shaking out. All sat themselves down for the meal and while they were eating, Seán Fada arrived.

"You have come at just the right time," said Tom Redden, "sit down and have a mug of tay. You must let a few súgáin for us because we are going wynding."

"No free meal, I notice," joked Seán Fada, taking a mug of tea from Rebecca.

At that time all the wynds of hay would be tied with súgáin and Seán Fada was adept at letting them.

"Where is the twister?" he asked, as he handed back the empty mug to Rebecca.

The 'twister' was a homemade tool made of strong wire in the shape of a modern day car wheel brace. Seán Fada ordered a small cock of hay to be made and then sat down beside it with Mickeen Muldoon standing in front of him with the twister in his hand, ready to start. Soon Mickeen was twisting and Seán was letting from the hay in the cock. All was going according to plan, and Tom Redden arrived and sat himself down alongside Seán Fada. As the work was going ahead, the two were swapping yarns and soon several balls of súgáin were made. As Muldoon backed away when the súgán was being let, he was facing the hill and, all of a sudden, he shouted to Redden, "Tom, throw your eye at the hill". Tom looked around at the hill and, to his dismay, he saw fog tumbling down. He knew that in a short time it would be upon them and the day's work would be in vain. In a pensive mood, looking at the hill and then at Seán Fada, he said, "What must have happened to Tom Seán's sea-pigs?" With a wily smile, Seán Fada answered, "They must have turned back".

Cutting the corn was also a major operation on the Redden farm and again the meitheal would be involved. Mowed with a scythe – the reaping hook had been discarded some years previously – three or four men were kept busy taking the corn and making it into sheaves which they laid out in rows. The binders, very often women, would then come along and bind each sheaf using four or five straws from the sheaf itself. In the evening, the whole crew would combine and make stooks of the sheaves. Then, to add further protection from the weather, the stooks would be headed. The heading consisted of placing four or five sheaves in an upright position on top of the stook with the grain end towards the ground. This had the effect of protecting the grain from weather damage and was very effective. After a few weeks the corn would be drawn in to the haggard and made into a rick. The rick would then be thatched using straw from the preceeding year.

Rushes were used if straw was not available. Later on in the year when the hay was in and the spuds dug and pitted and the mangolds and turnips secured as well, the threshing would be done. Threshing corn was a major operation that entailed hard work. Done inside with flails on a barn floor, and sometimes on the kitchen floor, two men, stripped to their waist, would beat the sheaf until all of its grain was shed. The grain and chaff would then be bagged and, in due course, winnowed. The flails consisted of two sticks or handles, roughly four foot long, tied together with a leather thong. Swung with the necessary articulation, they were effective in getting all the grain off the sheaf. The winnowing, that is the separating of the grain from the chaff, would have to be undertaken on a windy day. It was done between two open doors, the back door and the front door of the barn or between the kitchen doors. The operation was simple – just let the draft blow the lighter chaff away from the heavier grain. It could cause big problems in the kitchen for the woman of the house but there was no other way at the time. In later years, hand-operated winnowing machines came on stream and were a big step forward.

The first attempt at mechanical threshing of corn came in the form of a horse-powered machine. It was very simple. The threshing drum was fitted in a barn loft. Outside on a bank of earth, which was on a level with the floor of the loft, gear wheels were positioned which were connected by a shaft to the threshing drum in the loft and also to equipment to which two horses were attached. Tackled at opposite ends of a steel frame and walking around in a circle, the equipment was geared so that the walking speed of the horses would give the required speed on the threshing drum. The sheaves, which were already stored in the loft, would be fed into the machine and the straw fell to the barn below, while the grain was conveyed by chute, also to the barn, where it was bagged directly from the chute. Later again came the portable threshing mill, which was pulled from farm to farm by horses and was driven by a steam engine, which also had to be pulled by horses. Next came the traction steam engine and later the oil-fuelled tractor. Nowadays all threshing equipment has been superseded by the combine harvester, a long way from the flail.

During one summer, on a beautiful July evening, a strange noise was heard. Everyone in Ballymachad heard it but none could discern what it was or where it came from. Sometimes it would stop and, just when people thought it was gone, it would start up again. The noise continued all evening, sometimes stopping and then starting up again. Everyone was intrigued by it. It would get louder at times and sometimes get lower and lower and then stop. Old women stood looking out over their half-doors, bewildered. They wondered whether it was an omen of something bad about to happen, as some of them felt it was a lonesome kind of a noise. Men were standing up on ditches trying to ascertain where it was coming from. It was late in the evening when the mystery was solved. The noise was coming from Redden's place. Dan McGurk, on his way home to the slate house, ended the speculation. The noise was coming from a gadget Tom Redden was after buying for mowing hay, a thing pulled by two horses which had cost a heap of money – £8!

It was the first mowing machine in Ballymachad. The news spread quickly and it was the subject of much discussion for several days. When Jimeen the Man, Small Peter and all the other local mowers heard about it, they were devastated. They felt it was the beginning of the end of their business. And so it was, because soon other small farmers got interested in the idea and two friendly farmers would join in the purchase of a machine and it would easily cut the hay for both of them. Then one enterprising small farmer bought a mowing machine to cut hay on hire for his neighbours. This really hit the traditional mowers and, in the course of a few years, the men with the scythes were redundant. It was the end of an era. Strangely enough, some farmers were very much opposed to the idea, They argued that it wasn't right to have horses walking on the cut hay, "dunging and urinating on it and then feeding it to cows". But their objections were shortlived. Farm mechanisation had begun and it was impossible to turn back the clock.

But Tom Redden soon found that the mechanical mowing of hay had its problems too. Mowing the headlands of the Cross Field, called that because it was near a crossroads, the knife hit a six inch bolt which must have been dropped there sometime previously. Disappointed, Tom Redden sent fourteen-year-old Mikey John, who was helping out on the farm during the summer holidays, to the forge for the loan of a file to repair the damage to the knife of the mowing machine. Mikey John duly ran the shortcut across the fields and, panting, shouted to the smith, "Tom Redden sent me over for a file, sir". The smith, just to have a bit of craic with Redden, letting on that he thought Mikey John had said 'a while' replied, "Oh, that's fine with me. Sit down there and make yourself comfortable". Every few minutes the poor boy would say, "Tom Redden sent me down for a file, sir". And every time he would get the same reply from the smith: "Make yourself comfortable, stay as long as you like gorsoon, sure there is no one saying a word to you." That continued until Redden galloped into the forge yard on horseback and shouted, "Where is that young lad?"

"Oh, the boy," the smith calmly replied, "he said you sent him down for a while so I told him stay as long as he liked, thinking you wanted him out of the way for a few hours."

"You bloody rogue, you knew well what I wanted. Give me that file and let me out of here. Come on boy and jump up behind me, you have a lot to learn," said Redden irritably.

Smothering a smile, the smith handed over the file. Mikey John jumped up on a barrel that was in the forge yard and Redden drove over near him. He mounted bareback behind the saddle, Redden telling him to 'hold on tight' and they cantered home at a lively gait. Having dismounted, Redden placed his hand on the boy's head and said, "My dear boy, you have learned a lesson today that I hope you will never forget". When Redden had a chance to consider the deliberate ploy by the Smith to vex him in front of his customers, who were also Redden's neighbours, he vowed, with a smile, to get him at his own game and win next time round.

The Pig in the Tub

In the aftermath of the handing back of the land to its rightful owners, the plain people of Ireland, times were harsh and money almost non-existent. But, being the resilient people that they were, rural people survived by hard work which made them more or less self-sufficient. On the average farm, the 'farm machinery' consisted of the spade, the shovel, the scythe and the reaping hook. Some farms would boast a plough which would be loaned to neighbouring farmers because there were few who could afford the plough which cost £4. Power was supplied by the ass, the pony and the horse. The common car for the respective animals would transport all farm needs. There was an old saying which said 'necessity compels an old woman to trot' and necessity compelled farmers of that era to be self-sufficient and consequently to take on jobs that might be alien to their calling.

One of those jobs was the killing of the pig. Most farmers, big or small, would have a sow or two that would produce banbhs. The farmer who didn't keep a sow would buy in two banbhs to fatten, one to sell and one to kill for home consumption. There were two reasons why two would be bought. Firstly, a lone banbh was, for some reason, slow to fatten, and secondly because one banbh was for commercial purposes and would be sold. This sale would cover all the costs involved so the meat in the tub would cost nothing. The pigs would be fed on homegrown produce such as potatoes, turnips and mangolds laced with crushed oats or barley and often a little Indian meal, just to make the meat 'sweet' they would say. Some farmers mastered the technique of slaughtering their own pig and these would oblige a neighbour to slaughter theirs.

One such farmer in Ballymachad was Seamuseen Gray, a gobby little man of few words and great ability. Considered very clean and tasty, he was the preferred man by most people to kill their pig. The Nevins, Jack and Mary, claimed that he was the best butcher of all time and he would slaughter two pigs every year for them, one in the spring and one in the fall of the year. The day appointed for the slaughter of the pig, usually a Friday, meant early rising. A big barrel of water would have to be boiled, and that would entail boiling several big pots which would then be discharged into a steel barrel also placed near the fire to help keep the temperature up. As the turf fire was kept at its best with constant refuelling, regularly supplemented with faggots, the pots boiled quickly. This procedure would continue until the barrel was full. In the meantime, outside in the yard, the wheels would be taken off the pony's car and it would be parked as near to the door as possible to facilitate the drawing out of the boiling water to scald the pig.

Seamuseen would arrive walking across the fields, but if the river was in flood, he'd come by ass and car around the road. He'd usually arrive about eleven o'clock, bringing his own equipment. This would consist of two knives, one of which was exceptionally sharp and was used to do the actual killing. The minute the pig was dead, Seamuseen would wash that knife and put it carefully into a special sheath not to be used again until the next killing. He'd also have a selection of ropes of specific sizes for the purpose of tying up the pig prior to killing. This was a job that had to be done with great care and precision because, if the pig broke loose as he was being killed, it would be a disaster. Adept at his job, Seamuseen would tie up the pig in such a way that when he'd pull tightly on one rope, the pig's four legs would be automatically tied together and the animal would land on its back. Usually three men would be there to help and they would lift the pig onto the pony's car. The animal was tied to the shaft of the car with a rope around its jaw and was held on its back by the men.

Seamuseen would take off his coat and fold up his sleeves in preparation for the actual killing. Bessie, the servant girl of many years, knew the routine well and would come out from the kitchen with a big, flat-bottomed basin to collect the blood. Having covered the bottom of the basin with a sprinkling of salt and pepper, Bessie would also have two kitchen knives in the shape of a cross in its centre. This was to disperse the blood evenly around the bottom of the basin. Mary, the woman of the house, would be in bed, her head covered in pillows, as she couldn't bear to hear the screeching of the pig in its death throes. Bessie had no such inhibitions and if the men helping made any mistake and some of the blood was lost, she would give them a tongue-lashing they would never forget, and that would even include her boss Jack Nevin. "Are you ready, Bessie?"

Seamuseen would ask and when Bessie indicated that she was, he would turn his attention to the men saying, "Right lads, hold her firm, dead straight on her back and when I say 'turn' turn her towards the basin".

Then, clutching the knife, he would make a slight incision the length of the throat and then, reversing the knife in his hand, he would plunge it straight in and sever the jugular vein and shout "Turn". Immediately the blood would splash into the basin, which was rigidly held by Bessie despite her being spattered with blood. The pig's moans would grow fainter and in two minutes he would be dead. Bessie would immediately take in the basin of blood and place it on the kitchen table and, sticking her head in the room door, would shout, "Come on out, Mary, 'tis all over". From under the pillows, Mary would inquire, "Is he dead?"

"As dead as a stone," Bessie would reply, "come on out. I'll be stirring the blood."

This was a very important chore, as it kept the blood thin and helped to get it to the right consistency for making puddings.

In the meantime, the men would be busy drawing out the boiling hot water and pouring it into a wooden barrel in readiness to scald the pig. Seamuseen was very exact about the temperature of the water for scalding, which he would ascertain by dipping his finger into the barrel, and directing to add cold or hot water as he deemed necessary. The procedure of scalding was done by dipping the carcase into the barrel of hot water and then reversing it and dropping in the other end, lifting the carcase up and down for a few minutes. The carcase was lifted out of the barrel and stretched out on the pony's car and, as time was of the essence for this operation, the men would attack with knives. With Seamuseen continuously pouring saucepans of hot water over the pig, in a short time all the hair was cleaned off. The pig was then washed in cold water and would be spotless.

The rush now over, Seamuseen and the couple of neighbours who were helping would relax for a few minutes and would be given a mug of porter for their efforts. Looking at the carcase, they would remark on the fine pig he was and guess that he was well over two hundredweight. Mary, now out of her shell, was delighted, as it was she that fed him and she looked upon praise for the pig as praise for the hand that fed him. Next move was to get the ladder with a spar nailed across the top and to place it in the pony's car. Then the pig would be lifted onto it and put on its back, with its hind legs hitched to the spar at the top, and it would be taken into the kitchen and the ladder put standing inside the back door. The next part of the process was to open the pig, but first a small bath would have to be put at the foot of the ladder to catch the entrails and blood as the pig was slit down the middle of the belly.

This was an operation that Seamuseen would have to do with great care, as Mary, her inhibitions now forgotten, would be waiting close at hand with a pan to collect the intestines. The intestines were used to make the blood puddings' casings and the butcher was expected to deliver the whole lot of them into the pan without damaging them with the knife as holes or cuts would render them useless. In order to make sure that no damage would be done, Seamuseen would deliver all the entrails onto the kitchen table and then go through the procedure of separating the intestines under Mary's watchful eye. He would also make sure to retrieve the bladder and give it to young Tommy, who, when it was dried out, would get endless hours of pleasure from it playing football. The intestines secured, Mary and Bessie would spend a long time cleaning them. This was done with great precision and care, as they had to be thoroughly cleaned without damaging them and making them porous. The carcase, now minus all its entrails, would have to be kept open, so Jack would go out and cut two lengths of a sally, each about nine inches long. They were pointed at both ends and would be used to keep the carcase open by pulling it apart and inserting them. The carcase would then be thoroughly washed down with cold water and be left hanging on the ladder for twenty-four hours.

As disorder reigned in the kitchen, a meal of bacon, cabbage and spuds would be served in the back porch, preceded by mugs of porter for the men. The meal over, Seamuseen, collecting his 'traps', would arrange a time to come the next day to cut up the pig. Just as he was about to leave, Mary would invariably ask him to do her a favour, would he cut a bit of fat off the carcase as she needed it for the puddings. Jokingly retorting, "'Tis a wonder you didn't wait until I was halfway home," he would take out his knife again and cut a big section of the fat from inside the pig. This would immediately be put into a skillet with water and boiled. Having washed the intestines and cut them in suitable lengths to make nice sized puddings, Mary and Bessie would commence preparing the blood for the filling of the puddings. This chore would determine the flavour and wholesomeness of the finished product. The women took great pride in their ability in this field, especially as it was the custom at the time to divide puddings and pork steak with the neighbours, who, when they killed a pig, would reciprocate. This practice generated a friendly rivalry among neighbouring women as to who made the best and nicest puddings.

Sorting out all the ingredients to be added to the blood, Mary and Bessie would sometimes have an argument concerning the amounts to be used to give the proper flavour. Bessie would usually get her way and she would add spice, finely chopped onions, salt and pepper and pinhead oatmeal. Then, taking the boiled fat from the skillet, she would chop it into minute bits and add it to the big basin of blood. She would then stir and mix until a desired consistency was obtained. The actual filling of the puddings would now commence. Mary's role was to tie one end of the length of intestine with cord which she would then hand to Bessie. Taking the future pudding case, Bessie would stick two fingers into the open end and, stretching the opening, she would pour in the prepared blood between her two fingers to within about an inch and a half of the top. This allowance had to be made for expansion to prevent the pudding from bursting in the cooking. Still held by Bessie, Mary would then tie that end with cord and also tie the two ends together to form a circle – it was called a ring of pudding. This procedure would continue until all the lengths of intestines and all the blood was used. If too much blood was at hand it would be baked and would be cut into sections and, like the puddings, was very nutritious. The raw puddings would then be boiled in a pot of water and would be taken out when they were cooked and then placed in a row on the handle of a brush suspended between two chairs until they cooled down. They were then ready for consumption.

Next day Seamuseen would arrive at about three o'clock to cut up the pig and also to salt and barrel the meat. Again a few of the neighbours would be at hand to take the pig off the ladder and lay it on the kitchen table. The first thing Seamuseen would do was to cut off the head. Then, on his orders, the pig would be held on its back while Seamuseen retrieved a small hatchet from his bag of equipment. He would cut the rib bones along both sides of the backbone on the inside of the pig and this allowed the two sides of meat to lay flat on the table. With his knife he would then sever the two sides from each other and remove the backbone. One side would then be taken off and laid on two wooden chairs. Again with the hatchet, Seamuseen would chop the backbone into sections of about four inches. Jack would place them in a wooden box for the time-being until the salting commenced.

Removing the legs and then cutting the side of meat into sections, Mary would ask him to cut more and more pork steak from each section as she had a big divide to make. Seamuseen always grumbled that he was going too bare as it was, but still, he would always oblige. Remembering her list of all the people that had sent her pork steak and puddings, Mary was delighted to be able to return the compliment and had a golden rule of sending bigger portions to where there were big families. A kind-hearted woman, she also included poorer neighbours who could never afford to kill a pig but who were good friends. Her big worry was the possibility of forgetting somebody.

The table was then cleared, the meat placed down on the floor on a sheet and the salting would commence. But first the meat barrel, already washed and scalded and its bottom covered with salt, would be put in position under the ladder to the loft. A bag of salt would be put standing on a chair near the table and each section would get individual treatment. One man would be detailed to place the sections of meat on the table at the desired pace. Seamuseen would then cut pockets for the salt on the inside of the meat and he would stab the outside skin in several places. The meat would then be pushed across the table where two men would do the salting under the eagle eye of Seamuseen. The salt would have to be rubbed very hard on to the skin side first. The piece would then be reversed and, after it had got the same rubbing treatment, the pockets would be filled with salt. That section was then placed in the barrel and after a second section had been placed alongside it, both were covered in salt. As the meat was being put into the barrel, the salted pieces of the backbone, the crubeens and the head – now cut in portions, would also be laid into the vacant places between the pieces of meat.

With all the meat now in the barrel and covered with salt, Seamuseen would give it a sprinkling of saltpeter – not too much, just a small amount – judged by his own intuition. A wide flat board was then placed on top of the meat and all would be weighted down with a big stone. In a short time the salt would be in pickle and in three weeks or perhaps a month, the meat would be 'cured'. The job successfully completed, the kitchen table would be cleaned and washed of any residue and, with a large frying pan of pork steak sizzling on the brand by the open fire, giving off an aroma that would create ferocious appetites, the entire crew would be treated to a meal of pork steak and puddings, washed down with buttermilk and maybe a mug of porter – if there was a drop left. When it was taken out of the barrel in due course, the cured bacon would be placed on wooden laths over a bath or some similar container to drip and dry out. Afterwards it would hang on hooks from the rafters where, over a period of time it would become the much-loved yellow bacon. Great men were fed on it and generations of families were reared on it as part of their staple diet.

The pig was almost a part of the family. Indeed, when she was about to give birth, the sow would be taken into the kitchen where a bed of straw had been prepared for her. Some member of the family would have to stay up that night to oversee her giving birth to perhaps sixteen or even eighteen banbhs. Following the birth, for every night the sow and banbhs were in the kitchen, a member of the family would have to do duty. The story is told about a farmer who, worn out from being up every night minding his banbhs, hired a man of the road to mind them for a night or two. At two o'clock in the morning he was awakened by the noise the banbhs were making in the kitchen. He pulled on his pants and came down to the kitchen to see what was wrong. The big litter of banbhs were fighting each other as they all tried to get a teat from the sow who hadn't enough teats for the number of banbhs. The farmer was dismayed that his man didn't intervene and sort things out so he gave out to him in harsh language and asked, "Why did you not sort out them banbhs?"

"How could I do that, sir," the man said, "sure I was always told never interfere in a family affair."

He was sacked in the morning!

The Fair and the Gamble

The Fair

Cattle fairs were usually held on a fortnightly basis in the town and farmers with animals to sell would have to walk them there. There were no lorries or trailers in those days and on fair mornings cattle from a fifteen-mile radius would converge on the town. Farmers who lived about ten miles or more from town would have to commence the journey to the fair at three o'clock in the morning so as to arrive there by six o'clock in the morning. One particular year the weather was exceptionally wet during the hay-making season and consequently hay was scarce and of inferior quality, with the result that some farmers were over-stocked for the amount of hay they had succeeded in saving. One such farmer was Mickey Pat Seán, a low-sized, hardy, little man sporting a big, bushy moustache that eclipsed his mouth. He decided that he had no option but to reduce stock. Having considered all his options, he reluctantly decided that Dolly, a very old and uneconomic cow, would have to go. He was reluctant because she had been an excellent 'milker' for many years, so there was a certain nostalgia in parting with her. But then, he decided that he couldn't let his heart rule his head so he forced himself to dismiss those sentiments insofar as he was able. After all, Dolly was producing nothing, so it didn't make any economic sense to keep her in times of scarce fodder.

Mickey had her out grazing in the 'long meadow' for a few weeks in an attempt to spare fodder. This meant that Dolly was grazing on the commonage along the side of the road and every day she was moving further from home. Come Wednesday, he'd take her to the fair and maybe, just maybe, she could make four pounds, an amount not to be scoffed at in those days. On Tuesday evening Mickey commenced his preparations for the road. First, he had to fashion a halter from a rope he had purchased that morning. Next, he drove Dolly into the byre to fit the halter and to make sure it was the right size. He wanted to avoid delays in the morning as he hoped to get off to an early start. Then he gave the cow a rub of the currycomb, a device used for grooming the horse or a colt to be sold. As he said, if it did a good job on the horse and put a shine on its skin, it should also do a good job on the cow and the jobbers were always attracted to animals with a shine on their skin. Then Mickey brought in a pike of hay and put it at Dolly's head, a sop specially chosen from the reek so that she'd be sure to eat it. He pulped a turnip into a bucket, topping it up with a few fistfuls of yellow meal and threw the entire mixture on top of the hay.

This was done to get Dolly to fill her belly so that she would be well-able for the long trek to the fair and would look her best on arrival there. Mickey then closed the byre door, went in home, had his supper, shaved himself, gave a slight trimming to his moustache and, after a pull of the pipe, he set the alarm clock for two o'clock in the morning and retired early to bed. His sleep, however, was fitful as he didn't trust the alarm clock, a gadget that an old aunt had sent him from America long before any such contraptions were available in Ireland. It had let him down on two occasions before – once when he wound it too tight and the second time when he didn't wind it enough. Tonight he felt fairly confident the he had hit a happy medium, but you could never know with these figgey-me-gigs.

Mickey woke at half past one and nudged his wife, Nora, to get up and prepare the breakfast. She duly obliged and when he presented himself a short time later, he sat down to a feed of cold fat bacon, homemade brown bread and plenty of their own butter washed down with a mug of buttermilk, all of which was polished off in a hurry. Ready for the road, Mickey now lit the storm lantern which his wife took out to the byre to give him light to put the halter on the cow. In a few minutes, armed with a blackthorn stick, he led Dolly out and was on his way to the fair. Nora made her way into the house with the lantern and, as she opened the door, the alarm clock went off – it was twenty past two in the morning!

Mickey steered Dolly up the boreen and was soon out on the public road. At Fiddlers Cross he met the Spike Casey and his son Billeen driving three yearling bullocks. Wild little animals they were, and as they galloped and bucklepped, the Spike and Billeen soon left Mickey and Dolly in their wake. Another mile on they met up with Jackeen Tom Mick, a man, like himself, leading a cow on a halter. The pair stayed together and enjoyed each other's company, swapping yarns to the extent that they didn't feel the remainder of the journey until they finally reached the town. By then the poor old cows had a lather of sweat on them and, indeed, the two men weren't cold either. As they reached the railway bridge, a train of cattle wagons was passing underneath, leaving a swirling cloud of black smoke as it approached the local station. Coughing from the inhalation of the smoke, a blocker approached Mickey. A 'blocker' was a man hired by a big cattle dealer to meet farmers as they arrived with their cattle to the outskirts of the town. He would offer them a very low price for their stock. These blockers were professionals in their approach and if they happened to meet a softie, they would leave him with the impression that his cattle were worth very little and make him easy prey for the big dealer.

The blocker approached Mickey and opened the proceedings by asking, "How much for the auld frame?"

"A fiver," answered Mickey.

The blocker was now examining her horns and said, "She's ancient".

"Well, I can't make her any younger," retorted Mickey.

Pulling a pound note out of his pocket and pressing it up against Mickey's chest, the blocker shouted, "Will you take that for her?"

"Indeed I will not then," said Mickey, with a bit of temper in his voice.

"And what will you take for her?" the blocker persevered.

"I told you, a fiver," said Mickey.

"Would thirty shillings buy her?" the blocker insisted.

"It would not," answered Mickey in a peevish sort of voice.

"Would ye cut it?" intervened Jackeen Tom Mick.

"Ah, the difference is too much to cut it," said Mickey.

Then the blocker changed tactics.

"Tell me now, is there a calf in her?" he asked.

"There is not," was the reply.

"Ah, she's no use to me so," remarked the blocker and immediately turned his attention to Jackeen Tom Mick.

Mickey walked away with Dolly in tow, but he hadn't gone thirty yards when another blocker hailed him with, "Hey there, how much for the auld skin?" A bit taken aback by the nasty way he asked the price, Mickey answered, "A fiver" and kept going. But the blocker walked with him and caught the halter, bringing Dolly to a halt.

"You're asking strong," he said, "ask me right and we'll make a deal."

"Bid me and let me know the colour of you money," suggested Mickey.

"Thirty shillings and that's a rob," declared the blocker.

"What do you mane by a rob, sure that would be giving her away," retorted Mickey.

"Tell me," asked the blocker, "is there a calf inside in her?"

Remembering what the first man had said to him when he said she wasn't incalf, he replied, "Oh, a calf in her is it? Yerra no, there isn't a calf in the world in her," and walked away towards towards the Square.

He hadn't gone far when he was accosted by another of these blockers who shouted, "How much for the auld lady?"

"I'm giving her away for a fiver," Mickey replied impatiently, by now fed-up of the blockers and anxious to get to the Square and the fair proper.

"Well," said the blocker, "I suppose there is no harm in asking."

"No harm at all. If you don't ask you won't get," replied an irritated Mickey, giving Dolly a tip of the blackthorn stick.

"Hold on, mister, I'm anxious to do business with you if you ask me right," coaxed the blocker.

"I'm after telling you my price and she's there for sale, it's up to you to bid for her," retorted a now extremely impatient Mickey.

The blocker pulled a wad of notes out of his inside pocket and selected a pound note. He waved it in front of Mickey's face saying, "Take that for her, you can give me what you like out of it". 'What you like out of it' was 'luck money' he expected to get back out of the pound. This drove Mickey livid and when the blocker asked him again if he'd take the pound, he responded with temper, saying, "You can stick it where I won't say" and he hit the cow with the blackthorn and drove her down to the Square.

As he entered the Square, Mickey thought of his father, God rest him, who used to say that if you had only a goat to sell, be in the middle of the fair with it. Thinking these thoughts, he led Dolly to a spot which he felt would be a good 'stand' as many buyers would be passing that way and he'd have a better chance of a sale. And he was right – about the buyers at any rate. But as for a sale, he had no joy. Several buyers came, just looked at Dolly and passed on. Hungry and tired after the ten mile walk and standing all day, at one o'clock he tethered Dolly to a lamp post and went into a pub for a pint of porter and a sandwich.

When he came out there was a fellow looking at Dolly. He seemed interested as he was opening her mouth and checking her teeth – good sound teeth were very important in a cow so that she'd be able eat well, otherwise she'd waste away. Knowing that her teeth were good, Mickey's spirits rose – maybe after all, he might still sell. So, in rather upbeat mood, he went over to the cow and began releasing the rope from around the lamppost.

The fellow said, "Is this auld girl yours?"

"She is indeed, then," said Mickey, his hopes rising.

"You didn't sell?" he remarked.

"Not yet," said Mickey.

"Ah sure, the fair is over now," was the fellow's response, "what would you be asking for her now?"

"Is it how you are interested in her?" enquired Mickey.

"I am and I'm not," was the strange reply.

"And what's the reason for your dilemma?" inquired Mickey.

"Well, 'tis like this, I'd be buying her to feed dogs and she hasn't enough flesh on her at present, so I was toying with the idea of buying her and feeding her for a month or two, but I've changed my mind, it would take too long to put flesh on her," the fellow explained.

"You're perfectly right," said Mickey, who wouldn't sell Dolly to be fed to dogs for love nor money.

Tying Dolly to the lamppost again, he decided to have another pint and buy a quarter pound of cheese to be chewing on the long trek home. As he was driving out of the Square he was accosted by an auld fellow who asked him, "How much for the horns?" Feeling bitter and smart-aleckey, he answered, "I'm selling her all together", and kept moving towards the railway bridge.

At that time, all cattle sold at the fairs to buyers from 'up the country' would be transported by train and the onus was on the seller to drive them to the station and load them onto a wagon. Each buyer would have a representative on duty at the station and he would have to certify that the animal was loaded by signing the docket that the seller would have received from the dealer at the time of purchase, otherwise the farmer would not get paid. As Mickey came near the railway bridge on his way home he met Jackeen Tom Mick on his way down from the train station with a rope in his hand.

"You sold?" asked Mickey.

The Fair and the Gamble

"I did," answered Jackeen, adding, "it was a tough battle though. How did you fare out, were you satisfied?"

"Satisfied is it! There isn't a man here today satisfied, but what can you do? You cannot make a market of your own," Mickey said, adding, "no, the best I could get was thirty shillings and I wouldn't let her go for that. I'd rather let her take her chance on the long meadow. Anyway, things might be better in the springtime."

"I got the two pounds alright but I had to give him a half crown for luck money out of it," groaned Jackeen.

"Ah well, you did all right. You had more flesh than me, that was the difference," Mickey said, enquiring, "have you a drive home, Jackeen?"

"Tom Redden is in the market yard with a rail of banbhs so I hope to get a lift from him. You have a long walk before you, Mickey," Jackeen answered.

"Yerra, I won't feel it. I drank a few pints and they'll keep me going. I should be home with the daylight, that is if the lady don't get tired. Good luck Jackeen, the sooner I start, the sooner I'll get home," said Mickey, as he crossed the railway bridge for home and Jackeen went towards the market yard to secure a drive home from Tom Redden.

Mickey arrived home as it was getting dusk. Dolly barely made the journey as she got foundered, meaning she got very lame from the long walk on the hard road. Mickey put her into the small field near the house where there was a nice pick of grass. Seán Fada called in on his way home from work to inquire how Mickey had got on and expressed his disappointment when he was told he didn't sell. Seán wasn't long gone when Paddy the Lad arrived. In the course of conversation he asked Mickey what was he going to do with Dolly now.

"What can I do with her, only take the chance that she'll survive the winter. Maybe prices will be better in the spring if I could put a bit of flesh on her," came the reply.

"The spring is a long way away," said the Lad, "and the fodder is bad and scarce."

"Sure, I know that. Everyone knows that but what can we do about it only take your chance. Anyhow, we never died a winter yet," joked Mickey.

"If I were you I'd be taking no chances with her, she's as old as the hills," said the Lad.

"And as you are so smart, what would you do with her?" asked Mickey in a sarcastic tone.

The Lad thought for a moment and Mickey felt he had him in a corner, that he was stuck for an answer.

"I'd gamble her," said the Lad, as cool as a breeze.

"What!" exclaimed Mickey, jumping to his feet, "what do you mean 'gamble' her?"

"What I mean is, gamble her in the cards and you'd make a fortune," counseled the Lad.

"Says you," retorted Mickey in a rather derisory tone.

"Please yourself. You asked my advice so I gave it to you," replied the Lad, making for the door.

"Come back a minute," suggested Mickey.

"Think about it and I'll be back later. You're not in the mood for thinking at the minute. Cheerio for now," said the Lad and, with a smirk on his face, he pulled the door shut after him.

Mickey paced the floor, head down, thinking. Nora, who was out looking after the hens, came in the back door and, as Mickey continued pacing the floor half talking to himself, she remarked, "You'd think you'd have enough walking done for one day". He ignored her presence entirely so she confronted him as he walked towards the fire, saying, "What's wrong with you? Had you too much to drink?" Catching him by the arm, Nora got Mickey to sit down at the head of the table and said, "I'll make a fresh cup of tay and you'll be all right".

"I don't want any tay. I'm just thinking about what the Lad said," Mickey said.

"Was the Lad here?" asked Nora.

"He was. He's just gone out the front door," droned Mickey as if his mind was miles away.

"And what blackguarding was he up to that upset you so much? He always seems to brew trouble," said Nora.

"No, no, no, he done nothing wrong," said Mickey, "but I think I kind of half hunted him."

"You did?" said Nora, "and what made you do that?"

"Well, we were talking about Dolly and about how would she survive the winter and do you know what he said to do with her?" said Mickey.

"No, what did he say?" asked Nora.

"He said to gamble her," answered Mickey.

"Gamble her," said Nora in amazement.

"That's what he said. 'Gamble her on the cards' says he and you'll make a fortune," said Mickey.

"I wish 'twas true for him," said Nora and jokingly added, "we could do with a fortune."

"I think I insulted him when he said it. It sounded so awful, but when I come to think about it, isn't it better than burying her?" said Mickey.

"Who said you'd have to bury her, did the Lad say it?" asked Nora.

"Oh, he didn't say that but he said the risk was there and, no doubt, the risk is there," warned Mickey.

"Please yourself. I suppose you would have sold her for three or four pounds and she'll surely make that in a gamble," said Nora.

At that minute the latch lifted on the front door and the Lad walked in followed by Seán Fada.

"Well," said the Lad, "did you think about what I was saying?"

"Indeed I thought of nothing else since," confessed Mickey, "and do you know, I think you're right. She'll surely make three or four pounds in a gamble."

"Three or four pounds is it? She will, and make twenty-four. Wait and you'll see, if we do our job right," said the Lad. "We have Seán Fada here – won't you throw in your weight Seán?"

"Why not," said Seán.

"That's the form," enthused the Lad, "and we'll rope in several more and get tables played in maybe twenty houses or even more. I must go now. We'll meet tomorrow night to pick a date and, in the meantime, let ye be spreading the news every chance ye get. This will be the greatest gamble ever played around here. It will go down in history. See ye tomorrow night."

With that, he was out the door brimming with enthusiasm about the craic ahead.

The Gamble

The card game of 41 was one the most prevalent forms of entertainment in the community, especially during the winter months. No night was long enough for the real gambler and games often spilled into the broad daylight of the morning. So in this particular atmosphere, the gambling of a cow would be greeted with relish. Never before was there such a prize. The usual prize would be about four shillings and that would be if it were a table of eight players at sixpence a man and pro rata if the table just consisted of six. The stake would then be divided between the two partners so it wasn't for the money they were playing, just for camaraderie and the sheer love for the game.

Telephones or radios didn't exist and yet Seán Fada and Paddy the Lad, both avid gamblers themselves, soon had the news of the gamble of a cow spreading like wildfire by 'bush telegraph'. And it worked with unbelievable efficiency. As a matter of fact it worked too well, because on that historic evening a crowd of people descended on Ballymachad the likes of which was never seen before. They came astride mules, jennets and asses. Some came riding dandy horses with creaking saddles. "A touch of the gentry," remarked a smiling Seán Fada. They came walking on the highways and byways, across fields and paths, across shortcuts and stiles and they all congregated at the crossroads. Soon the news arrived that two canoes from Clare, loaded to the gunwales with passengers, had landed on the strand and those aboard were heading towards the cross. As the crowd initially began to gather there had been broad smiles on the faces of Seán Fada and the Lad, the instigators of the affair. But now, deluged with such numbers, the smiles were gone, as the pair had the problem of getting some place for all of them to play. The locals were getting very worried too. Big Moll Sharp, surveying the scene from inside her half-door declared, "What will feed 'em all, they'll ate us out of house and home".

As Seán Fada and the Lad were contemplating their options, they were disturbed by an unusual noise coming down from the hill. It seemed to be coming closer by the second and finally it did arrive at the cross. The likes of this yoke was never seen or heard before. It was a thing with two wheels and two young fellows astride it. How they balanced themselves on it was considered a miracle. But the frightening thing about it was that it made a desperate noise, and it was spitting flames from a pipe jutting out from the back of it that would nearly set fire to the road. Furthermore, it upset all the dandy horses and some of them reared up on their hind legs. One of the jockeys even fell off. The jennets, the mules and the asses that were tethered to the fence were also in a panic as they brayed and kicked to get loose. Some of them pulled the furze bushes and the sallies they were tied to from the roots and bolted off home. Seán Fada decided that he'd interview the two riders for fear they were spies of some sort. Who would have a yoke like that only the army, he thought. Approaching the two and followed by the Lad, he noticed their peculiar dress. Both wore gaiters, but the curious thing was that while one fellow wore black shoes and brown gaiters, the other fellow wore brown shoes and black gaiters. They both wore heavy jackets and a scarf around their necks.

"Good evening, boys," he commenced.

Nice and mannerly, the boys replied, "Good evening, sir".

"Will you tell me now what's that yoke ye have?" inquired Seán.

Again with impeccable manners, one of the riders answered, "This is a motorbicycle, sir. It's about two horsepower and can travel thirty miles in an hour".

At the time there wasn't even a bicycle in Ballymachad!

"We came to play in the gamble for the cow, sir," the young fellow said.

"Where did ye come from?" asked the Lad.

"O'Dorney, sir," was the answer.

"Where is that place?" said the Lad.

"'Tis where we came from," was the reply.

"I know 'tis where ye came from, but where is it near?" inquired Seán.

"'Tis near no place, sir," said one of the boys.

Innocent young lads Seán thought, so he changed the subject.

"And where did ye get the whatever ye called it?"

"My father was in the army and he got it. He's away for a few days so we said we'd take it for a spin," the young rider admitted.

"And who told ye about the gamble here?" asked Seán.

"Ah sure, everyone heard about it at the fair and pattern day in O'Dorney," was the reply.

Satisfied that the two were just innocent youngsters who stole out on a joyride, Seán turned his attention to the pressing business at hand, namely finding houses to accommodate the unexpected numbers and getting them all sitting down at tables playing cards. Enlisting the help of anyone who was willing to cooperate, Seán soon had an army of helpers. While outlining his problem of getting all of the would-be gamblers 'billeted' around some table, the Ducker Casey, a small, old man sporting a goatie beard, said, "If I may spake, Seán".

"Spake away, Ducker, if you have anything good on your mind," exhorted Seán.

"Well, what I'm thinking," said the Ducker, "is that you'll never get houses and tables for all that army of gamblers simply because the number of houses aren't there. But, as it is a beautiful fine evening, why not put them playing out in the open while 'tis bright and by the time it gets dark a lot of them will, shall we say, be eliminated."

"Good thinking," said Seán, "but we will still need tables."

"For what?" asked the Ducker, "couldn't they play on a tay-chest, or in an ass's car, or a horse's car for that matter? Take the wheels off them if you like, to make it handy for them."

"I don't know would they be too happy at that carry-on, Ducker. Gamblers like a bit of comfort, you know," said Seán Fada. "Gamblers only want a deck of cards and when them cards are dealt out, they forget where they are," argued the Ducker. "Anyhow," he continued, "most of the tables in the houses around here wouldn't stand up to the pounding they would get in the heat of a game. Imagine the likes of the Porpoise Brady hitting the table with the knave or the five – he'd drive his fist straight down through any of the tables around here." "And another thing," added the Ducker, "Suppose they start a fight inside in a house, wouldn't they wreck the house, table and all. If I were you, Seán, I'd walk through the crowd and I'd pick out all the fairly well-dressed men that you think would be used to tables and direct them into the houses. For the rest you could bring out the tay-chest, or, as I was saying, the cars with the wheels off. You see, the beauty of the card game is that it can be played any place – throw your coat on the ground and play away on it, or on the battlement of the bridge, or even on a piece of timber across your knees."

Prompted by the Lad and the Ducker, Seán soon plucked up enough courage to stand up on the ditch to address the crowd, a thing he had never done before. Shaking like an ivy leaf, he cleared his throat and spoke.

"Men and women or who ever else is listening, I must say ye were great to come. I hope ye all brought a deck of cards with ye and that ye will all find some place to play as the crowd is very big."

At this there was a bit of a murmur from the crowd but, oblivious to any grumbles, Seán continued.

"Ye'll all have to find a place to play – if ye get into a house well and good, but all we have is twenty or so houses. So with a table of eight at each house that would cater for wan hundred and sixty of ye. Therefore ye won't all get into a house so ye can play outside in the yard. We will get all the tay-chests we can for ye. And if some of ye are still stuck for a place to play, there is a car of some description in every haggard and ye have permission to take off the wheels if ye so wish."

Getting the feeling that the vast majority of those present were happy enough with the arrangements, Seán decided to broach the subject of money.

"Now ye all know that the fantastic prize for the winner is a cow," he said.

"Where is the cow?" roared some fellow with a big crop of hair on his head and a bushy moustache, "ye should have her here you know."

"The cow," retorted Seán as cool as a breeze, "is as snug as a bug in a rug inside in her stall and there she'll stay until the winner puts a halter on her and leads her out on her journey to her new home."

Of course, if the truth was told, the cow was such a bad specimen of a bovine that they dare not show her for fear of a riot.

"Now, I must explain the rules and regulations for the gamble," said Seán.

"What rules?" shouted a middle-aged man. "We know all the rules, we didn't come here to be listening to a man up on a ditch talking. We want to get started."

Unperturbed, Seán continued.

"Rule number wan – the charge for to enter the gamble is two shillings a man," he said.

"Two shillings!" shouted someone, "sure that's robbery."

"What do you mean by robbery?" shouted back Paddy the Lad, "don't you know that the prize is a dairy cow."

"He knows that well, what do you think brought him?" said Seán, and he continued, "the money will be collected as soon as ye start playing, whether 'tis at a table or a tay-chest, or a horse's car or whatever. And I must tell ye we have twenty able-bodied men with blackthorn walking sticks."

"What?" roared a small man with a big hat from the back of the crowd.

"It isn't what you're thinking at all now," Seán replied quickly, "when these twenty gents raise their sticks straight up into the air, ye'll all recognise them. Then eight gather around each man and he will lead them to a house, is that fair enough?"

"Fair enough," was the response from the vast majority, although a few seemed to have reservations.

"Raise 'em lads," ordered Seán and, like an army presenting arms, the twenty sticks shot up in unison and the stampede began.

Still on the ditch surveying the scene, Seán cautioned, "Take it handy now, we will accommodate ye all if ye give us a chance".

"Ye will, with yer tay chests and ass's cars," shouted a disgruntled gambler.

Ignoring the remark, Seán continued, "The first rubber will be three sticks and all the rubbers after that will be three sticks". A 'stick' is one game and there can be any number of games or 'sticks' in a 'rubber' as determined by whoever is in charge. Given the go-ahead, the players quickly fanned out through the community. In the meantime, the Lad and Seán Fada, in consultation and with the approval Mickey, had picked out twenty trustworthy men to collect the two shillings fee from each of the players. They immediately sprung into action, and it must be remembered that the success or failure of the whole exercise depended on their ability to collect from every single player. Ten more were appointed to collect from those playing outdoors. Afterwards, the consensus of opinion was that, in spite of the huge number of players, the collectors did a thorough job.

All the local gamblers were playing and, indeed, locals who never played cards before came to support the venture. Two local teenagers, Ted Manion and his cousin, Freddie Conway, arrived somewhat late, saying that they saw all the people passing through the village and so decided to follow on. They were just in time to be accommodated with another group who were also latecomers. Ted and Freddie had never played in a gamble before but they paid their two shillings each and joined in the craic playing in the body of an ass's car. Soon there were winners from the first rubbers and, to their own amazement, Ted and Freddie qualified to go forward to the second round. The two motorbicycle boys qualified also and they soon found themselves playing, in the company of others, opposite Ted and Freddie. After this round it was felt that there would be plenty of room in the houses, as many of the players would be on their way home having failed to make it onto the third round. It so happened the two motor riders were eliminated. The pair of them strolled down the road to where they had parked their bike in Matt McCracken's yard.

It was just midnight and, even though a lively card game was in progress in his house, Matt was outside standing near the bike, as someone had warned him that it could set fire to his cock of hay.

"I'm waiting for ye all night," he exclaimed as the two boys approached. "Take that thing out of my yard and don't burn my hay," he demanded.

The boys were all apologies and assured him that there was no fear of his hay been burned. Matt wasn't convinced and told them to go away about their business – which they did. They pushed the bike out onto the road and both sat up on it. The driver tried to kick-start it, but no way would it start. The rider on the back jumped off and ran into Matt's and asked if they could bring the bike into the kitchen so that they would have light to fix it. Matt looked at him and said, "Do ye want to burn the house on me?"

"Ah, there's no fear of that, sir, it must be only a wire that got loose or fell off," pleaded the boy.

Matt felt a bit guilty as he had been messing with the bike, pulling this thing and that thing while he was 'minding' his cock of hay. Therefore he said they could bring it in as soon as the card game in progress was over.

Smiling, the boy thanked Matt and, assuring him that there was no danger whatsoever, he went out to inform his colleague. They pushed the bike into Matt's yard again. The card game over, pushing back the table against the wall to make room, Matt indicated to the boys to bring in the bike. They reversed it into the centre of the kitchen floor and proceeded to examine it. Quickly they found the offending wire and refitted it and, in their anxiety to test it, one of them sat astride it and gave a kick to the starter. It started immediately with a terrible roar. Sparks shot out the pipe at the back along with a gush of wind that blew the fire out of the hearth and drove a cloud of ashes all over the house. Quickly, the second fellow mounted and they shot out the door like a rocket. As they put up speed, the ashes were soon blown off their clothes by the wind. As for Matt and his house, the whole place was strewn in ashes – the table and chairs were all covered and it took an hour to make the place half presentable for the next game of cards. But to be fair to Matt, he took it in his stride, mainly because he knew he had tampered with the bike.

The night wore on and people were leaving as they were eliminated while others stayed on to watch the final destination of the cow unfold. At the Briar's house, excitement was building as it was now down to two tables of just sixteen players, all of them strangers except for the two locals, Ted and Freddie, who were still in the hunt. At five in the morning, it was down to just one table and eight players. Now the excitement was at fever pitch. The eight players, having discarded their bawneens and stripped to their shirts, were now hammering the table. One of the eight would be the owner of the cow in a very short time. With the table in the centre of the kitchen floor and the house packed, the atmosphere was electric and the heat intense. All the onlookers had their favourites to win and bets were exchanged as to the eventual winner. Seán Fada felt sorry for the two teenagers "thrown to the lions" as he said, trying to hold their place among such seasoned gamblers. The battle increased in intensity when two players were dispatched for reneging. One of the rules of the game of 41 is that you must 'hit with the fall of the lift' – this means that the last player in a game must play the card that will win that hand if he or she has a card with the capacity to do so. If a player fails to do so his hand is turned, that is, if the omission is spotted, and seasoned gamblers are very quick to spot such omissions and pounce without mercy. To turn means that the offending player has to actually turn his hand of cards on the table for everyone to see and cease playing for the remainder of that game.

With only six players in contention, new battle lines were again drawn and the two local representatives still held out under the pressure. Playing with great gusto and the crowd sensing that they had a good hand of cards, every trick they won was applauded. And so the battle raged until finally, and rather abruptly, two of the 'foreign' players threw their cards on the table in disgust at their poor hand. Shortly after, their two colleagues followed suit and Ted and Freddie were declared the winners. They couldn't believe they had won and, when it was suggested that they would have to single it out to find the individual winner, they refused point blank and said that they didn't even want the cow. It was real beginners' luck for them as every hand of cards they got won it for them with great simplicity against some of the great gamblers of the era. Realising the hour of the morning, their priority was to get home and into bed before their fathers were up. So without further ado, they departed and walked briskly home by the shortcut through the fields. Noiselessly stealing into there respective homes, they were in bed just half an hour when their fathers were calling them and they had no option but to get up.

As the gamble was held on a Friday night, the two met on the Saturday evening to discuss their win of the night before.

"You can have the cow if you wish, I'm certain my old man wouldn't let her inside the gate," said Ted.

"Oh, not a hope," answered Freddie, "my old man would be the exact same. Let 'em keep her. I heard she was foundered anyway. What I'm hoping is that no one will tell them that we won her."

But on Sunday there was an unusual sequel to events and it happened as follows. At about seven o'clock on Sunday evening Freddie and Ted met and were just about to go up the shortcut to the village when they saw a group of young people coming around the bend of the road, driving before them what looked like an animal of some sort. When they came closer they saw that it was like a cow. Coming closer again, they saw that it was a cow all right and that she was festooned with flags and bunting. Chains of flowers and leaves encircled Dolly's body and flags flew from both her horns and when she swished her tail she waved the national flag.

The two boys walked down to meet them and there was their prize, all dressed up. She was led from a halter by Paddy the Lad, himself festooned with a garland of flowers diagonally across his shoulder, and followed by a crowd of cheering youngsters, all decorated with flowers and bunting. With a big smile across his face, Paddy greeted them by saying, "How lucky to meet the two of you together. It gives me great pleasure to present you with your prize". The two boys were flabbergasted. If their fathers saw this sight, they thought, they'd have to leave. What would they do with her was the burning question? Suddenly Ted had a brainwave – supposing they put her into Small Danny's lot? Small Danny lived in a little thatched cottage within a few yards of where they were standing and, it being Sunday evening, he would have gone to the pub for a pint. When they approached Small Danny's gate, Ted said, "We will let her in here. There's a nice pick of grass there".

"Thank God," whispered Freddie to Ted, "how did you think of it?"

"Drastic situations need drastic remedies. 'Twill give us time to think," responded Ted.

So they led Dolly into Small Danny's lot and, ripping the rope off the halter, they left her to graze there, complete with flags, flowers and bunting. Small Danny came home from the pub late that night and went to bed, oblivious to the fact that he had a cow grazing in his lot. Next morning as he looked out his kitchen window he couldn't believe his eyes! He rubbed the windowpane and then rubbed his eyes a second and third time. Trying to convince himself that he wasn't drunk, he went out the back door and there she was in reality – a cow. Moving closer he put his hand on her back as if to convince himself that she was really there.

"A cow," he shouted at the top of his voice, even though no one was listening, "a cow and it must be God Himself that sent her to me. Who else could give a cow wearing such finery?"

Small Danny spent the most of that day admiring his cow and told everyone he met about his good fortune in the fact that God had sent him a miraculous cow and that her likes were never seen before. He invited all and sundry to come and view the apparition.

Alas, when he went out to see her the next morning he found her dead. When the sad news spread, Ted and Freddie were the first to arrive to offer their 'condolences'. They notified Paddy the Lad and, sure enough, himself and Seán Fada arrived in haste, armed with picks, spades and shovels. They found Small Danny in a semi-shocked state, lamenting the loss of his 'Heavenly Cow' as he called her.

"What do you want to do with her now?" asked Ted. Small Danny thought for a few moments and, looking down at the cow, he whispered in a broken voice, "I suppose we should give her a dacent burial". These were the words they wanted to hear and they immediately commenced digging a grave for her. Soon they had it ready and they laid her into it, complete with flags and flowers and ribbons. After closing the grave they got a timber board and, painting the outline of a cow on it, they wrote the inscription: 'Here lies Dolly the Heavenly Cow'.

"Wasn't it more natural than feeding her to dogs," remarked Mickey when he heard about the escapade.

Turkeys

The turkey played an important role in the economy of the farms of the era. In the weeks before Christmas turkey markets would be held in every town and village, giving a welcome financial boost to hard-pressed farmers' wives. In this field, the women took control, as this was their chance to make some money that they could call their own. And they earned it, as it was a long, hard battle over many months, often strewn with casualties, to ensure the birds survived until market time. Work would commence in early spring and be ongoing until the Christmas market. A frail type of bird, turkeys were susceptible to many diseases and, as research was scant or non-existent, and with remedies such as antibiotics unavailable, there was always the danger of losing some animals right up to market day. But that did not deter the farming women from trying year after year to produce turkeys and, as the years went by, they became adept at treating them with remedies which became available from various sources and, even though the success rate was limited, it still gave them great encouragement. Every little helped and in time most producers were cutting down the casualty list.

But there were other dangers a well. The fox was a constant prowler and a serious threat, even daring enough to attack a flock in broad daylight. The weasel, too, was to be feared, but not to the same extent as the fox. The hawk was also a constant danger to young chicks, but the big danger with the fox was that he could decimate a flock right up to market day and that would be a real disaster. The season of turkey rearing commenced when the hen turkey would be seen 'lying'. This was the sign that she was in the process of producing eggs. It also meant that for the eggs to be fertile she would have to be 'mated' and this entailed taking her to the cock. Now it must be said that the taking of the turkey to the cock was a social affair of sorts.

Bessie Johnny was the proud proprietor of turkey cocks for hire. A middle-aged mother of two sons and three daughters, she would give a detailed account of the bloodline of her cocks to anyone who would care to listen. And the general consensus of opinion among her clientele was that she always had the best bird around. That judgement was based on the high percentage of fertile eggs obtained and of course that was the bottom line as far as the turkey owners were concerned. They didn't want 'gluggers', the title given to non–fertile eggs. Molly Keogh and Biddy Jones were two of Bessie's faithful customers of many years and the two of them always travelled together. Near neighbours, they travelled by ass and car, Molly would take her ass one turn and Biddy would take hers the next time, a partnership that lasted a lifetime. Sitting on either side of the car with their legs dangling, in the body of the car would be their two hen turkeys inside sacks with their longs necks and gaping heads sticking out surveying the passing scene. Each year this routine continued on a regular basis during the whole turkey-breeding season. And it was a familiar sight as all breeders, and that was the vast majority of small farmers, made the same trek with their turkeys to the cock.

Always anxious to get the 'first of the cock', the two friends would usually travel early in the day. On arrival they would be greeted by Bessie and, after short preliminaries, they would get down to business. Her husband, Johnny, would tie the ass to a ring on the gable end wall of the house – the ring was there especially for that purpose. That would end Johnny's involvement in the business at hand and he would immediately disappear to do some work on his own small farm. A bad mixer, he was never happy chatting to all these women as all they would talk about was their turkeys. In the meantime, Bessie, helped by the two women, would take the birds to the rear of the house. Here she had two long, somewhat narrow, pens enclosed with wire. These she called her two 'lovers lanes'. In each was a turkey cock and, as they paraded up and down with their wings spreadeagled, touching the ground and their heads erect, they looked majestic. Opening a small entrance, Bessie pushed one of the hen turkeys into each pen. She then explained to Molly and Biddy that the cocks are very shy of onlookers and wouldn't operate under their gaze (even the turkey cocks at that time had moral standards!). So she would invite the women to adjourn to the house to give the birds a chance to do the business.

This was the social end of the job, as Bessie, a great cook, would have a big currant loaf and a variety of goodies on the table. As currant bread and goodies of any sort were a rarity in that era, they would be eaten with relish. The tay made, Bessie would cut the currant loaf, which the two women would enjoy, and she would insist on their sampling all the goodies. Of course, this treatment was reserved for her best customers, who used her cocks exclusively, and she had no time for anyone who would take their birds to other cocks and only come to her now and again. Discussing the gossip of the place over the tay, time would slip by and, as Molly and Biddy had to be home in time to milk the cows, they would pay Bessie her fee of one shilling each for the service of the cock. Bessie would then retrieve the two hens from the pens and put them back into their sacks, with their heads out, of course. Johnny would appear, as if by magic, from nowhere, and load the birds onto the ass's car. Untying the ass, he'd hold him by the head until the two were safely aboard and ready for the road home.

One day as Molly and Biddy were driving leisurely on their way to Bessie's with their birds, on came Mickeen Seán, bareback astride a pony, with a turkey in a sack strapped onto his back. With her head out, stretching away above his head, and bobbing as if timing the stepping pony, he passed them by. With a grin on his face, and a wave of his hand, he saluted the two women and left them in his wake. Barely acknowledging his salute and hitting the poor ass a clip of the stick, Molly and Biddy got very excited. When they regained their composure, Biddy exclaimed, "He'll have the first of the cock!"

"That's the trouble," moaned Molly, "and we'll have a nest of gluggers. And as well as that, he'll have all the currant loaf ate."

"Nothing surer," agreed Biddy, "there won't be a goodie left. Sure that wife of his never gave him enough to ate in his life so you can be sure he'll fill up when he gets the chance."

"And that's the truest word you ever said. The poor man, he has seen a lot more dinner times than dinners," agreed Molly.

But when they arrived at Bessie's they were relieved of their anxiety – there was no trace of Mickeen Seán, but then, on second thoughts, couldn't he have come and gone?

They broached the question with Bessie, asking if Mickeen Seán had been there with a turkey.

"He was," Bessie answered.

Their hearts sank. He had the first of the cock and that could spell disaster. After a moment's hesitation Bessie said, "He's a mane bacach. He asked me what I was charging and I said only a shilling and what do you think he said to me?"

"No," blurted the two in unison.

"He told me that he could get a finer cock altogether from the Pedler Casey's wife for nine pence," said Bessie.

"And what did you say to him?" they asked, expectantly.

"I said peddle away for yourself and away he went," Bessie explained.

"So you didn't give him the cock at all?" asked the pair.

"Not at all," replied Bessie angrily.

And with a sigh of relief the two women blurted out, "And that was the right thing to do with him". Suppressing a desire to give her a clap on the back, their depression immediately lifted and they felt on top of the world – they would have the first of the cock!

There would be great excitement when the turkey laid her first egg of the season and, laying one every day, the numbers would accumulate rapidly. Molly and Biddy would then be watching their flock of hens to spot any of them hatching. If, after a certain length of time, none of their own hens went into hatching mode, they would ask the neighbours for the loan of a hatcher, if anyone happened to have one. And usually someone in the locality would come forward with one and lend her with a heart and a half. When the chicks were hatched and out of their shells for a week or two, the hatcher would be gratefully returned to its owner. This was general practice at the time and it is an instance of the co-operative, neighbourly and community spirit that existed at that period. The turkeys themselves would also hatch at a certain time and, being the big birds that they are, they would cover several more eggs than the ordinary hen.

Some cock owners created a type of status for their birds by charging one shilling and six pence instead of the usual shilling. People being somewhat innocent in those times, this would create petty jealousies. On market day, as they would be looking into each others' rail of turkeys, the comment would be made – "Sure they are only off the cheap cock" – and fast would come the reply – "And wouldn't you know in 'em". A tender type of chick, the rearing of the infant turkey was painstaking and demanded great skill and attention. Casualties were always a possibility and very often a reality. As the birds got older they wouldn't require as much attention and by day they would potter around the haggard or in a specially prepared compound where they would be safe from dogs or foxes. They would always be housed at night. The housing for turkeys at that time was very mediocre and that mediocrity cost poor Mrs Tom Seán dearly one year.

Going out to feed her flock of turkeys on the morning of market day, as she pushed in the door, a fox rushed out and almost knocked her. Recovering her composure after the initial shock, she entered the bothán to find all her flock killed except three. Two cocks and one hen was all that was left. Shock and despair alternated in her mind and the children too were uppermost in her thoughts as she surveyed the carnage. How would she buy some little things for them from Santa Claus? Depressed and dejected, she went to the cow byre to tell her husband the awful news. Sitting on a three-legged stool milking a cow, he listened. Tom Seán made some involuntary movement that upset the cow she kicked the bucket of milk from between his knees, which added to their distress. Tom Seán figured that the fox pushed in the door and that it slammed closed when he got in, so he couldn't get out. If he could have got out he might only have killed one.

The bad news soon spread throughout the community and, as they were a nice and popular family, there was widespread sympathy for them on their great loss. Seán Fada heard about it as he was going to Paddy Mikes to build a wall. He related the sad news to the woman of the house and her first reaction was to run out the back door to check her own flock. Satisfied that all was well with her flock, she soon had Paddy and Seán Fada sitting down to breakfast and, of course, the conversation was about the terrible loss suffered by Tom Seán and his wife, Mary. They speculated that the family might owe a big bill for the feeding stuff to the local shop. The breakfast over, Paddy Mike asked Seán Fada if he know how many birds were killed, to which the latter replied that he thought it was fifteen.

"Fifteen," uttered Paddy Mike thoughtfully and then added, "it's a big loss for them."

"It is all that then," agreed Seán Fada, "isn't it a pity something couldn't be done for them."

"That's what I was just thinking," said Paddy Mike. "You know, fifteen is a lot but, in another way, it isn't an awful lot. Look at it this way, how many rails of turkeys will be at the market?"

"About fifty," answered Seán Fada.

"Fifty," repeated Paddy Mike, "surely it would be possible to get one turkey from fifteen dacent people out of the fifty."

"I honestly believe it would," agreed Seán Fada, "and what would you think of giving a run around to a few people to test the response?"

"It might be a good idea," said Paddy Mike, "we'll forget about the wall. You'll come with me, I'll tackle the pony and we'll test the temperature. As a matter of fact I'll put on the rail and we'll collect as we go along, if we happen to get birds."

For starters, Paddy Mike took a turkey from his own flock, causing Seán Fada to remark, "We only need fourteen now". Suffice it is to say that in the course of an hour and a half they had collected the fifteen birds and when they drove into Tom Seán's yard, there was disbelief and then tears of joy and many words of thanks. Even the child felt the elation, saying, "Will Santa come now Mom?" Soon the two men had the birds dropped off and were ready for home. Standing up inside the rail with Seán Fada also aboard, Paddy Mike turned the pony towards the gate for home. As he was turning, Tom Seán ran across the yard and asked them to come in for a mug of tay but they declined, saying, "We'll see you at the turkey market". Tom Seán then reached up his hand and Paddy Mike reached down and the two shook hands. Clasping Paddy Mike's hand in a vice-like grip and looking up at him with tears in his eyes, he said, "I can never thank you enough. You saved us from ruin".

"Well, 'tis like this," replied Paddy Mike, "one good turn always deserves another."

"What do you mean? I never did you a favour in my life," said a surprised Tom Seán.

"It is going back a long, long time, sixty years or maybe more," said Paddy Mike, with a faraway look in his eyes.

"What are you talking about?" muttered a perplexed Tom Seán.

"It is a long time ago all right," continued Paddy Mike, "my father's rick of hay was burned, every sop of it. It was a real disaster for our family and several times he told me that the first man into his haggard with a load of hay was your father. As I said, one good turn deserves another."

Full of emotion, he hit the pony with the whip and drove out the yard gate, leaving Tom Seán standing motionless in the middle of the yard gazing after them, perplexed by the events of the day.

As the market date approached and as the turkeys were sold by weight, their feeding routine would be stepped up as it was imperative that they put on as much weight as possible to ensure a worthwhile profit from the enterprise. On the week before the market day, the topic of conversation among the womenfolk wherever they met, whether after Mass on a Sunday or at the well for water or selling the eggs on a Friday in the local grocer's shop, would be turkeys. The more inquisitive would ask all kinds of questions, especially of a more docile neighbour. They'd ask, "How many have you? How many cocks are in 'em? Did you lose many? Whose cock did you take them to? What did you feed them on? Where did you get it? Was it dear?" The litany of questions would continue until the 'victim's' husband would arrive on the scene, then the conversation would be brought to an abrupt end. Driving home in the pony and car, the woman would, invariably, give out to the husband saying, "I thought you would never come. She had me driven demented". With a knowing smile on his face, the husband would just remark, "I partly guessed you were under cross-examination".

Market day saw a hive of activity in the village from early morning. The early birds, pardon the pun, would arrive about eight o'clock, hoping to have an early sale. They were often disappointed because, when they first arrived, the buyers would feign complete lack of interest in buying stating that they were over-supplied. This attitude often sparked off angry scenes with disgruntled producers shouting "What brought you so?", and far more explicit obscenities. This conduct was an instance of the abuse and pressures hard-pressed farming folk were subject to and had to endure to earn a meagre living. In the meantime, the line of cars would be getting longer and longer, and every type of animal would be brought into service. There would be horses and ponies, asses, jennets and mules, all harnessed to some type of car, with creels covered with sacking from meal bags. Some would be covered with old quilts and these would add a bit of colour to the scene. Others would have old black shawls for cover or a discarded woman's dress might cover an ass's car. All in all, it was a motley selection of cover and its purpose was to stop the birds from flying out of the creel. However, after hours of arguing and abuse, with some of the farmers blaming the government and this causing more confrontation due to inflamed tempers by farmers of differing political allegiance, the buyers would take out their weighing scales and commence business.

The crowd would at once become subdued but not for long. The buyers would claim that the majority of the turkeys had 'crooked breasts' and consequently would be worth less money per pound. Naturally, this would cause further uproar and the farmers would call a strike and agree among themselves that no birds would be sold, crooked breasts or straight breasts! Bessie, knowing that a large number of the turkeys on sale were the progeny of her cocks, would also attack the buyers and state categorically that none of her cocks bred crooked breasted turkeys. She would be supported by the proprietors of the several cocks in the area who would form an alliance for the day to combat this outrage about their cocks breeding birds with crooked breasts. This standoff would continue for hours and, in the end, the buyers would be as frustrated as the farmers. It was only when the farmers would give the impression the they had decided to take their turkeys home that the buyers would eventually give in and buying would commence, in earnest this time, and all would be forgotten when the money started changing hands.

The parish priest of Ballymachad at the time was a man well into his eighties and on the Sunday before a general election, after reciting the Deprofundis at the foot of the altar, he turned towards the congregation and said, "As you all know, we are on the eve of a general election and I sincerely hope you will not return to power that man that has brought ruination to our little country". One parishioner nudged the other and said, "The poor man, he is doting at last". Of course, the priest was told what was said about him but he took no notice of it and never mentioned it again. After the election, the same man was returned to power. In due course the turkey market was held in the village as usual. There was a mile of cars in each direction from the village, but the buyers were offering very small money and the producers wouldn't sell. This went on all day and, in the afternoon, the parish priest was out for his walk. Walking sprightly up and down the row of cars, twirling his walking stick and noting that there was no sale for the turkeys, he kept saying out loud, for all to hear, "Who's doting now, who's doting now, who's doting now? However, the next year the flocks of turkeys would be produced again in the hope the market would be better. No doubt, hope springs eternal in the human heart.

The Stepping Match

In good times or bad times farmers always gave pride of place to the horse. The horse was their pride and joy. They would jealously boast about their horse and it would be considered a cardinal sin against its owner for anyone to criticize his horse.

There was a maxim which said 'you can criticize a man's wife but don't criticize his horse'. Stabled in the winter, the horse would get the best of the hay and a generous feed of oats every day. As the horse would be more or less idle during the winter he'd be restricted to the one feed of oats but when work commenced in the spring that would be increased to two or three feeds a day, according to the type of work at hand. An annual chore during winter was the clipping of the horse – that is cutting the hair off the lower part of the body and belly. The tail would also be cut short to prevent it from getting dirty while the animal was stabled. This job was always done by a professional for a specified fee. In Ballymachad the man who undertook this work was known as Bob the Clipper. He did this chore for many years and had his own routine. He would arrive at the same time of the year, every year, to each of his many customers. He would usually be given a meal washed down with a tumbler of porter, either before or after his job was done. A well-known and very likable character, sometimes Bob would arrive half groggy, compliments of the generosity of his customers. Some farmers wouldn't let him touch their horse in such a condition for fear he'd leave a hair out of place, so particular were they about the appearance of their horse.

There was also the pony and the cob, the latter being an animal that was bigger than a pony and smaller than a horse. Both had their uses, especially cobs which were ideal for smaller farms as they wouldn't eat as much grass as a horse but would be strong enough to do most of the work on the farm, including ploughing when coupled to a horse which might be loaned to the farmer by a neighbour. For the man with a handy farm, the pony was ideal for light work. Ponies were also lively on the road, being good travellers and, most important of all, light on grass in comparison to the horse. On smaller farms it was considered more profitable to have extra cows than a horse, as it was reckoned that a horse would eat as much grass as three cows, hence the value of the pony or the cob.

On Sunday evenings in Ballymachad many of the neighbours would meet in the Shanty. The Shanty was a type of room built on to the gable-end of the pub. As the public house was also a grocery shop where the women purchased their groceries and, as the counter continued to the drink section, the women would have full view of the men drinking. Many of the men customers resented this and some of them changed their allegiance. They went to other pubs for their drink. The local publican took a serious view of this trend and, after due deliberation, he decided to build a temporary structure onto the gable-end wall of the shop to accommodate the men. He then made a hatch in the wall to serve the drinks. With a thatched roof, it was fairly comfortable and the men took to it immediately – a little haven away from the glare of the women. He called it the Shanty and the name stuck. In time it became a meeting place for men who had business to transact, such as making a match for a daughter or a son and indeed, many a horse and cow were bought and sold there over the years as men sipped their pints.

There was never a night in the Shanty that a discussion on horses didn't take place – the horse could be called the common denominator in the community. One such Sunday evening, when, as usual, the conversation turned to horses, a discussion started between Mickey Tom Seán and Patcheen the Gambler about the good and bad points of their respective horses. What started as just a friendly appraisal of the two animals culminated in very noisy, abusive and fiery exchanges between the two neighbours. Tom Redden and Paddy the Lad walked in when the argument was at its peak. The two called for their drinks, pretending to be oblivious to what was going on. In an effort to drag Redden into the argument Mickey Tom Seán said, "In the word of an honest man, Tom Redden, what do you think of Patcheen's old mare? Sure she has no timber under her". Paddy the Lad, sipping his drink, was enjoying the fact that Tom Redden was caught, he'd never get out of this situation without making enemies, he thought.

With relish, he took a slug of his porter and nearly choked on it when he heard Redden say, as cool as a breeze, "Test them together. No use in talking here about one horse being better than another except ye put the two of them to the test. Then ye can come back and talk, when ye know what ye are talking about".

"What do you mane by a test?" questioned Mickey Tom Seán, a small, peevish, elderly man with eyebrows like a blue terrier. "What I mean," retorted Redden, "is put the two of them at the same job and see which one will come out tops."

"What kind of a job would that be?" questioned Mickey Tom Seán.

After a moment's thought, and in a roguish voice, Redden said, "What I have in mind is a stepping match."

"Well now, fair play to you Tom," cut in Paddy the Lad, "that would be the right test of them, cut and dried, one is faster, the other is slower. You would soon find out which of them has the best timber".

There was a deafening silence. Eventually it was Patcheen who broke the silence declaring, "I'm game". He wasn't called the Gambler for nothing.

Again you'd hear a pin dropping. Mickey Tom Seán picked his cap off the floor where it had fallen and, making for the door, gave a scornful look at the Lad and shouted as he passed him, "What the blazes do you know about horses, all you ever had was a jennet. You were always only a bloody troublemaker," and walked out the door in a huff. Paddy the Lad nearly choked laughing, it really made his day to knock such a rise out of Mickey Tom Seán. Controlling his laughter, the Lad said to Tom Redden, "I think that's a great idea of yours but why don't you leave it open to anyone who wants to compete? Make a parish thing of it and give us all a day out".

"And who says otherwise?" countered Tom, "that's exactly what I had in mind," adding in a mischievous voice, "'twas you who made a one-to-one of it and upset poor Mickey Tom Seán. Anyone in the parish that wants to can compete, the more the merrier. And to show that I'm serious," continued Tom, "I'll put up a ten-stone bag of oats for the winner."

"Here! Here!" shouted the crowd in the Shanty.

"That's the form," said Patcheen, "I suppose you're thinking the horse that will win is worth a bag of oats."

Ever the joker, the Lad mused: "I'm just wondering will Mickey Tom Seán compete."

"He's as welcome as the flowers in May if he does," responded Redden, "no one with a four-legged animal will be ruled out."

"May I ask when are ye holding it? I'd like to be involved if I may," said a grey-haired man in a cultured voice who was relaxing with a pint of porter in his hand. He was sporting a colourful scarf around his neck and a big brown hat on his knee. All eyes turned in his direction but no one knew him as he was a complete stranger. Redden got a bit of a start when he heard this, but quick enough, he turned towards the stranger and in his unique mannerly way, said, "Sir, we haven't a date fixed yet but I assure you, we will be giving it a lot of publicity when we do. To answer your other question – thank you, sir, we will need all the help we can get". The trio – Redden, Patcheen and the Lad – went out the back door to the yard with Tom Redden remarking, "It's hard to do business in there". Out in the open space the question as to when the event would take place was raised. After a short discussion, Patcheen's proposal to hold it on a Sunday afternoon was unanimously agreed to. Tom Redden then suggested that day fortnight as that would give all the local horsemen ample time to prepare. It was also agreed to charge an entrance fee of two shillings, as putting a price on it would make it sound 'uppish' and there was never any 'meas' on something for nothing.

Immediately, the trio retraced their steps to the Shanty and Redden announced that the date of the stepping match was fixed for "this day fortnight". Turning to the grey-haired stranger and using his best vocabulary, Tom Redden politely said, "Your help would be much appreciated, sir, if it is forthcoming". To give more volunteers an opportunity to come forward a meeting was arranged for the next Tuesday night, not in the Shanty, but in Patcheen's farmhouse because of, among other things, its big kitchen. Some of the 'other things' were the noise and the chatter in the Shanty, the lack of privacy there and hangers-on who had no interest in the stepping match but who would try to throw a spanner into the works by asking awkward questions and upsetting the proceedings.

The meeting duly took place on the appointed night. Patcheen's wife, Bessie, had the big kitchen table cleared of all crockery and covered with a white linen cloth that was never before used for anything except the Stations. First to arrive was Tom Redden, closely followed by the stranger with the colourful scarf and the big brown hat. Who he was, no one knew. The thought that he could be an English spy infiltrating the local scene crossed Redden's mind, who was now half sorry for allowing him onto the committee. He decided it would be better to play it by ear for the moment, but if he got the slightest suspicion that anything was awry, the stranger would get the road, or maybe worse. Paddy the Lad arrived late, as usual, for which he got a friendly admonishment from Redden, which, of course, fell on deaf ears. Patsy the 'Lark' O'Brien was the only newcomer to the meeting, arriving just as the meeting was about to get under way. Patcheen insisted on Tom Redden sitting at the head of the table, Redden protesting that the man of the house should sit there, but to no avail. When they were all seated on súgán chairs around the table with Tom Redden sitting on an armchair at the head of the table, he opened the meeting with the words, "Any suggestions from anybody?" There was an uneasy silence broken when Tom said, in a questioning voice, "Well?"

"Mr Redden," commenced the stranger.

"Tom," interrupted Redden.

"Fine," smiled the stranger, "you may call me Mortimer."

The ice was broken and all were now on first name terms. Mortimer's first question was, "How many horses do ye expect to have?"

"Any number from ten to twenty," suggested the Lad.

"Ten to twelve would be more likely," said the man of the house, Patcheen.

The Lark O'Brien agreed. Tom Redden said it was hard to predict as some could be holding their cards close to their chests, sizing up the opposition and maybe planning to spring a surprise on the day.

"You could counteract that," suggested Mortimer, "by stipulating that all runners will have to be declared two days in advance."

"A good idea," declared Redden, "I propose we adopt that."

They all concurred.

"Any prize for second place?" asked Patsy the Lark O'Brien.

"No, do you think we should?" inquired Redden.

"Well, it would look nice," was the Lark's opinion, "I would give a bag of turnips if ye like."

"Well, that's mighty dacent of you," said Redden, "what do ye think, lads?"

All agreed that it was a generous gesture and felt it would add to the prize-giving ceremony.

"Any more suggestions?" asked Tom, looking at each one of them around the table. Mortimer took the cue.

"We will have to appoint a judge. Have ye anyone in mind?" he asked.

"A judge! For what?" gulped the Lad.

"We will have to have a judge on horseback checking that none of them break into a gallop," explained Mortimer.

He seemed to be well-versed in this sport and continued to explain that the penalty for a horse that breaks is to be turned, which meant he would have to turn around in a full circle on the road, thus losing valuable time.

"And if he don't turn?" inquired the Lad.

"He will be disqualified immediately," answered Mortimer in an authoritative voice.

Patcheen suggested that they take time to think about a judge as they'd want a sound man for that job.

The Lark O'Brien suggested that all the horses entered should have a name. Tom Redden agreed, saying he'd call his mare 'Rebecca's Pride'. All agreed that they had a week to get the names in and, most important of all, to appoint a judge. As the meeting was about to end, the stranger, Mortimer, delivered a bombshell. If they all agreed, he would judge the stepping match. He would bring his own horse and, being a stranger in the place, he would be totally impartial. It took a few minutes for the reality of the offer to sink in. But then, one by one, all agreed that Mortimer's offer should be accepted as it would exonerate them from potential charges of perceived partiality to friends or neighbours. Silence prevailed while the men were thinking about this fellow and where he might have his horse. Where did he come from or where did he live? How did they know he even had a horse? Reading their thoughts, Mortimer gazed across the table at Redden and said in a low voice, "May I introduce myself to you?" After a short uneasy silence, Tom Redden said, "You may, of course".

"Thank you," responded Mortimer. "Firstly, I'm retired, a retired court judge."

Eyes opened at this revelation and none wider than Tom Redden's. In that era, judges were considered persona non grata and that would be the line taken by Tom Redden and indeed his colleagues around the table. Mortimer continued.

"I retired, not because of my age, but in protest at certain laws in force in this country which judges are forced to implement. I'll say no more about that. You know where I stand."

"Certainly," said a relieved Redden.

Mortimer continued in a lighter tone of voice, as if he, too, was relieved of an enormous weight.

"I am living just outside the town where I bought a rundown house which I am in the process of renovating. Being from a farming background I keep a horse and a cow on about six acres of land. I am deeply grateful to you all for giving me the honour of appointing me the judge of your stepping match. I guarantee to you I will be totally fair."

Redden graciously replied, "We have the utmost confidence in your integrity".

"Thank you," said Mortimer.

Bessie had the kettle 'singing' on the crane over a blazing turf fire. She made the tay and served it in her best china which was never used except for the priest at the Station every five or six years. With a fresh currant loaf and plenty of homemade butter, it became a lovely social evening, and when Patcheen uncorked a bottle of poitín, in a short time there was more than the kettle singing!

The word spread rapidly throughout the parish that a stepping match was organised and the response came just as rapidly. On the Monday evening, several men commenced riding their horses on the roads, bareback or otherwise, in training for the event. Others soon followed suit and this continued nightly right up to the Saturday night before the match. The training attracted onlookers at the crossroads who enjoyed the sparks off the road from the steel shoes on the horses on the dark night, as well as betting with each other as to who the eventual winner would be. In the meantime, the word went out that all the horses entered would have to have a name. The names were to be handed to Paddy the Lad as soon as possible with two shillings to confirm the entry. This gave them all food for thought and caused a certain amount of jealously. Men like Paddy Dan Tobin who, when he heard that Redden was calling his horse 'Rebecca's Pride' – obviously honouring his wife Rebecca – declared openly, "If Redden can name his horse after his wife so can I, after my wife, Molly".

"What will you be calling her so?" asked the Lad with a smirk on his face.

Without a moment's hesitation Paddy Dan replied, "I'll be calling her 'Molly's Dolly'". Tom Jim Cronin named his horse 'Ballymac Lady' while Long John Casey christened his mare 'Lady Jane' after his eldest daughter. Duncan Shorte, a relic of the gentry, entered a horse which he nostalgically named 'Glory Days'. The Fowler Carey named his horse 'Crack Shot Daisy' while Timmy Pat Landers chose 'Dandy Lad' for his newly-trained colt. Mickeen Seán called his piebald mare 'The Colourful Lady' while Nedeen Murphy from the hill came in with 'Hilly Billy' for his four-year-old chestnut. Good timber or bad timber under her, Patcheen entered his mare and, just for the craic, called her 'Wooden Legs'.

Mickey Tom Seán laid low and wasn't seen out for a week and he didn't enter his horse for the match. Paddy the Lad accosted him after Mass on Sunday, a week before the event, but he walked away. But the Lad kept walking with him and asked him was he entering his horse, to which Mickey Tom Seán brusquely replied, "I think too much of my horse to put him at that kind of a caper". The last entry was from a woman, a widow woman at that, called Mary Kate Muldowney. A very resilient woman, Mary Kate was left with seven children but eked out a living on a small farm of stubborn soil through sheer hard work, with sheep and farmyard enterprises of turkeys, geese, ducks and hens.

"What name will you put on him?" asked the Lad.

Mary Kate thought for a few minutes.

"I'll call him 'Hurricane Boy' because he was foaled the night of a terrible storm seven years ago," Mary Kate said.

"Well, that's as good a reason as ever I heard and as classy a name. I wish you luck on the day," exclaimed the Lad.

"Thank you," responded Mary Kate, "I'll get young Connor to ride him, Mickey Pat's son, a great little cratur and as tough as wax. He'd take no notice of falling off, he'd just make a sweep and up on his back again and off."

So that was the field of certain starters whose names plus the entry fee of two shillings had been given to the Lad. There were several other horses tested on the nightly runs, but one by one they dropped out as their owners felt they hadn't what it would take.

Patcheen remarked to the Lad in idle conversation that it was a pity someone didn't take bets on the day as 'twould add to the excitement of the race. The Lad didn't answer but it sparked an idea in his brain and two hours later he accosted Patcheen as he was driving in his cows to be milked. However, Patcheen kept going so the Lad followed him into the yard.

"Is there something wrong?" inquired Patcheen, noticing that he seemed fidgety.

"Oh, there is nothing wrong, but do you remember what you said to me today about someone taking bets?" asked the Lad.

"Oh, for the stepping match is it? Yerra, I do. Did you hear of some gambler coming?" said Patcheen.

"No, I heard of no one but I was thinking I might have a go at it myself," said the Lad.

"Yerra, why not. Sure it could set you up to be a mighty big gambler. That's the way all the millionaires started out – small," declared Patcheen, laughing his way to the cow byre.

Excited about his brainwave, the Lad shouted to Patcheen, "Go away and milk your cows", and he exited the yard with his head in the air and his mind calculating all the money he was going to make. It could top a hundred pounds, he thought. Presently he let it be known that he would be taking bets on the stepping match. He advised people that he would make himself available in the Shanty up to any hour on the Friday and Saturday evenings before the race to accommodate them to place their bets in comfort and to avoid the rush on Sunday. Still on a high, the next port of call for the Lad was Pat's shop.

Pat was serving a customer but the Lad intruded saying, "I'm in a dangerous hurry Pat, would you have a tay chest cover by any chance?"

"Well, now, this is the first time I ever saw you in a hurry," remarked Pat, "what would you want that for?"

"Did you hear the news at all?" asked the Lad.

"Hear what?" asked Pat.

"I'm going to be taking bets on the horses for the stepping match and the reason I'm in a hurry is that I'm taking the tay chest cover up to the Master at the school to write the names of the horses on it with chalk before he closes. You must do things right in this job you know," the Lad explained proudly.

"Oh, I suppose you must," chuckled Pat, going out the back door and returning in a jiffy with a lovely clean tay chest cover. "Will that do the job?" asked Pat, handing him the cover.

"Perfect. Just what the doctor ordered," enthused the Lad.

"What kind of odds will you be giving?" asked Pat.

Pointing to the chest cover in his hand, the Lad replied, "You'll have to watch the board", and he ran out the door.

The Master did a neat job on the chest cover for him, fitting the names of five horses in one row and six in the second and leaving plenty of space for the odds to be filled in. He then gave the Lad a few sticks of chalk to put in the odds himself. Then, however, a big impediment presented itself, something the Lad should have foreseen – he wasn't good at figures. On the contrary, he was very bad. In the euphoria of the thought of getting rich quick, he never realised what it entailed but now reality struck. A master at improvising, he realised immediately he would have to get help so he decided he would approach Jackeen Casey. An elderly man, Jackeen was a fiddle player of note but what was more important to the Lad was that his father and grandfather before him were hedge-school masters, and Jackeen himself was reputed to have been well educated in his youth. Without further ado, the Lad made a beeline for Jackeen's house across the fields where he found the old man busy teaching a young boy a tune on the fiddle. Smiling slightly, Jackeen listened intently as Paddy the Lad explained his dilemma and after listening to a long list of explicits, Jackeen said, "All you want is a fellow with a jotter, me boy".

"A jotter!" exclaimed the Lad.

"That's what you want," confirmed Jackeen, "and someone to mark in the transactions."

With a puzzled look on his face, the Lad asked, "What do you mane by trans... whatever you called 'em?"

"You'll have to keep an account of what you take in and what you pay out, otherwise you could go broke," explained Jackeen.

"Broke?" queried the Lad.

Sensing that the Lad hadn't a clue of what he was about, Jackeen decided to help him.

"Paddy," he advised, "go down to the village, go into Pat's shop, ask him for a penny jotter and I'll help you out on Friday. I'll be down to you about two o'clock and, sure, we might make our fortune together."

Racing back across the fields, the Lad arrived, panting, at Pat's shop.

"A penny jotter, Pat," he panted, oblivious to the fact that Pat was serving an old woman who was buying snuff.

"Still in a hurry?" laughed Pat, noticing the Lad's breathing exertions as he handed him the jotter.

"Here is your penny," blurted the Lad as he laid the coin on the counter, "I must be off to be ready for Friday night, it's very important to have everything right, you know, in this job."

As he exited Pat shouted after him, "Best of luck. I hope you'll make a fortune".

The Lad didn't look back, just raised his hand in the air in acknowledgement.

Friday afternoon arrived, a lovely warm afternoon with clear blue skies and singing birds. It was that sort of evening when men going home after a day in the bog would have an insatiable thirst and that's the way Jackeen Casey felt when he hit the village that same evening. Paddy the Lad met him just outside the school gate and immediately pulled the jotter from the inside pocket of his coat, saying, "You're late! I thought you had forgotten".

"Put that thing back into your pocket, my boy, I have a most desperate thirst and I won't be able to look at a thing until 'tis quenched," said Jackeen.

The Lad had no better to do but to take him into the Shanty and stand him three pints of porter, one after another, which Jackeen downed in quick time. When he had the last drop drained, he emitted a belch of gas, turned towards the Lad and, licking his lips, he said, "If you have that jotter handy we'll do a bit of business now". Hurriedly the Lad handed Jackeen the jotter and explained to him that there were eleven runners so he was thinking of giving odds of two to one on all of them, so as to keep the payout as small as possible, no matter who would win.

"Wrong," exclaimed Jackeen, "if you know of horses that you think have no chance of winning you should put odds of five or six to one on them because some will take the chance that an outsider might win. And if you know one that you would consider a certain loser, you could put ten to one on him and guaranteed you would get gullible people to put plenty money on him just to take the chance of making big money, so it's your call."

The Lad was more puzzled than ever – what he thought was a simple way to make big money fast was now getting more and more complicated. After ten minutes or so of soul-searching, he said, "Jackeen, maybe we should play it by ear".

"As I said, it's your call," replied Jackeen, "but come what may, Paddy, we should go back into the Shanty before the crowd comes and hang the tay-chest cover on the wall to display the names of the runners, odds and all, and stand by for results."

The Lad agreed.

Back into the Shanty they went and the Lad pulled a length of string and a small nail out of his pocket. Going out to the yard he returned with a stone the size of a big spud with which he hammered the small nail onto the tay-chest cover. Tying the string with a black knot to the nail, Jackeen warned him to have it just the right height – high enough to ensure that you would have to stand on a small stool to change the odds if the need arose.

"If it was hanging too low some scoundrel with a drop too much taken could blot out all the names and the odds and make us look very silly," counseled Jackeen.

When the board was ready, Jackeen opened the jotter. Copying the names of the horses off the board, he gave a page to each horse, which worked out perfect as there were just twelve pages in the jotter.

"Now," said Jackeen, clearing his throat, "we will have to take the bull by the horns – what are the odds going to be?"

The Lad, in spite of all his cod-acting, was forlorn and completely out of his depth. The thought that there was a possibility he could go broke completely knocked the wind out of his sails and he wondered how he would ever live it down.

"Cheer up auld stock," urged Jackeen, still flushed from the three quick pints, "we'll start off with Rebecca's Pride. What odds are you giving on her, will we say two to one?"

"At the very most," said the Lad.

"Next, we have Molly's Dolly, what will you give on her, Paddy?"

"Put all the rest of 'em down at two to wan except maybe, Hurricane Boy. Young Connor will be riding him and he is sure to fall off so you could give ten to wan on him and you could even give eight to wan on Wooden Legs and Glory Days," said the Lad.

"I'll do that," agreed Jackeen, "as I said, 'tis your call."

The board was now complete with the odds marked in after each horse's name. Standing on a stool, the Lad tied the cord to the nail almost up to the thatch where it was safe from any interference. Standing back, the two men admired the board, agreeing that it certainly looked the part.

"We forgot something," declared Jackeen.

"What did we forget?" inquired the Lad with worry written all over his face.

"How will we know who bet what? I mean, if a fellow comes up to you after the event and says that he had two shillings on the winner, how will you know whether he had or hadn't?" questioned Jackeen.

"I never thought of that," said the Lad with dismay, "I thought you were going to write them down, that that was what the jotter was for."

"I must admit that was my plan," Jackeen replied, "but I now feel it would be unworkable. At the time I didn't realise it would be such a big affair."

"What will happen at all now?" asked a very go brónach Paddy the Lad.

Oozing confidence, Jackeen declared, "I have been hatching a plan inside in my head for the last couple of hours and 'tis this – you go over now, this very minute, to Pat's shop and get a sheet of wrapping paper from him, white if possible but brown would do as well, it needs to be fairly strong stuff".

"What will that do for us?" asked a very sceptical Lad.

"What it will do for us is this – we have eleven horses so we will give each horse a number, from one to eleven. We will cut the sheet of paper in small pieces just big enough to write in the number of the horse and the odds. For example, Rebecca's Pride would read 1 at 2/1 and Hurricane Boy would read 10 at 10/1," explained Jackeen.

"That's all?" wondered the Lad.

"That's all, me boy," said Jackeen, "we'll call them 'tickets' so run away as quick as you can and be sure to bring a scissors back with you."

Muttering a nasty expletive and blaming Patcheen for having mentioned the idea of bets on the stepping match in the first place, Paddy the Lad scurried out the door, still talking to himself, and ran up the street to Pat's shop. When he noticed people watching his unusual demeanour, he slowed down and walked into Pat's shop in as relaxed a manner as he could put on.

"Well, Paddy, what can I do today for you?" Pat asked politely.

"Could you give me a big sheet of wrapping paper, strong stuff if you have it," asked the Lad.

"Wrapping paper? What do you want that for?" questioned Pat.

"For to make betting tickets for the stepping match," answered the Lad, putting on a business-like air as best he could.

Pat went into his store room and, standing in the doorway, held up a sheet of what appeared to be very light cardboard, he asked, "Did you say you were making tickets?"

"That's right," answered the Lad.

"Well, feel this stuff, it came covering boxes. I imagine it would be ideal for that purpose," said Pat.

The Lad felt it with his thumb and forefinger and agreed that it would be much better than paper. He said he'd take a couple of sheets of it, hoping it would suit Jackeen.

"What's the damage?" inquired the Lad.

"No charge," replied Pat, "I'd be only burning it."

"Better again," smiled the Lad, putting in under his oxter and walking out the door.

But he retuned again within a minute, saying as he walked in the door, "I forgot Pat, have you a scissors? Jackeen warned me to bring a scissors". Pat went inside the counter and handed him a new scissors, saying, "That will cost you one and six". "Sounds dear," the Lad grumbled.

Pat just smiled.

Jackeen was delighted with the cardboard and he immediately cut out what he considered would be the correct size for a ticket. Then, handing the prototype and the scissors to the Lad, he ordered him to cut out tickets as fast as he could, but warned him to be sure to always use the original for measuring. The Lad sat down on the floor and did as he was told, while Jackeen commenced writing in the numbers of the horses and the relevant odds. Then he suddenly stopped.

"Wrong," he shouted to no one in particular but it gave the Lad a start.

"What is wrong now, Jackeen?" asked the Lad in a worried tone.

"Work away you. It just suddenly struck me that the right time to fill in the ticket is when the bet is made, otherwise we could end up in a heap," explained Jackeen.

The Lad worked silently for several hours until all the cardboard was used and when he counted there was over two hundred tickets. Jackeen was very happy with the number but the Lad, to add to his woes, had a swelled thumb and finger from the scissors. He got no sympathy from Jackeen who said with a grunt, "The young lads nowadays are mighty soft".

The Lad felt hungry and asked Jackeen if he would drink another pint before the business would start. Jackeen replied that he would but said he would like "something solid with it". Tapping on the shutter to the bar and then leaning his elbow on the bit of a counter, the Lad gazed in admiration at the board hanging almost from the thatch, while waiting for Mrs Muldoon to open the shutter.

The Stepping Match

"Two pints, Molly, and would you give a couple of slices of bread with 'em?" the Lad requested.

"I certainly will," Molly replied, "and if ye are hungry, I have lovely fat bacon cooked and I'll put a slice of it between the bread for ye."

"Oh, bless your heart, that's better again," extolled the Lad, licking his lips in anticipation.

The two pints were soon handed out, followed by a tin plate containing four thick slices of homemade bread with the promised slice of fat bacon about an inch thick between the slices. Jackeen and the Lad ate with a desperate appetite and soon there was fat from the meat flowing down Jackeen's jaw, off his unkempt moustache. As soon as the bacon, the bread and the pints were put away the pair were ready to take on the punters.

Patiently they waited and the first to arrive were men going home after a day in the bog. Naturally, those men didn't have much money on them but at least they opened the betting. A few of them bet a shilling on Rebecca's Pride, others bet sixpence, all on the same horse. This was worrying for the Lad as it became a trend that was to continue for the remainder the night. He did his best to change the trend by pointing out to punters that there were horses at eight to one and even ten to one, all to no avail. His takings for the night came to four pounds, sixteen shillings and six pence – every penny of it on Rebecca's Pride. The Lad carefully put the money into the inside pocket of his coat, amid jibes from all in the Shanty of the wealthy man he'd be on Sunday evening. He himself was thinking differently and didn't sleep a wink that night, only twisting and turning and thinking that if Rebecca's Pride won, and he was convinced she would, he'd have to show a clean pair of heels and where he'd go to, he didn't know. In his fitful dozing, the Lad thought he could hear some of them laughing at him and more of them swearing at him, all looking for their money. What a predicament to be in and no one would have pity for him, not one.

Saturday evening, Jackeen and himself arrived at the Shanty, as arranged, about five o'clock. It was a warm, hazy evening that tempted the larks to sing their sweet refrain and that made Jackeen thirsty. He immediately rapped on the shutter to the bar and when the jovial Molly opened it he ordered "a pint of the best porter you have" to which Molly cheerily replied "all my porter is the best". When the Lad arrived, Jackeen turned towards him and said, "You'll have a pint?"

"Not a hope," answered the Lad, "I must keep my senses."

"Begor," retorted Jackeen, "I never knew you even had senses."

"My worry is how will we stop 'em of betting on Rebecca's Pride," moaned the Lad.

"Don't know," was Jackeen's curt reply.

Just then three men entered. Their faces seemed foreign. Neither Jackeen nor the Lad had ever seen them before. One of them ordered three pints of the black stuff. Sipping their drink in subdued conversation, their attention was suddenly focussed on the betting board. This led Jackeen to whisper to the Lad, "I'd swear these are punters, wherever they came from". And he was right.

Talking between themselves, they discussed every one of the horses named on the board as if they knew them well. One of them, a tall sandy-haired fellow, said loud and clear, "I would be inclined to put my money on Wooden Legs". Turning to Jackeen and the Lad he said, "I'll put ten pounds on Wooden Legs". Before they could answer a second fellow, a big, sallow-faced, rough-looking character with an overgrown black moustache that you could sweep the floor with, declared, after a thorough perusal of the board, "I'll go for Hurricane Boy, win or lose, I'll chance twenty pounds on him. The name fascinates me. What will you do Simon?" Simon, the only name mentioned, was the third man. A tall, blonde-haired fellow with a clear complexion and nicely-spoken, he complained that the only horse left for him was Glory Days. The Lad refrained from saying there were several others.

"Yes," said Simon after due deliberation, "I'll put a ten pound note on him."

Addressing the Lad and Jackeen, the fellow with the black moustache said in a very gruff manner, "Gentlemen, are we on or off?"

"How do you mane?" asked the Lad.

Incredulously, the trio looked at the two and the two were gazing back at them in awe and with wonder in their eyes, thinking how could anyone have all that money to bet. The nicely-spoken one, Simon, broke the impasse asking, "What we want to know is, are ye taking our bets?"

"Oh, the bets. Ah, no, sure we have nothing to do with bets," said the Lad and, pointing to the board, he added, "sure that auld thing is hanging up there for ages."

"Come on, we are only wasting our time here," said the sandy-haired fellow, "we should be gone out of here long ago."

The Lad stole out after them to satisfy himself that they were really gone and was amazed to see that they had a horse tethered to a ring on the end wall of the shop where there was also a trough of water. Obviously they were on a long journey and just stopped to rest, water and feed their horse. But what really dazzled him was the beautiful harness, festooned with all kinds of polished ornaments that would blind you with reflections from the sun. With the horse tackled to a massive sidecar that had multi-coloured cushioned seats and a big long whip standing erect in a special holder, it was the most luxurious means of transport ever seen in Ballymachad. Bewildered by it all, the Lad couldn't understand how they still had money to burn. Jackeen didn't even go out to see it, nonchalantly saying that they were government agents or big landlords, adding, "Not our class at all".

"Paddy," said Jackeen, looking him straight in the eyeballs, "what kind of a gom are you?"

"How?" asked the Lad.

"How could you be such an ejit to refuse forty pounds from the three strangers, a sum of money that you never, ever, had in your pocket, or never will. You got wan bite at the cherry, me boy. When will you get it again – never!" said Jackeen.

"Ah, 'tis all right for you to talk, Jackeen, you have no responsibility. You'd be above at home playing your fiddle and I'd be inside in jail," said the Lad.

With a scart of a laugh, Jackeen exclaimed, "In jail! What would carry you to jail?"

"The boys with the dandy horse and the big side-car, that's who would carry me if they happened to win and I couldn't pay up," said the Lad. "Imagine if the fellow that wanted to bet twenty pounds on Hurricane Boy at ten to wan won, how much would I have to pay him?"

"I suppose two hundred pounds," calmly answered Jackeen, pulling on his pipe.

"Two hundred pounds," shouted the Lad, 'the price of the biggest farm around here! They would just lock me up and throw away the key."

"But didn't you tell me that young Connor was riding him and that he'd fall off," argued Jackeen.

"I did. But that's the very time he wouldn't, the time you'd want him to fall off, that's the time he'd stick on like a leech and let you down in a bang," answered the Lad, "we'll stick with the local, small punters and see what happens."

"Ah, my dear boy, you'll never make a gambler because you are afraid to take chances," opined Jackeen.

The Lad made no reply and just shook his head.

"Paddy," said Jackeen, in a plaintive voice, "do you know why me and you have no money?"

"I dunno, why?" asked a puzzled Lad. "Because them English scroungers that were here waving twenty and ten pound notes at us a few minutes ago have it all, that's why! They took over our land, our houses, our money, and what scorns me is that you got the chance of taking forty pounds off of them and you funked it. You haven't the guts of a mouse. There was a time around here and if them fellows appeared they would be shot, shot stone dead, Paddy."

Paddy the Lad never felt as humiliated in his life and thanked God there was no one listening.

After that outburst, there was an eerie silence between them and when his temper cooled, Jackeen took a few sips from his pint. Sucking the froth from his overgrown moustache, he looked towards a forlorn Paddy the Lad. Then, walking over to him, he put his hand on his shoulder, saying, "I'm sorry, Paddy, 'tis just when I see any symbol of British rule my blood boils. They dispossessed my grandfather, killed my uncle and evicted my neighbours, as well as my father and mother, when we were childers. But we survived in spite of them". Again there was a period of eerie silence. The only sound was Jackeen pulling on his pipe. Then, taking the pipe out of his mouth and looking sideways at the Lad, he cleared his throat and in an apologetic voice said, "But then, Paddy, thinking with a clear head, I must admit you were right to refuse their dirty, ill-gotten money because into jail they would throw you if things went wrong. All they want is an excuse to lock up the likes of us". The Lad responded positively, so, in a coaxing voice, Jackeen said, "Now let us get our act together and get back to business, there is some few coming in".

The latch on the Shanty door lifted and in walked Tom Redden and Mortimer, closely followed by Patcheen and the Lark O'Brien.

"Oh, begor, but the right punters have arrived," declared Jackeen, "scan the board, boys."

"We are no good to ye," declared Redden, "the committee have decided to refrain from betting in the interest of the integrity of the race and therefore we must stay neutral."

They just had one drink and departed hurriedly, excusing themselves by saying they were on "official business". Presently, the locals arrived, first in ones and twos, but later it looked as if they all were coming in together and the Shanty was full. Soon Paddy the Lad and Jackeen were doing brisk business but the trend continued with most of the money going on Rebecca's Pride. Strangely enough, a share of money was bet on Hilly Billy and also on Hurricane Boy with just a few bob on Wooden Legs and Glory Days. As the night wore on every horse received some bit of backing, but by far the lion's share was on Rebecca's Pride, increasing the tension on the Lad to almost breaking point. Jackeen estimated that if she won, and there was a strong possibility that she would, the Lad would be down by the tune of several pounds – a lot of money in those days. And to make matters worse, the takings on the pre-race hours on Sunday could increase that figure further.

"Live in hope," cautioned Jackeen, "maybe a crowd of strangers tomorrow will turn the tables around."

But such sentiments were no consolation to the Lad who could see no way out for himself, only to disappear.

Sunday dawned overcast and showery but Jackeen forecast that the day would clear up because, when he was driving in his cows at six o'clock in the morning, a cock robin was singing his heart out on the top of a tall fir tree in the haggard, a sure sign of a fine day. A half an hour before the ten o'clock Mass it was noticeable that a bigger crowd than usual was congregating and at five minutes to ten the church was already packed. Paddy Mike Trant, a man with a very loud voice, was in his usual position with his box at the church gate collecting a penny from each of the worshippers. He noticed improved takings as the crowd outside the door got bigger and bigger. Molly Seán arrived, late as usual, and when she saw the crowd outside the door, she exclaimed, "Glory to God in the highest, Mike, will I get a seat?"

"Not a hope, Molly, why didn't you come in time? You won't even get in," he replied.

"Well, if I can't go in, I'll only give you a ha'penny," threatened Molly.

"Give me out my penny and go in to hell out of here," roared Mike in his rasping voice that carried all the way to the altar and caused the priest to stop as he read the gospel and visibly try to control his laughter. Reluctantly Molly threw in her penny, under inaudible protestations.

Before the final blessing the affable parish priest welcomed all the visitors and wished everyone an enjoyable afternoon. The priest was the proud owner of a lovely brown horse which was his only means of transport and he was a familiar figure on the saddle doing his rounds of the parish.

The sun was peeping through the clouds as the congregation dispersed around the village. As the race wasn't scheduled to start until two o'clock most of the locals went home while visitors went to the Shanty. On account of the occasion the pub was allowed to open for a certain number of hours and here the visitors staved off hunger and thirst, while being treated to Molly's speciality of fat bacon between slices of homemade bread with their drinks. With porter selling at two pence a pint and the food mostly free, it was a cheap lunch and Molly did a roaring trade. It was a day reminiscent of a football match day, with flags of all colours flying from every vantage point in the village and at various places along the route of the race. There was an especially large display at the starting point, Bessy's Cross, three miles away. With all the local musicians and bodhrán players marshalled into an impromptu band, they marched up and down the village to great acclaim. And to add to the gaiety, when they stopped in the centre of the village and played a reel, suddenly there were several groups dancing eight-hand reels and changing to sets as the music dictated. They were oblivious to the cloud of dust they were rising off the road. It was all good fun and it took the people's minds, if only for a day, off their otherwise harsh existence.

Paddy the Lad was now suffering a harsh existence of a different kind as, aided by Jackeen, he displayed his board by hanging it on the school gate. They were immediately surrounded by the crowd and money was soon changing hands but the panic continued for the Lad as the most of it was going on Rebecca's Pride. Suddenly there seemed to be a change and people began placing their money on different horses. Lady Jane, Ballymac Lady and Dandy Lad were attracting a lot of money with Lady Jane getting by far the most. To a lesser extent Hurricane Boy, Molly's Dolly, Hilly Billy, and even Wooden Legs, were coming into the reckoning. As the clock moved closer to the starting time, all the runners had been backed to a certain extent. Jackeen reckoned that it was strangers who didn't know the scene that brought about the change. Suddenly the dancing had to stop as the horses and riders prepared to march through the village. Tom Redden approached the musicians and asked them to line up in front of the horses and play them through the village which they did to thunderous acclaim from a massive crowd. The applause continued for each horse and rider, with the greatest applause of all reserved for the youngest rider – the Connor boy on Hurricane Boy. Last in the parade was Mortimer, the judge.

Riding his own horse, a beautiful steel grey mare, he really cut a dash. With her mane and tail beautifully plaited and a shine on her skin, someone remarked that she was like a picture in a book. Astride her, on a massive creaking saddle, Mortimer looked the part. Dressed in knickerbockers with black shining gaiters and black boots that you could see yourself in, he wore a three-quarter length black coat and on his head was a black hardy hat, held in place by a strap under his jaw. He looked aristocratic and all eyes were on this prancing horse and rider as they brought up the rear. Redden, who proudly saluted his son, Tom Óg, as he rode Rebecca's Pride in the parade, was speechless. When the horses reached the outskirts of the village the band about-turned and played their way back through the village again and then dispersed. The scene was now set. As Jackeen had forecast, the day cleared up and the sun was now shining – the cock robin on top of the tree was right.

Back at the starting point, Bessy's Cross, two men designated by the committee were in place with a rope which they were to hold across the road as the starting line. To allow the race to go through the village, two others were detailed to hold a rope across the road at the far end of the village, to denote the finishing line. Two men were also appointed to stand there, one at each side of the road, to judge the winner and the second horse home. One of those was the schoolteacher, Master Quigley, and the other was Paddy the Quack. At Bessy's Cross Mortimer ordered all the riders to line up their horses abreast across the road. Astride his horse he faced them and in an authoritative voice explained the rules of the race. He told them, in no uncertain manner, that any horse that would break, that is rise in a gallop, would be turned, and any rider that failed to obey the judge's ruling would be disqualified. He further explained that 'to turn' meant that the offending horse would have to be turned full circle on the road and then continue the race as normal, albeit losing valuable time.

"I wish you all the best of luck," he concluded.

Moving behind the line of horses, he ordered the two designated men to hold the rope taut within a foot of the line of horses, adding, "When I say 'off' drop it immediately". This worked a dream and the race was on! About half a mile into it, Wooden Legs was the first to be turned. A short time later, Hilly Billy had to do the 'circle', as it was now being called by the riders.

As most punters had predicted, in a short time Rebecca's Pride was leading the field, closely followed by young Connor on Hurricane Boy. But then the eagle eye of Mortimer caught Rebecca rising and Tom Óg was immediately ordered to turn by Mortimer. This turn of events left Hurricane Boy in the lead, with Ballymachad Lady in second place and Lady Jane third. The turn left Rebecca's Pride in fifth place just behind Glory Days. There was still nearly two miles to run and it must be said that Tom Óg, cool and unperturbed, showed great horsemanship, and was soon, slowly but surely, clawing his way back into contention. When Glory Days was pushed trying to keep ahead of Rebecca's Pride and ordered to turn, Tom Óg found his mount was now smelling the tail of Lady Jane. A battle royal developed between the two and soon they were riding abreast. Stepping beautifully, side by side, and almost touching each other, they parted as they overtook Ballymachad Lady, one at each side of her, and then the three of them were riding abreast. Bravely, the Lady stayed the pace with them for a good distance but gradually they left her in their wake.

It was now down to a three horse race – Rebecca's Pride, Lady Jane and Hurricane Boy. Now in the last half mile, young Connor took a squint behind him and saw the other two in hot pursuit. Slowly they overtook him and, using the same tactics, they came abreast of him, one on either side. All Mortimer's attention was now focussed on the three leaders, as what was happening backfield didn't matter at this stage. Young Connor, now under pressure, displayed horsemanship beyond his years by pushing Hurricane Boy to the very limits without letting him rise, and was head to head with the other two going into the last quarter mile. The excitement was immense with the crowd lining the road and shouting, "Come on Connor! Come on the Hurricane! Come on young Connor! You're a pure hurricane. Keep it up".

Then the unthinkable happened – Rebecca's Pride picked up a rambler and ran lame and had to be pulled up. A 'rambler' is a loose stone and it got wedged between the horse shoe and the hoof, a common happening in those days when roads were kept repaired with broken stone. Tom Óg jumped off and did his best to dislodge the stone but it took too long and, disappointed, he retired from the race. In the meantime, Hurricane Boy and Lady Jane were still battling it out. When they entered the village, Paddy the Lad, perspiring profusely from worry and excitement, couldn't believe his eyes – there was no trace of Rebecca's Pride. Jumping to his feet like a man inspired, he shouted and cheered the two horses who were still head to head. Cheers from the waiting throng for both riders rent the air amid palpable excitement as to who would be the first to 'hit' the rope. Up through the village they raced, still under the eagle gaze of Mortimer, doing their best to ensure their horse wouldn't rise, as then all would be lost. But to their credit, both riders kept their nerve, their discipline and their concentration on the task, oblivious to the cheering crowds.

Into the last hundred yards, Lady Jane started to gain on Hurricane Boy. Into the last fifty yards, she was just a head in front and when she hit the rope at the finishing line, Hurricane Boy's nose was at her stirrup. 'Twas that close! Long John Casey and his wife Biddy were in the throng at the finishing line. In a welter of excitement Long John rushed in, took the horse by the head and patted his sweat-soaked neck. Biddy, accompanied by her daughter, Jane, in whose honour the horse was named, was shaking her son's hand. Their happiness couldn't have been greater if they had won the Grand National today.

In the meantime, the very popular young Jimmy Connor was being feted by the crowd and hugged by his mother, Mary Kate when she arrived breathless, after running up the length of the village. Oblivious to his sweaty face, she placed a kiss on the forehead of her Hurricane Boy. One of the first to congratulate them was Paddy the Lad as he swaggered around with his head in the clouds, all fears of going broke having disappeared as he now knew he was in the money, how much no one ever knew, not even Jackeen, with all his smartness. The two riders were then asked to present themselves and their horses at the school gate for the official confirmation of the winner and the runner-up and the prize-giving ceremony. All the other riders, still on their horses, formed a semi-circle around the two winning horses and with them was Mortimer, the judge, still resplendent on his steel grey. He indicated to Tom Redden that he would like to say a few words to what he described as "a great bunch of horsemen".

Standing on the school wall, Tom Redden congratulated the winner and asked the owner to come forward to collect the first prize of a ten-stone bag of oats. Amid great applause Long John came forward and, shyly saying "Thanks", he put it on his back and took it across the road where he had his pony and car. Again, there was great acclaim when Redden congratulated the runner-up, Mary Kate Muldowney, with her Hurricane Boy. Presently, Mary Kate drove into the circle of riders with her ass and car and the Lark O'Brien, who donated the second prize, was on hand to place the bag of turnips into the car for her, amid great clapping and cheering. Tom Redden then said he had one more chore to perform after which he would hand them over to Mortimer. This was greeted with applause and, calling for attention, Tom reminded the contestants that each of them had paid two shillings to enter their horses. This came to twenty-two shillings and the committee had agreed to divide it between the riders who came first and second, so each received eleven shillings. This proved to be a very popular decision and there was prolonged applause as the two riders rode their horses up to the school wall to collect, what was to them, the biggest amount of money they ever had in their pockets.

Still standing on the school wall, Redden then said, "Over to you, Mortimer". Mortimer backed his horse against the school wall and faced the assembled riders and the general public. In his cultured voice he said, "I couldn't let the occasion go without paying sincere compliments to the horsemen, who are as good as any I have ever had the privilege to meet. I would also like to compliment them on how honourable they were when asked to 'turn'. This showed their extraordinary discipline and I hope to have the pleasure of more outings with them in the future". He concluded by saying that they "were all winners on the day". He got tremendous applause and, to his own surprise, found that he had won the hearts of the community with what the people felt were words from the judge's heart. So ended a sporting event that came about as the result of an argument over a horse in the Shanty. It became an annual event for many years and brought life, excitement and cheer into the lives of the people of Ballymachad.

The Handball and the Goat

The social life of country people long ago centred round the rambling house, crossroad dancing and especially sports. Handball and football were played, but it was some time before they came to competitive standard. Handball was a game that was played by the young, and not so young, boys of the parish. The game of twenty-one was the usual one played and it would be hotly contested. The biggest problem with this game was with the ball going over the wall and being lost. A new ball cost nine pence, a lot of money to young boys at the time. They usually put their pennies together and even at that, they would sometimes be short and have to go home dejected. Some boys were prepared to go to extremes to think of great ideas to get the price of a ball.

The most unusual idea of all was the brainchild of Mickie Óg Casey. A very likeable and obliging nine-year-old, he used to run errands for several of his elderly neighbours, one of whom was Biddy Mike. Always delighted to oblige, Mickie Óg would rush to her beck and call. She was good to pay – he'd be sure to get two or maybe three pence and, on occasions, depending on the errand, she would give him a tanner, that is six pence, big money to Mickie Óg. There was one very special job he used to do for her on an annual basis for which he'd get even bigger money, a silver shilling, and, needless to say, he always looked forward to it.

Biddy kept a goat for milk and she called her Lucy. A real pet, Biddy need only call Lucy by her name and the goat would gallop from afar to her front door. Mickie Óg's annual job was to take her to the puck goat or, as Biddy would say, "Take her to see the gentleman goat". Delighted to oblige, he'd have a head collar made for her in quick time. Once upon a time he'd have a far journey to take her but now, with Dan McGurk installed in the slate house and he being the proprietor of a fine specimen of a puck goat, Lucy would be with the 'love of her life' in fifteen minutes.

It transpired that on a beautiful sunny day Mickie Óg and his friend, Charley Burke, met in the village. Charley had a handball in his pocket so the two nine year olds proceeded to the alley for a game. With the score reading Charley 12 and Mickie Óg trailing by two points at 10, they were really enjoying themselves. But then disaster struck. In an effort to overhaul Charley, Mickie Óg decided to try a hard shot at the top of the alley wall but to his great embarrassment and disappointment the ball went over the top and fell into the nearby river where it was swept away. Dejected, the pair walked up the village to Pat's shop.

Looking in the shop window they could see a carton of beautiful multi-coloured handballs with the price tag on the carton reading ten pence each. Grumbling to themselves about the price increase of one penny over the usual nine pence, the boys began searching their pockets but whatever way they turned them inside out and outside in, all they could muster was five pence between the two of them – just half the price.

"Come on," said Charley dolefully, "there is no use looking at bread in another man's window. We'll go home."

"Just as well," Mickie Óg ruefully agreed and they commenced the silent journey home.

As they approached Biddy Mike's the silence was suddenly broken. Lucy the goat was up on the roadside fence. Mickie Óg called her by her name and, being the pet that she was, she responded in her goatey language and then he added in a barely audible voice, "A pity you don't want to see the gentleman goat". It was then the thought struck him – suppose he could make her 'want' to see the gentleman.

Swearing Charley to secrecy, Mickie Óg ordered him to go up on the fence and catch Lucy by the smeg. Being a maol goat, the smeg was the best way to hold her. Charley obliged and when he had her secured by the smeg, he shouted, "I have her". Never telling Charley what he was about to do, Mickie Óg took a small straight pin from the cape of his coat and, ordering Charley to hold on to her tight, he lifted up her tail and stuck the pin into it. Lucy went berserk and galloped off to her mistress's house leaving Charley stretched inside in the field in her wake.

"What did you do to her?" asked Charley when he got out on the road.

"Yerra, nothing. Keep your mouth shut and we will soon have a handball," said Mickie Óg.

"How?" questioned Charley.

"Shut your trap and you'll soon find out," ordered Mickie Óg in a haughty tone.

In the meantime, Lucy, making noises no goat had ever made before, galloped over to the front door of Biddy Mike's cottage. Swishing her tail in all directions, she reared up on her hind legs and placed her two front legs on top of the half door and her goatey gibberish echoed around the kitchen. Biddy Mike rushed to find out what was wrong and, patting the goat on the face and gently stroking her smeg, exclaimed in a soothing tone, "Poor Lucy, poor Lucy, what's wrong with my pet?" This scenario continued for a few minutes until Biddy Mike realised the goat was furiously swishing her tail. Continuing to pet the goat she confidently predicted, "I know what you want, Lucy my pet, indeed I do. Every thing will be all right Lucy. I know you want to see the gentleman goat".

At that very moment, accidentally on purpose, the two boys walked past, Mickie Óg in the van. When Biddy Mike saw them arriving her face lit up and she immediately hailed them, saying, "Come in boys, I need ye badly". Feigning ignorance of the situation, Mickie Óg asked her, "Can we do something for you, Biddy?" Smiling she answered, "Indeed ye can. It's a miracle that ye happened to come along. 'Twas God that sent ye to me in my hour of need". Like a soldier standing to attention, Mickie Óg looked her straight in the eye and with all the emotion in his voice that he could muster, he calmly said, "One thing my parents taught me was always to come to the aid of a lady in distress, so whatever problem you have we will do our best to help you".

Charley muttered something like, "Don't you know what happened", but he was quickly silenced with a slap across the gob from Mickie Óg, followed by an admonishment in an audible whisper – "Keep that gob of yours closed." "Well, I was only thinking," commenced Charley but with a look that would stop a clock, Mickie Óg cut in, "Well, stop thinking now this very minute if you want to get your handball back".

In the meantime Biddy Mike and the goat disappeared into the kitchen and in a short time Biddy reappeared again holding a rope in her hand, closely followed by Lucy. "Well," said Biddy Mike, "what's troubling me is that Lucy wants to see the gentleman goat and I would be very much obliged, Mickie Óg, if you would do the honours as you always do."

"I will of course, Biddy, sure I never let you down yet," responded Mickie Óg.

"Fair play to you. You did not indeed. Come into the kitchen so and get Lucy ready," said a delighted Biddy Mike.

In the trio went, the two boys and the goat, and Biddy went into the lower room. In the middle of the kitchen floor and with her tail still swishing, presumably with the excitement, Lucy did the unthinkable – she covered the floor with her 'marvels'. Ordering Charley to brush them out the door, he took the rope that Biddy Mike had laid across a chair and made a head collar for Lucy.

Returning from the room, Biddy handed Mickie Óg three silver shillings – one for himself, one for Dan McGurk for the use of the puck and, as she didn't want to make exceptions, one for Charley. Promising to have Lucy with the gentleman goat in quick time, Mickie Óg was ready to depart when Biddy Mike stooped down and kissed Lucy on the forehead. Leading Lucy out, Mickie Óg made a beeline across the road and then down the boreen with Charley bringing up the rear. Halfway down he came to an abrupt halt.

"What's wrong?" inquired Charley.

"Hold her there while I do something," said Mickie Óg.

"Like what?" asked Charley.

"Just hold her and keep your eye on that bull inside the fence," retorted Mickey Óg. While Charley's attention was on the bull, Mickie Óg pulled out the pin that he had stuck in the goat's tail. If Charley knew, he might spill the beans was Mickie Óg's thinking, so he left him in the dark. Taking the rope from Charley, he led a more subdued Lucy all the way to the slate house.

On arrival they were greeted by Dan McGurk himself and, after a chat about the goat and her owner Biddy Mike, Dan said they would introduce her to the puck. Walking before them, Dan guided them to the paddock where the puck was grazing. As soon as they entered, the puck ran towards them. Soon he was serenading Lucy in his own unique way, but, as Mickie Óg expected, she didn't want anything to do with him and rebuffed his advances. Finally, Dan lost patience and said to Mickie Óg – "What made ye bring down that bloody goat, sure she isn't ruttin' at all."

As cool as a breeze, Mickie Óg replied, "Biddy Mike thought she was, because she was swishing her tail".

"I didn't see her swishing any tail," said Dan, "and anyhow, it isn't because a goat swishes her tail that she is ruttin'. Tell that to Biddy."

"Here is a shilling she gave me for you," said Mickie Óg, taking a shilling out of his pocket.

"I won't take that at all, bring her again when she's ruttin' properly and tell her to forget the codology of the swishing of the tail," said Dan.

Retacing their steps, they arrived back at Biddy Mike's in fifteen minutes. Their big worry was would she leave them the shilling she had given each of them? Mickie Óg believed she would and he was right. Biddy Mike was very disappointed and even upbraided Lucy for not been "nice to the gentleman goat". The two boys made a beeline to Pat's shop where they purchased a handball and a penny worth of sweets each – at that time you'd get ten or twelve sweets for a penny and there were two hundred and forty pence in a pound – and resumed their game.

This is an illustration of how scarce money was at that time and the way youngsters had to use their wits just to get an item, even one as small as a handball. If they asked their parents for the price of a handball the answer would probably be "No", the reasoning being that it would only be lost like previous ones. And it has to be said, that would almost certainly be its fate. Charley never suspected anything and it was only years later that Mickie Óg told him about putting the pin in Lucy's tail.

Toaching and Poaching

Toaching

Three brothers, Billeen, Seáno and Tadhgeen, lived with their sister, Biddy, in a small thatched cabin comprising a kitchen, two small bedrooms and a loft. Biddy always slept in the front room and Seáno occupied the back room. When they grew up and because they were always working for farmers, Billeen and Tadhgeen would only return home at Christmas or maybe a day or two at Easter. They would then be billeted in the loft as it was as big as the other two rooms put together. A fine, bright room it was, with a big window on the gable-end wall that gave plenty of light. However, it had to be kept closed permanently because the birds had a habit of flying in thinking they could build their nests there which, of course, Biddy would not tolerate.

When the two boys would return home at Christmas, Seáno and Biddy would expect that they would have a bit of money spared and that they would give them a donation to cover the cost of their keep over the Christmas. Sometimes the donation would be grudgingly forthcoming but there were occasions when the two boys would be after spending a day or two on the spree on their way home and arrive with an empty kitty. The reception wouldn't be great on those occasions, as two extra mouths to feed, and two big mouths at that, would put a great strain on the family's meagre resources.

Soon Biddy's larder would be almost empty and there was no money to replenish it. Seáno worked most of the time with a neighbouring farmer and his wages would be small as the farmer's cash flow would be small too. But he would get a bottle of milk a few evenings each week which was a great help. During the winter months milk was scarce as the cows would be dry so the done thing was that any farmer who would happen to have a cow calved early, would give a bottle of milk to any family that needed it. There would be no charge for the milk as there was an unwritten rule by farmers of the period never to refuse anyone for a bottle of milk.

But, as the saying goes 'one good turn deserves another' and when that farmer would be saving hay in the summer, the recipients of the bottles of milk, without been asked, would arrive to help wynd the hay and, needless to say, the farmer would be delighted as the extra help was invaluable. But people could not live on milk alone, so Biddy would put pressure on the boys to do something. The hunger was bad, but listening to a tongue-lashing from Biddy was worse so, to keep the peace, and, of course, to fill their bellies, they would decide to go 'toaching'. How this particular practice was called 'toaching' was unknown, perhaps it was derived from the word 'torch' as it entailed using a lamp of some sort. At about ten o'clock at night the three brothers would sally forth to seek their prey, armed with a blackthorn stick, a storm lamp and a bag for the catch. Knowing well the haunts of their prey, they would take the shortcut across the fields, cross the stile into a field of Tom Redden where there was a high, whitethorn hedge.

Here they would commence operations. The prey, mostly blackbirds and thrushes, would be asleep in certain places in the hedge. The first man would shine the lamp on the sleeping birds and the man with the stick would kill them with a blow to the head and hand them to the third man. He would pluck the dead birds and bag them as they went along. If the birds were plentiful he wouldn't get time to pluck all of them, so he'd just bag them and they would be plucked at home. When the brothers arrived home well after midnight, tired, hungry and often wet, Biddy would have the frying pan on the brand and well-embellished with goose grease. She, too, would be smacking her lips in anticipation of a midnight feast. The bag would be emptied on to the table and immediately Biddy would commence gutting the birds and washing them in spring water. The entrails would be stored in a bucket to be fed to the dog the next day.

As can be imagined, when the bird was dressed and ready for the pan, the amount of meat on each one was small. Therefore, to satisfy big appetites, several birds had to be cooked at the one time. Luckily the pan was big and soon the aroma of cooking flesh filled the kitchen, sharpening up the appetites even further. With 'pointers' of mixed bread of flour and Indian meal, as well as goats' milk to wash it down, the family would soon have a nutritious meal. Immediately afterwards, Billeen and Tadhgeen would climb the ladder to the loft leaving Seáno and Biddy to do the washing up, which they would do straight away as

Biddy always said she couldn't get up to a dirty kitchen. Before the chores were completed, the snoring from the loft would commence and would be so loud that Biddy and Seáno would have to close their room doors tight to shut out the noise.

Tensions were often high between the family but they reached a record high on one particular night. It happened like this – Tadhgeen was missing, presumably gone on the batter. Billeen and Seáno decided to go toaching but as it happened they hadn't much success so they arrived home with just six little birds. Biddy, as usual, had the frying pan ready. She dressed the birds and, just as she put them into the pan to cook, Tadhgeen staggered in the door, drunk and starved with the hunger. He sat down on the form along the back wall of the kitchen and shortly his nostrils perceived that there was something cooking. His hunger was immediately increased by the smell of the cooking birds as it wafted around the kitchen so he stood up and, with an unsteady gait, he made his way to the fire to see what was in the pan. With greedy and hungry eyes, Tadhgeen gazed at the six little birds in the pan while at the same time inhaling the beautiful aroma. Then, casting his bleary eyes around the kitchen, in spite of his condition, he made a mental assessment of the situation.

He felt that six little birds among three men and a woman would give none of them enough and he was hungry, very hungry. He decided to do the unthinkable! He walked over to the fire again as Biddy was turning the meat with a fork and, just as she completed that chore, he dropped the biggest spit ever to come from the mouth of a man right into the middle of the pan. Disgusted, the two brothers walked out the door and a disheartened Biddy went to bed, leaving Tadhgeen alone with his ill-gotten meal. It took some time before he was allowed back into the fold. He betrayed their trust, a serious offence within a family and he was barred from home for a period, albeit a short spell, but he was never left near the frying pan again.

Seáno always kept a few goats and a puck. The puck always earned his keep because there were a lot of goats in the neighbourhood and charging a fee of one shilling for every goat served, Seáno would be laughing all the way to the pub. Not that he was a heavy drinker, he liked his pint on a Sunday night and he'd also take home a drop for Biddy who would have the tongs reddened in the fire in anticipation as she liked her porter mulled. He'd complete his purchases with an ounce of snuff, also for Biddy, and that would be his spending for the week. As Biddy kept a number of hens, when she would sell the eggs she would do the bit of shopping for her own needs and, if the price of the eggs allowed after the groceries were paid for, she would reciprocate Seáno's generosity.

One of his customers was a neighbour, Mickie Pat, who kept one goat but was no real advantage to him because he'd never pay the shilling. Mickie Pat's goat was a real pet that always slept in the kitchen every night. Each morning, Mickie Pat would be seen brushing out the kitchen floor after the goat's night in. One night Seáno's puck broke out of the haggard where he was grazing and rambled up the road to Mickie Pat's cottage. Presumably he smelled the goat inside in the kitchen and commenced pucking the door so hard with his big twisted horns that he woke up Mickie Pat. Taking a very serious view of the puck's misconduct, he drove him back down the road to where he came from and, obligingly, the puck jumped back into the haggard from whence he had rambled. A peevish little man at the best of times, now, at about five in the morning, disturbed from his sleep and his door almost pucked in, Mickie Pat's temper was razor sharp as he knocked on Seáno's bedroom window.

"Who's there?" asked Seáno in a sleepy tone.

"'Tis me," answered Mickie Pat.

"Who are you?" mumbled Seáno.

"You'll know soon who I am because your puck pucked my door, me boy, but I'll puck, puck you with a summons," complained Mickie Pat.

Now realising who was there, fast came the reply from Seáno.

"And why wouldn't he – sure 'twas only looking for his fee he was."

He had pulled the rug from under Mickie Pat, who walked away muttering something to himself. The episode was never again mentioned by either of them.

The Shotgun

Dickeen was a well-to-do bachelor farmer who lived across the river from Seáno's house. A regular caller, he enjoyed their carry-on and often went toaching with the brothers. He was good to them and would give them the odd butt of spuds and a goose sometimes for Christmas. A man who always kept a shotgun, Dickeen enjoyed fowling in his spare time and he would often take Seáno with him for company. If he shot a pheasant or a wild duck, he would usually give it to Biddy, who would be delighted. To thank Dickeen, she would keep a thigh of the bird to give to him when he'd call again. Dickeen would prefer not to get it but he wouldn't want to insult her either.

As Dickeen grew older he gave up the fowling and would lend the gun to Seáno. This was a godsend as they were never again short of something to eat. Seáno proved to be a good shot and kept the table supplied with wild duck, plover, pheasants, wild geese, the odd snipe and, now and again, a rabbit. Then one day Dickeen dropped in and in the course of conversation he told Seáno he could keep the gun. Himself and Biddy were over the moon with this news.

It wasn't all sunshine either, however. Having expended all the cartridges he had received from Dickeen when he gave him the gun, Seáno soon found that ammunition was expensive and he had to walk to town to get it. But then, after a few journeys he got smart and made it a point to go only on fair days, when it would be easy to get a lift from a farmer who would be going to the fair with a horse and car. Encouraged by Dickeen, he commenced taking a few rabbits or pheasants, or any game he may have shot, to town, where he found a ready market. This helped cover the cost of the cartridges. Knowing his dilemma over the cost of cartridges, Dickeen suggested to Seáno to keep all the expended cartridge cases, saying that he had an idea how to make the powder and that he could cut nails into small pieces, or better again he could pick up a lump of discarded lead and make little balls of it to refill the cases. Needless to say, Seáno was delighted.

True to his word, Dickeen arrived one night with a bag of secret ingredients to make the powder. Biddy had a big fire of brusna (also called faggots) on and a cake of griddle bread almost baked.

"Will that be long more?" asked Dickeen, pointing to the griddle of bread.

"Only a few more minutes. Why so?" questioned Biddy.

"Because I want the griddle," said Dickeen, "I'm going to make the powder for Seáno."

Just then Seáno arrived into the kitchen with the gun in his hand and a brace of duck across his shoulder.

"Were they plentiful?" inquired Dickeen, pointing to the duck.

"Ah, there was a few around all right but they all flew off when I shot these," said Seáno.

"Who'd blame them," commented Dickeen, adding "I'm going to have a go at making the powder the very minute she takes the bread off the griddle."

"Great," enthused Seáno, "I'll be able to shoot all round me now."

"Don't be too certain now. Maybe it mightn't work out at all. I never did this since I was a young gaffer and that's more than a few years ago. Back then we couldn't legally have guns and cartridges were not available, so we had to improvise at the risk of been jailed, of course," said a reminiscing Dickeen, smiling at the memory. Presently, Biddy took the bread off the griddle, saying, "The griddle is all yours now, Dick".

"Seáno, take it outside and throw a bucket of water on it to cool it down," ordered Dickeen, settling a chair for himself in the corner, under the lamp, as it was now getting dusk.

Seáno arrived in with the griddle and placed it on Dickeen's lap, who by now was comfortably seated on the súgán chair, ready for action. Wiping the griddle dry with one of Biddy's towels, he commenced pulling small packages of ingredients from a bag that he had brought with him.

Soon he had the griddle covered with powdery substances in separate heaps. Sitting under the lamp, Dickeen found as it got dark that he was sitting in his own light so he stood up and, lifting the griddle carefully with both hands, he got Seáno to turn his chair around so that he would be facing the lamp. Murmuring "that's better", he sat on the chair and commenced mixing the powders. Half an hour went by and not a word was spoken as Dickeen worked intently – a spoon of this, then a spoon of that, then half a spoon of something else and now and again, two heaped spoonfuls of another ingredient, and all the time the heap in the middle of the griddle was getting bigger and bigger. Standing behind Dickeen, looking over his shoulder as he mixed the ingredients, Seáno watched in fascination, thinking of all the birds he'd bring down with that heap of powder. Finally, after an hour, and having mixed all the ingredients with great care, Dickeen, rubbing his hands together to clean them of any residue of the powder, broke the silence with two words, "'Tis ready."

"Glory on you," shouted Seáno, "wouldn't I love to have your brains."

"Now, this is the moment of truth," declared Dickeen, "we will do a test."

Carefully moving the heap of powder to one side of the griddle, he then took a spoon of it from the heap and placed it on the other side of the griddle as far as possible from the main heap. Reaching into the fire he picked up one of the burning faggots and, with great deliberation, he pushed it closer and closer to the spoon of powder. Eventually it touched it and ignited into a ball of fire that started spreading towards the main heap on the residue of powder on the steel. Dickeen saw the danger, pushed back the chair and threw the griddle onto the floor, moving back as fast as he could. Suddenly there was a mighty explosion. It quenched the lamp and the room was plunged into total darkness that was made worse by the smoke. Seáno ran for the back room. Poor Biddy had the same idea and, not knowing that Seáno was in front of her, she ran against his back and, hitting him at speed, she knocked him prone on his face and fell on top of him.

There was an eerie silence for a few seconds that felt like an eternity before Biddy, in a plaintive voice, said, "Am I alive?"

"You must be," whispered Seáno, "because you're talking."

All of a sudden, Seáno shouted, "What about Dickeen, what about Dickeen?"

"I suppose he's dead, God rest him," murmured Biddy.

"Dead!" shouted Seáno and that was the catalyst that brought them to their senses. Struggling to their feet in the smoke-filled room, still in great darkness and coughing from the smell of the exploded powder, they felt their way along by the wall and they soon came to the door. Nervously, they walked through the door into the kitchen, afraid of what they would find. Shuffling along, they were startled when a voice said, "Where were ye?" Suddenly there was light as the man behind the voice lit a piece of paper from what was left of the fire that was scattered around the hearth.

"Who are you?" asked Seáno.

"Who do you think?" countered the man.

"I don't know, I never saw you before. There was never a black man in this house, sure there wasn't, Biddy?" said Seáno.

"Have you lost you senses or your eyesight? Where is there a black man?" said the voice.

It was then Seáno recognised Dickeen's voice.

"Glory be to God, Dickeen, is it you? Don't tell me you're dead," said Seáno.

"Dead," said Dickeen with a chuckle, "I'm very lucky to be alive whether I'm black or white."

"Well 'pon my soul, you are as black as the black man that was at the pattern a few years ago. Isn't he Biddy?" declared Seáno.

"Ah, sure what harm," said Biddy, "sure plenty of soap and water will bring out the white in him again."

Biddy set about putting the fire together and when the brusna lit up, the extent of the devastation began to unfold. When they checked the lamp, they found that the globe was in smithereens. All the walls were black and the griddle, which took the full force of the explosion, was, as Seáno described it "in four halves". He'd have to take it to the forge that day to be repaired by the blacksmith. Now almost midnight, Dickeen declared that he'd be making tracks for home.

"Oh, no, no, no!" exclaimed Biddy, "you can't walk into Maggie in that state. She'd have a fit, you have to wait 'till your own colour comes back. I'll make tay."

Maggie was Dickeen's sister and she was known to be of a nervous disposition. Biddy felt, with a woman's intuition, that if Dickeen walked into her, as black as soot, she could drop down dead from the shock.

Biddy soon found the relic of a Christmas candle which she lit and Seáno got the fire going with a gabhal of brusna and a few sods of turf brought in from the haggard. Shortly there was a blazing fire and Biddy hung a skillet of water on the crane over it to wash Dickeen and make him white again before he went home to Maggie. Then, standing in the middle of the floor, with her hands on her hips, she solemnly declared that she would never again allow experimentation in her house. Presently Dickeen was washed and, having regained his natural colour, confessed that it was all his fault and that it was very bad judgement on his part to test the mixture on the griddle so near to the main heap. A very unhappy Dickeen then left for home, taking the shortcut across the fields. Thus ended Seáno's hope of free ammunition!

The Two Boys

Christmas was around the corner and Seáno and Biddy were expecting the two boys to arrive any day now. Money was scarce and Biddy had only a few turkeys to sell at the Christmas market as that particular year the birds had gone against her. Seáno blamed Biddy herself for the loss, as he had advised her after the first clutch of gluggers to change the cock, but she adamantly kept taking her turkey to Nellie Pat's cock. As Seáno said, it took a few more clutches of gluggers to bring her to her senses but by the time she changed cocks, the turkey-laying season was almost over. However, their spirits changed somewhat when they saw the two boys, seemingly sober, walking down the boreen at one o'clock on the Saturday before Christmas, Their usual time of arrival would be midnight and they would usually be drunk.

Arriving in to the kitchen, both as sober as judges, with not even a smell of drink of any description from them, they seemed to be in great form. Biddy filled the kettle and hung it with the pot-hooks on the crane, noticing that all the greetings and exchanges were exceptionally cordial. There has to be something wrong, she thought, as she made the tay and placed four mugs and a plate of hot bread on the table. She got the crock of homemade blackberry jam from the press and invited the two boys to sit out, which they did with manners such as Biddy had never experienced before. The conversation was unusually subdued and just to say something, Biddy asked when they would be going back to work again. They replied that they did not know.

Billeen quickly changed the conversation, saying that they were after a Mission in the parish where they worked.

"Did ye go to it?" asked Biddy.

"We did of course," replied Billeen.

"We had no choice anyway," added Tadhgeen, "the woman of the house would have gone mad if we didn't go."

"Well, now, that's a change," said Biddy, "if the woman of this house went berserk, ye wouldn't go. 'Tis amazing what some women can make men do."

"How was it?" asked Seáno.

"Well, you could say there was two halves to it," volunteered Billeen, "wan of the preachers was a right tough man. I'm telling you he would frighten the daylights out of you with his stories of burning in hell if we didn't watch ourselves."

Tadhgeen then took up the story.

"Ah, the other man was different altogether, a nice, quiet kind of a man who told us all to go to Confession and to say our prayers and to make sure to go to Mass every Sunday. That must be very important because the two of them were very strict on that."

"Did ye go to confession?" inquired Biddy.

"Oh we did. The two of us went but Tadhgeen got fooled though," laughed Billeen. "How was that?" asked Seáno.

"Well, 'twas like this," said Billeen, "he wanted to go to the quiet man as he was kind of afraid to go to the tough man, with the drinking you know. The tough man used to make a show about lads getting drunk, he called them some kind of a name. What's that he called 'em, Tadhgeen?"

"Yerra, gluttons, or something like that, whatever that meant," Tadhgeen answered shyly.

"But do you know what happened?" said Billeen, "when Tadhgeen was next in line to go into the box, didn't the missioner come out and go off about his business and left Tadhgeen stranded. He had no better to do but cross over the chapel floor and go to the hard man."

"So there we were," continued Billeen, "me at wan side of the confession box and Tadhgeen at the other side and you'd never believe it, but weren't the two of us inside in the box together. Well, when I went in and knelt down, whatever Tadhgeen was after telling him – what did you tell him at all Tadhgeen?"

"'Tis none of your business," Tadhgeen replied gruffly.

"Well, whatever it was anyhow," continued Billeen, "but the holy Father was giving him a fierce dressin' down. 'Twas so bad that I started shivering in a way that the box was beginning to shake. Then, after a bit, things quietened down at the other side of the box and I said to myself, says I – 'Billeen, you better stop this shiverin' and shakin' and be ready to face the music my boy and just play your cards as good as you can with him.' By the time he was finished with Tadhgeen, I felt I was ready for him. Then the shutter opened with a bang and I saw a red face, 'twas like a ball of fire and I blessed myself and said, 'Bless me Father, for I have sinned.' I saw his hand blessing me and then he asked me 'How long since your last confession?'

"'Tis a good bit then, Father', says I. 'How long is a good bit?' 'Well, about twelve months, Father, would be the outside of it,' I answered. 'Do you drink?' said he. 'Well, I would take the odd pint, Father.' 'How many odd pints would you drink?' he asked me. 'Well, now, 'tis like this, Father,' I said, 'if I was after a hard day in the bog or a hot day wynding hay with a farmer, I'd love a pint of porter or maybe two that evening, according to the sweat I'd have lost.' 'Is that all?' he asked me. 'Upon my word, Father that's all,' says I. 'Well, now, that's what I'd call sensible drinking,' he said, and then do you know what he said? He said as a young fellow growing up he had often spent a day in the bog with his father and a meitheal and his father would always take the men into a pub for a drink on the way home and have a pint himself. 'And maybe wan yourself,' I joked. 'No, nothing stronger than a mineral water for me, ever,' he told me," said Billeen, as Biddy and Seáno listened, fascinated, to his story.

He continued with his tale.

"After a long chat about saving hay, making the rick, digging spuds and drawing home the turf – he was like wan of ourselves – all of a sudden he said, 'We'd better finish your confession. Tell me, are you company keeping?' 'What's that?' says I. 'It means are you friends with a girl,' says he. 'No, Father,' says I, 'to tell you the truth, I hate women.' He didn't like to hear that, so he said to me, 'Do you know it is a sin to hate women, or men for that matter, it is very wrong to hate anybody, especially women, because wasn't you mother a woman.' 'Well, do you know that never struck me, Father,' says I. 'Well, you know now, so amend you ways, if you want to live in the state of grace. Do you go to Mass every Sunday?' he asks me. 'I do of course,' says I, so he says, 'And what time is your Sunday Mass?' 'Well you have me there now, Father.' 'Are you telling me you go to Sunday Mass and you don't know what time its on?' he shouts at me and I just answered, 'I just goes by the bell, Father.' 'Oh, I see,' says he and left it at that. The hard man just broke out in him, so after a few more things that I can't tell ye about he gave me a stiff penance and then absolution. As I was leaving he said, 'God Bless you. You made a good confession and be sure to go to confession oftener.' 'I will of course, Father,' says I back to him as I was half-ways out of the box."

Seáno and Biddy were listening in awe as Billeen continued – "I was relieved it was over, but I must be a long time inside, because all the people were gaping at me when I came out. Paddy the Lad was at the end of the row as I passed up to say my penance, with a big smirk on his face. 'He'll knock that smirk off of you,' I shouted at him as I passed. I declare the priest must have heard me because he stuck his head out of the box and caught the Lad muttering something but I was just kneeling down."

"The last night was the hardest of all," declared Tadhgeen. "He even went back to the day we were baptised, a thing we remembered nothing about, but he made us say all the things that the wan that stood for us had said for us when we were babies. Isn't that the way he put it, Billeen?"

"Oh, that's what he said all right," agreed Billeen, "and then he blessed all rosary beads and crucifixes as well as statues and medals."

"Then he started about the drink again," remembered Tadhgeen, "and gave a fierce talk about the dangers of drinking and the big sin it was to get drunk because of the harm it does to your brain when you lose your senses and as well the harm it does to your insides. Isn't that what he said, Billeen?"

"You're dead right," agreed Billeen, "and then he finished up saying that the harm it does to the body is nothing compared to the harm it does to the soul and that's what frightened us. When he asked everywan to take the pledge, we were glad to get the chance and we never wet our lips since. Isn't that right, Tadhgeen?"

"That's right, Billeen, and that's the way we are going to stay," declared Tadhgeen.

"The very same here," promised Billeen.

Then the two boys delivered a bombshell to Biddy and Seáno. Billeen did the talking: "I must tell ye that the holy Fathers talked about an awful lot of things outside of drink. They talked for ages wan night about families fighting and arguing among themselves. They maintained that was an awful sin and it would have to be confessed. Myself and Tadhgeen were discussing this as we walked home along the road, but what we were saying is, if we start fighting again the following day, all the fat is in the fire and we would have to go to Confession again. Tadhgeen was saying if that was happening, sure you'd want a priest in the house with you and do you know, he wasn't far out."

"Well, that's what I was thinking," cut in Tadhgeen, and he continued, "Billeen, do you remember the holy Father saying something wan night – yerra he had a name for it, he had a name for everything – but it meant you shouldn't stay or even go to a place where you would be inclined to commit a sin, like going into a pub if you had enough money to get drunk. The danger was there, he said. He saw danger everywhere."

Seáno was sitting with his back to the wall near the fire, smoking his pipe, and was getting tired and fed up of listening to the two boys. Finally his patience was exhausted and he stood up and said, "Slow down a bit lads, I think the two of ye have gone cuckoo, yer a bit touched in the head". The two of them looked at him in disbelief. Billeen was the first to get his voice back and, looking Seáno straight in the eye, he said with great emotion, "Seáno, you didn't hear that holy Father, but if you did, you'd be running to confession quicker than any of us and my advice to you is to go anyway. Tell them what we have decided to do, Tadhgeen".

"What!" exclaimed Biddy, "Is it how yer going to go for the Church?"

"Ah no, Biddy," laughed Tadhgeen, "there isn't a hope they would take us! What we are going to do is to get a house of our own."

Biddy looked at them incredulously while Seáno just said, "Ye'll die with the hunger". The two boys took great offence from Seáno's remark and immediately went on the defensive. Billeen said with a house of their own, that they'd be their own bosses, that they would have a pig in the tub, that they would get a gun each and that they would never be short of a bob when they could shoot rabbits and pheasants and mallard and have time to poach a few salmon.

"Less the mercy of God ye'll shoot one another," said Seáno in a derisory tone. "There 'tis again now," declared Tadhgeen, "wasn't the missioner right? There's a danger of fights and arguments living in the same house and how could we be going to confession every second day?"

Biddy was crying and through her tears she said to the two, "Ye don't know the cost of running a house".

"Ah, but we'll learn," said Billeen, placing his hand on her shoulder, "Dry your tears girl. We'll make out all right – every bob we make will be our own."

"If ye make the bobs," sobbed Biddy.

"What's to stop us of making them," argued Billeen.

"I hope so', murmured Biddy, drying her eyes with her bib.

Then they shocked Biddy and Seáno again when they admitted they had already got a house. And how they enthused about it. It transpired, however, that it was just a kitchen with a big fireplace and a loft overhead.

"'Twill suit us down to the ground," said Billeen, "the loft is lovely and cosy, sealed and all with bags, and the walls and the ceiling are all whitewashed as white as snow."

"Is there beds in it?" asked Seáno.

"No, we will have to carry our own beds with us and the small table if ye can manage without it," said Billeen.

Seáno said he'd give them a goat for milk and Biddy said she'd bake a big loaf of bread in the oven as housewarming gifts. And so it transpired that on the following Tuesday, Seáno tackled the ass to the cart and he loaded up the beds and the small table for the two-mile journey over the road and down towards the sea. He also had to make room for the loaf of bread, two mugs, a few plates, knives and forks and a couple of spoons that Biddy insisted they carry. As he was about to leave, Seáno decided to throw a bag of turf on top of the beds to warm up the place. That night the two boys slept peacefully in their own little house.

A New Home

A few days later they walked to town and returned sporting two shotguns – a double barrel and a single barrel.

"They'll never stop until they'll do some harm with them guns, either to themselves or some other one," predicted Seáno.

When they told him that the single barrel cost four shillings and six pence and that Billeen paid six shillings for the double barrel, he told them that the guns must be as old as the hills and that they could blow up in their faces. The boys got very indignant and sour with Seáno for criticizing their equipment and countered by asking him: "How old do you think Dickeen's gun is?"

Seáno replied by saying, "I knew that gun though. I'll say no more to ye. Yer old enough now to run yer own affairs". That admission made the two boys happy. The following evening, the pair, armed with their guns, went down to the shore and, lying down on the bank, they patiently waited for game to appear. An hour passed and nothing appeared, then another hour and still nothing.

Taking the cartridges out of their guns, they decided to start for home. Just then a flock of ducks flew straight over them, but by the time they had reloaded the birds were safely out of range. Cursing their luck at having unloaded, they decided to stick it out for another hour in the hope that a second flock might fly the same route. Presently the boys were rewarded when they noticed four wild geese flying in formation towards them. When they thought the birds were within range, the two of them opened fire together but the geese just changed course when they heard the noise and flew out to sea.

Rather despondent, they turned for home. Up near their house they met Paddy Mike walking down against them. A tall man with a brown moustache and goatee beard, he was well-known locally as a joker who would delight in throwing spars at the likes of Tadhgeen and Billeen. An unusual man, sometimes he would come off the worst, but he would even enjoy that too, and would relate with great humour how he got caught. True to form, he decided to have craic with the two boys so, after a few pleasantries, he said something the boys considered unforgivable – "Ye shot nathin'." The two boys looked at each other and, being low in stature, they looked up at the tall man as if in shock. Their pride was hurt and Billeen responded, saying, "There was nathin' there, sure there wasn't, Tadhgeen?"

"Not a thing," agreed Tadhgeen.

"But I heard shots," insisted Paddy Mike.

Quick came the reply from Billeen – "We heard them too."

Paddy Mike had met his match.

Things went lovely for them for about a week or ten days, until Biddy's big loaf of bread was gone. Then, for the very first time in their lives, they had to think about shopping. Next they realised that to go shopping money was needed, so they decided to pool what funds they had. Searching every pocket that hadn't a hole in it, they found that they had the princely sum of two pounds, four shillings and three pence. After paying for the guns that's what they had left after their year's work They considered themselves well-off, thanks to the holy Fathers, because if they were still drinking they wouldn't have a bob at all. Which one of them would do the shopping was the next item on their agenda.

This was solved quickly and amicably when Billeen insisted that Tadhgeen do the needful. A true blue woman-hater, Billeen said he would rather die with the hunger than go into a shop, because it was always women inside the counter. However, Tadhgeen had no such inhibitions and was well-able to chat up the ladies inside the counter, or elsewhere for that matter. Tadhgeen took ten shillings from Billeen and, with ten shillings from his own pocket, whistling a merry tune, he went shopping. Making a conscious decision to avoid grocery shops attached to a pub, for fear the smell of the drink would overpower him, he made a beeline for the Yank's, a shop opened about five years back by a returned Yank named Willie Casey.

Mrs Casey was inside the counter and Tadhgeen and herself exchanged greetings. Then it got embarrassing as Tadhgeen stood there motionless. His mind went blank, as it was his first time inside in a shop, as distinct from a pub, and he couldn't think of anything he wanted. Mrs Casey spotted his dilemma and graciously said, "Can I help you, sir?" A big smile spread across his unshaven face, no one had ever addressed him as 'sir' before and it made him feel important.

"I just want stuff for the house, mam."

"Could you be more specific, sir?" Mrs Casey asked.

"Things you'd ate, mam," Tadhgeen said shyly.

"Well, sir," she said, "we have bread and meat and eggs. We also have tea, sugar, butter and jam. We also stock salty bacon, rashers and puddings."

"Anchor there, mam, that's the stuff I want, mam, the salty bacon, give me a junk of that and throw in a couple of puddin' as well. I'll take a grain of tay too, mam, and a few spoons of sugar, and a loaf of bread, if that's all right with you, mam," said Tadhgeen excitedly.

"No problem," she responded.

Businesslike, Mrs Casey set about fulfilling the order and as she cut the bacon, she asked him, "Is that enough?" to which he responded, saying, "A bit more". This happened on a few occasions, after which she asked no more and just added the two rings of pudding and parcelled up the lot. She then completed the order with a pound of tea, a pound of sugar and a loaf of bread. Placing the parcel on the counter, she politely asked if he needed anything else.

"Begor, as you said it, I could do with a half quarter of tobaccy," said Tadhgeen. "Very well," Mrs Casey said, reaching up to the second shelf and placing the tobacco on the counter.

"How much is the damage now, mam?" asked Tadhgeen, as he put his hand into his trouser pocket and took out ten shillings.

Mrs Casey added up the account with a pencil on a sheet of paper and then handed it to Billeen, but he handed it back to her, asking, "How much is it?" as he couldn't read. Looking at him almost pathetically, Mrs Casey said, "Nine shillings and four pence".

"'Tis dear," he remarked as he put the ten shillings he had in his hand on the counter and, taking coins from his pocket, he said, "Tell me when you have enough, mam." "Oh, this will do," she said, taking the ten shilling note.

She then handed Tadhgeen his change but he couldn't count money. Going home, he though of what Biddy had said about him and Billeen not knowing the cost of running a house. He had received his first, hard lesson. He consoled himself by thinking he could have drank it and have had nothing to show for it. At least he now had enough grub for a week or ten days, thanks to the holy Fathers.

Poaching

As time went on the boys got better with the guns and were soon bringing home some game from every outing. These they plucked, cleaned out and boiled. They were mad for soup and would describe the various birds by the quality of the soup they would produce. When asked what kind such a bird would be to eat, the answer would go like this, "Very good, lovely thick soup", or "Not up to much, thin watery soup", or another answer might be, "The finest soup you ever drank with big suillins floating around on it". In a short time, the boys' home became a rambling house frequented by all the locals. Some of the visitors would overstay their welcome by staying on until the small hours and then the two boys couldn't go to bed. They would get very wicked on those occasions and go into silent mode, letting the stragglers know in no uncertain terms that they would not be welcome back. However, after remaining absent for a few nights, they would ramble in again, as if nothing had happened, and the welcome would be gracious until they dirtied their copybook again.

A favourite visitor was young Jimmy. He was studying for the priesthood and during his holidays he used to enjoy visiting the two boys and he would often go on a shooting expedition with them. He enjoyed the eccentricity of their ways, and would relate with great mirth the happenings on a given expedition. The years rolled on and then one day Jimmy was ordained a priest. Arriving home the day after his ordination, his family had some friends in for a meal after his arrival. When the meal was over, the newly-ordained Fr Jimmy excused himself, saying he'd go out and give his blessing to the two boys. They were delighted to see him.

"Well, begor, Jimmy boy, you have the round collar," declared Billeen, "and it suits you down to the ground, Jimmy boy."

After chatting about various things for a while, Fr Jimmy said he had come to give his blessing.

"Oh, that's great altogether," said Tadhgeen, kneeling down and ordering Billeen to do the same.

Tadhgeen got his blessing and, as Fr Jimmy was about to shake hands, he looked up at him and said, "I can get up myself, Jimmy". Then he gave his blessing to Billeen and shook hands with him. Still down on his knees and holding the priest's hand, Billeen looked up at him and with great solemnity said, "You're a priest now, Jimmy".

"That's right, Billeen," said Fr Jimmy.

"Well, now, I'd like to give you wan bit of advice and 'tis this Jimmy."

"Yes," said Father Jimmy with a controlled smile on his face.

"When you are inside in the confession box don't be too hard on the poor men but give it to the bloody women though."

"I will of course, Billeen," joked Fr Jimmy.

"Ha, ha. That's the stuff to give 'em," said Billeen, rising from his knees, an unrepentant woman-hater.

There was some laughter when Father Jimmy told his family and their guests about the advice he had received from Billeen.

As time went on, the two boys realised the truth of Biddy's words – it was expensive to run a house. Every visit to the grocery shop took its toll on their meagre income from the sale of game and rabbits and the odd poached salmon. But sometimes they would have to eat the salmon, or any game they may have shot, as their larder would be empty. This became their way of life, and was later supplemented by working odd days for farmers, especially during the turf-cutting and hay-saving period. Still defiant about the wisdom of getting their own house, the boys would doggedly spend hours at the seashore in all kinds of weather, hoping to get a shot at wild duck or wild geese, or plover, or indeed anything that flew. Prepared to shoot at anything, Billeen was one day walking down the road towards the sea, gun in hand.

When he arrived at an acute bend of the road where the river flowed parallel with it, he spied a salmon resting in about four feet of clear water. Looking down at him with greedy eyes for a full five minutes, wondering how he could catch him, he suddenly pointed the gun at the salmon, aimed and fired, shattering the still water. When the water came back to normal, there was the salmon with his head blown off by the shot, lying on the stones at the bottom of the pool, his tail making an involuntary movement. Then there was stillness. He wondered how he was going to retrieve the dead fish. Laying the gun down on the grass margin and scratching his head for enlightenment, Billeen suddenly made a decision. He would strip off all his clothes, leave his shoes on, and go into the water. This is exactly what he did, jumping off the bank into the river.

Now up to his belly in water, Billeen waded towards his prey. Finding it deeper than anticipated where the salmon lay, he made a few vain attempts to snatch his tail. Then, in a do-or-die bid, he dived completely under the water and succeeded in grabbing the salmon's tail. He surfaced with water dripping from his hair and his moustache and coughing out more water, but with a triumphant air – he had his fish. Struggling towards the bank with the salmon in tow and sometimes stumbling over the stones on the riverbed, Billeen was just a few yards from the bank of the river when he saw something that should have given him the shock of his life. But not woman-hater Billeen!

Around the bend on the road appeared three young girls, chatting and laughing on their way to the beach for a swim. Suddenly they saw this apparition of a naked man pulling a salmon after him. Shocked and frightened, they gave a unanimous roar of horror, turned and fled the scene, while, unperturbed, Billeen waded ashore, threw the salmon onto the bank, climbed up and dressed. Afterwards, when asked about the episode, he used to say, "You can't do wan bloody thing without women interfering".

Tadhgeen and Billeen persevered in that lifestyle for many years, but eventually they were forced to return to the fold with Seáno and Biddy as their hard lifestyle took its toll. They never had a pig in the tub as they confidently said they would and they found it difficult to come to terms with the cost of running a house, as Biddy had predicted. However, in spite of all the hardship they endured and their rough meals and lifestyle, they lived to be of great age and then they died within twenty-four hours of each other, together in the afterlife as they had been on earth. Their likes will not be seen again.

A Day in the Bog and a Day in Court

For generations all homes in rural Ireland were heated with turf fires. With acres of bog scattered throughout the country, it was the natural thing at the time for all householders to cut their own supply of turf, save it, draw it home and reek it in the haggard in close proximity to the house. This was a hard-won crop as it entailed backbreaking work undertaken by a meitheal of local people. Assembling a meitheal was the easy part as it was the done thing at the time that country people were willing to help each other in the major jobs like cutting turf, saving hay and cutting corn. Saving the corn crop, be it oats, wheat or barley, was also labour-intensive as the crop was usually cut with a scythe and every sheaf had to be handmade, bound and stooked. The non-farming community supplied a lot of help as they in turn were dependent on the farmers to help them cut their turf, lend them a horse to draw it home, or plough a little garden for them and various others needs they may have. Help was forthcoming because all sections of the community needed each other simply because money was a very scarce commodity and very few could put their hands in their pockets and pay out money in wages.

A day in the bog was something special and unique. It involved a lot of people including the woman of the house. When a farmer, or indeed any householder, declared that he intended to cut his turf on a certain day, that was a signal for the housewife to swing into action. It was she who was responsible for preparing all the food to feed the men on the day. She would pester her husband asking how many men he was likely to have on the day and in most cases she would never get a straight answer. After asking him the same question perhaps twenty times, to get her off his back, he would eventually gruffly say, "Yerra, throw enough of it into the auld basket". This answer was neither here nor there to the worried housewife, as her good name was at stake – if there was a shortage of food for the hungry bogmen, it was she who would be blamed. And, as she well knew, the bog was a noted place for sharpening up the appetite. So she would set about her task with clear intent. She would indeed throw enough of it into the auld basket and give them nothing to say. It was a well-known fact that in the atmosphere of the boggy air, men did eat to excess and the housewife had to allow for that, as well as wastage. It was considered great fun for younger members of the meitheal to start throwing slices of bread at each other, oblivious to the fact that it was waste of a scarce enough commodity.

Arriving in the bog, perhaps at seven o'clock in the morning, all would immediately line out in their respective places, the sleans-man taking up his position at the top end of the turf-bank. The brancher would be beside him, ready and waiting. Two men would be on the bank, ready to pitch and spread. The first sods cut on the end of the bank might be brittle and would be dumped into the hole, then the work would commence in earnest and the householder would expect that they would cut a decent slean of turf during the day. A 'slean' of turf was reckoned to be the amount of turf that four men would cut and spread in a day. Slinging would not be acceptable, this was a job for the strong and the willing, but in spite of that, there was always some bit of craic.

There was the case of Johnny 'Townie', a teenager born and reared in town, who was holidaying with his aunt and uncle in the country. Having heard a lot about the bog and the cutting of the turf, he was delighted when his uncle decided to cut his turf and Johnny insisted on going along with the men. Full of excitement, he awoke early in the morning and was all fired up and ready before any of the men arrived. The men sat down to breakfast, but Johnny was so excited that he ate very little. Tomeen, one of the men, decided to bring his own ass and cart as he needed to bring home a handful of turf that evening. Johnny opted to travel in the ass and cart with him – another first for him – and he was delighted when Tomeen gave him the reins to guide the donkey up the bog road. The usual routine was followed and in a short time a fire was lit to boil the kettle for a midmorning break which consisted of tea, a duck egg, bread and butter. Johnny was fascinated with whole operation and gobbled down a blue duck egg and several slices of home-made bread plastered with homemade salty butter and drank several cups of strong, black tay coloured with goats' milk.

At one o'clock all work stopped and the meitheal partook of the main meal of the day. Johnny was all business handing around plates of bacon and

A Day in the Bog and a Day in Court

cabbage and spuds, followed by cups of strong black tay. Johnny was delighted to be allowed to do the honours and all the men were full of praise for him, saying what a nice, friendly boy he was, willing to do any job he was asked to do. Handing a mug to Tomeen, Johnny asked, "Tomeen, will you let me drive the ass home this evening?"

"I will of course, boy, why wouldn't I?" agreed Tomeen.

Johnny was on top of the world at the thought of the drive home that evening. The meitheal worked late to finish the bank and Johnny had already been detailed to restart the fire and have the kettle on the boil, which he did with great aplomb. He was also asked to have the bread sliced and buttered and all the cups rinsed and ready as the break would have to be as short as possible. When everything was ready, he beckoned to the men to come. They immediately dropped tools and descended round the fire and were back working again in ten minutes.

Tomeen was the last to leave and, as he passed Johnny on his way, he asked him would he do him a favour.

"I will of course, sure one good turn deserves another," said Johnny, "aren't you letting me drive the ass home."

Tomeen smiled and then asked him, "Is there any chance you would put a fire of turf into the cart for me so I'll have nothing to do but put the ass under it?"

"I will of course, no problem at all," replied Johnny.

"You're a great boy Johnny, you kept us fed all day and everything, you're great altogether," said Tomeen.

Johnny tidied up everything, and then proceeded to do Tomeen his favour. But at this point the lines of communication between town and country broke down. Johnny failed to interpret Tomeen's language when he asked him to "put a fire of turf in the cart". What Tomeen wanted was for Johnny to put some turf into the cart for him. Johnny, on the other hand, thought he was meant to put the fire he had going for the cooking into Tomeen's cart. This he proceeded to do, handling the blazing sods with a pike. The cart started to smoke and immediately someone of the men on the bank spotted what was happening and alerted Tomeen. Tomeen got into a rage and jumped off the bank and, with his pike raised, he ran, roaring, towards the cart and Johnny. He was very near before Johnny realised that something was wrong and when he saw that Tomeen was in a real temper, cursing and swearing vengeance on him, Johnny ran down the mountain as fast as he could.

Tomeen went to follow him, but as he passed by his burning cart he stopped and commenced throwing out the offending sods. Then one of the men brought water from the boghole and quenched it. The damage was negligible and, to give Tomeen his due, he soon forgot about it. The next time they met, Johnny said he was sorry, that he took him up wrong, and that he never meant to do any harm. Both of them then laughed at the memory. Many years later when Johnny was a vet he'd say to Tomeen every time they'd meet "do you remember the day I burned your cart?" and Tomeen would just give a scart of a laugh.

The turf, neatly spread, would be left in that position to dry for about two weeks. In dry weather it might be turned sooner, in wet weather it would be left longer. Sometimes the turf would be turned to aid the drying process, but if the weather had been good it would be footed directly from the spread position. 'Footing' was done by putting four or five sods standing supporting each other. Then two sods would be laid on the flat on top of them and, finally, one sod would be laid crossways on top of those. These were called 'criacógs' and making them was backbreaking work as it involved being in a constant stoop. The air and wind was able to circulate and in dry weather the drying process would be rapid. Two to three weeks later, again depending on the drying conditions, the turf would be re-footed.

This entailed putting two or three smaller criacógs into one big criacóg. This was designed to further the drying process and if the weather was favourable, in two to three weeks the turf would be saved and ready to be drawn out. The drawing out was usually done with an ass and cart, as in most cases the bog would be too soft to bear the weight of a horse or pony. Even the ass would sometimes go bogging, but he and his cart were light and it was easy to relieve them and get them back on terra firma to proceed with the work. The turf was then drawn out to dry solid ground where adverse weather conditions wouldn't hinder a horse from taking a full load home. This was important as turf cutting sometimes coincided with the haymaking season and usually the hay took precedence over all other farming operations.

It often happened that, owing to the pressure of work, the owner of a heap of turf wouldn't inspect his turf for a long period, and when he finally went to draw it home he would find that there was a hole in it which meant that some of it was stolen. This is exactly what happened to Mickie Tom Bessy who found that a quantity of his turf was stolen. Being a wicked little man with a very short fuse, he decided on a course of action. He decided that he would spend a night in the bog in the hope of apprehending the thief. True to his threat, he took down his shotgun on a Thursday night and, under cover of darkness, arrived at his heap of turf. He stayed there all night and when the birds started singing in the morning, he wearily made his way home. But that didn't deter him from pursuing his course of action and he continued going to his heap of turf at least one night, if not two nights, a week.

Eventually his perseverance paid off when, one morning about four o'clock, a man arrived and commenced filling a bag with turf. Mickie Tom Bessy loaded his gun and shouted to the man, "Stand your ground or I'll shoot". The poor man dropped the bag and ran.

"Stop running or I'll shoot," warned Mickie Tom Bessy, but to no avail – the man kept running.

Mickie Tom Bessy was true to his threat. He let him go a certain distance and then fired low. A marksman of repute, he knew what he wanted to do – just give the thief a few grains in the back of his legs. The man gave a roar but continued running. The man was from the next townland and his name was Danny Pat, a man that never cut turf but who always had a fire. He reported the incident to the RIC and in the afternoon Mickie Tom Bessy had a visit from a constable. He examined the gun and said he would have to confiscate it. The constable told Mickie Tom Bessy that he would be summoned to the next court, which happened to be in a week's time.

The summons duly arrived and a few days later Mickie Tom Bessy found himself in court. Danny Pat was the first to be called and the judge asked him, "What were you doing on the night in question?"

"Nathin' sir," came the reply.

"He was staling my turf, your honour," shouted Mickie Tom Bessy from the back of the courthouse.

"You will get your chance to explain, mister, but if you interrupt the court again I will hold you in contempt for which the penalty is two weeks in jail," warned the judge.

"That's the stuff to give him, your honour," shouted Danny Pat.

The judge looked at him out over his glasses and said, "I'm warning you too, if you interrupt the court again you will be inside in jail with him and the two of you will have two weeks to settle your differences".

"You said you were doing nothing on the night in question. Is that correct?" asked the judge.

"Well, 'twas like this sir, I mane your honour, sir," explained Danny Pat, "on that night a few of the neighbours called in and we started playing cards and we had a fine fire going all night, and didn't we run out of turf."

"So you used up all the turf you had?" queried the judge.

"That's right, your honour, and that left me in an awful predicament, your honour," groaned Danny Pat.

"Please explain how that caused you a 'predicament' as you call it," asked the judge.

"Well, 'twas like this, your honour, if the wife woke up in the morning and hadn't a sod of turf to boil the kettle to make a mug of tay, she'd go berserk. So can't you understand now the pressure that was on me that I had no way out, your honour, only to take a bag and run up across the mountain for a few sods of turf, just to keep the peace in the house," Danny Pat said in a pleading voice.

The judge was looking down on him with a controlled smile on his face and then asked, "Was it to your own rick of turf you went?"

One thing Danny Pat had in his favour was that he was a quick thinker and he immediately answered, "Your honour, the night was so dark it was impossible to see where you were going, and in the terrible black darkness didn't I go to the wrong heap".

"How did you know it was the wrong heap?" asked the judge.

"But I didn't, your honour, until I heard a man shout 'stand you ground or I'll shoot'."

"And what did you do?" asked the judge.

"I ran like a hare, your honour, and then I heard a shot of a gun and it felt like needles pinching the back of my legs," explained Danny Pat.

"So I presume you arrived home without any turf. What did your wife say the following morning when she had no turf to boil the kettle?" mused the judge.

"Ah, your honour, I was very lucky. Didn't I run into another heap of turf in the dark, and to save myself trouble, didn't I take a few sods from it – sure that wasn't any harm, your honour?"

The judge smiled.

Next to be called was Mr Michael Thomas O'Riordan. No one moved. Three times the judge called the name to no avail. What happened was that Mickie

Tom Bessy never realised it was him that was being called. He didn't know his proper name because he was never called it since the day he was baptised. A neighbour of his, Tangler Casey, who was in court on an assult charge, was standing near him and, nudging Mickie Tom, he whispered, "That's your name being called, you'd better go up". Immediately Mickie Tom straightened himself and walked up to the stand.

"Why did you not come up when your name was called, Mr O'Riordan?" asked the judge in an authoritative voice.

"Sure you didn't call me by my name, your honour, what I'm always called is Mickie Tom, sir."

"Surely you know your baptismal name, Mr O'Riordan?" questioned the judge.

"Your honour, as sure as I'm standing here in front of you I never heard it before," said Mickie Tom.

"Wonders will never cease," mused the judge with a chuckle in his voice. "Well now, Mr O'Riordan," the judge continued, fumbling with some papers, "you are here and that's the main thing. I have to tell you that there is a very serious charge against you, to wit, that you discharged a shotgun at a Mr Danny Pat Scanlon, wounding him in the legs. What have you to say for yourself?"

"I went up to inspect my heap of turf some weeks ago, your honour, and I found that some of it had been stolen. I stayed there several nights in the hope of finding out who the thief was. Then, about four o'clock one morning, under cover of darkness, a man arrived and was filling a bag of my turf. I called on him to stand his ground or I would shoot. The man choose to run away and to avoid causing him serious injury, I held my fire until he was almost out of range, then I fired simply for identification purposes, your honour. I knew he would only get a few grains and there would be no serious injury. That's my story, your honour," said Mickie Tom Bessy.

The judge then recalled Danny Pat and asked him if he had been hospitalised.

"Not at all," replied Danny Pat.

"And have you still the grains in your legs?" inquired the judge.

"Ah no, your honour, sure the wife picked all of them out with a needle," said Danny Pat.

Summing up the case, the judge said that both parties had broken the law, one man stole his neighbour's property while the other discharged a shotgun at him.

Discharging a shotgun at a person was a very serious offence, he explained, but in this case it had to be acknowledged that Mr Riordan showed great control and self-restraint and seemed to know just what was needed for identification purposes.

"However, I feel that Mr Scanlon is entitled to some compensation for the pain and the shock he suffered," the judge said.

"Excuse me, you honour, may I have permission to speak?" asked Mickie Tom.

"Yes, you may," agreed the judge.

"I'll give him a horse-load of turf if that would be acceptable," suggested Mickie Tom.

"What would you think of that, Mr Scanlon?" asked the judge.

"That would be famous, sure I never had a horse-load of turf in my life," said Danny Pat.

"Very well," declared the judge, "case settled. Next case."

The next case concerned two local men who were involved in a bout of fisticuffs, one of them being the aforementioned Tangler Casey, who was charged with assault. His real name was Jack Casey, but as he was involved in buying and selling cattle, pigs, horses, indeed anything with four legs, he was christened 'Tangler'. And no matter what price he paid for the animals, he always seemed to make a profit, often to the disgust of those who sold to him. It was like pouring salt into an open wound to tell a farmer that he had been fooled by the Tangler. The other man in court was Mossie Cartwell, a quiet, unassuming character who was never known to raise his fist to anyone. And indeed the same could be said for the Tangler. What caused the altercation between them, no one knew. It took place on sports day and the theory was that, as both men had sons running in the children's races, something happened, and the fathers took it up.

Whatever the reason, the two men squared up to each other and the Tangler, being the stronger of the two, hit Mossie on the side of the head. Mossie fell to the ground and couldn't get up. A doctor happened to be at the sports and after examining Mossie, he ordered that he be taken to hospital. He was immediately put into a trap and driven to the hospital where he was examined. The hospital doctors came to the conclusion that Mossie had sustained a crack in his skull as the result of a blow. They also found that he was a man with an unusually thin skull, so even a light blow could do him harm. When the case was called, the judge asked Mr Cartwell to take the stand. He immediately informed the judge that he had a doctor as a witness. Somehow there were no solicitors involved, a sign of the times as people couldn't afford them.

The judge asked him to tell his story, so he commenced by saying that himself and Mr Casey had an argument.

"An argument over what?" asked the judge.

"I don't know," replied Mossie.

The judge looked down at him and said incredulously, "You mean to tell the court you had an argument with a person and you don't know what it was about".

"I don't," repeated Mossie, adding, "I have a doctor here, your honour, as a witness."

"We have no need of a witness until the court is made aware of what the argument was about," said the judge, "Will you tell me or will I have to call on Mr Casey to inform the court?"

Mossie then said, "I'd better tell you so, your honour, because the Tangler could tell you the wrong story".

"Who did you say?" asked the judge.

"Yerra, Casey, sir, your honour, he has a nickname, sir," said Mossie.

The judge sternly said, "The court dose not allow nicknames. You will have to apologise to Mr Casey for calling him out of his name, do you understand that?"

"I do, your honour," said a chastised Mossie.

"Well, proceed and apologise to Mr Casey," urged the judge.

"I'm sorry, Tang…I mane Mr Casey," said Mossie.

'That's better," said the judge, smothering a smile.

"Proceed now Mr Cartwell, and tell me what the argument was about," directed the judge.

"Well," started Mossie, "twas the schools sports day, your honour, and my young lad and the, I mane Mr Casey's young lad, were running in a race, and didn't my young lad win, but didn't the judge give the medal to the Casey boy."

"So the Casey boy was the winner," said the judge.

"Well, he got the medal all right, but 'twas my boy won because he was ahead of the Casey boy for a long time," said Mossie. "And what happened then?" asked the judge.

"Out of pure blackguarding, your honour, didn't young Casey pass my boy out in the last fifty yards or less. My boy had it won, I tell you," explained Mossie.

"So the Casey boy passed him out and then what happened?" asked the judge.

"I gave out to the, I mane Mr Casey, for accepting the prize and I tried to take the medal off of him, so we had a tussle and he hit me in the side of the head. I had to be taken to hospital and do you know what they told me, the doctors said I had an awful thin skull and that he should never have hit me, your honour. The doctor will prove that my skull is thin, your honour," said an emotional Mossie.

The judge then asked Mr Casey to take the stand.

"Mr Casey, you have heard Mr Cartwell's evidence. You hit a man on the head and knocked him out. What's your defence?" asked the judge.

"Well, now, your honour, I must tell you first and foremost that I was acting in self defence – didn't Mr Cartwell admit that he attacked me to take the medal off me? My little boy won the race fair and square, your honour, and he was handed the medal and he gave it to me to put it in my pocket for safekeeping. Then on comes Mr Cartwell in a fighting attitude and caught me by the cape of the coat with wan hand, and tried to search my pocket for the medal with the other. Now I said to myself, your honour, that this was going too far so I pushed him away. But then he came at me again like a bull calf, with his head down and fists flying – and I can tell you he is fairly handy with the knuckles, your honour, shouting at me to 'Come on and fight, you cowardly so and so'. As you will understand, your honour, at this stage I had to really defend myself, so when he tried to give me a few more belts, I gave him a little tip on the side of the head, just to show him that he had a fight on his hands, and what did he do only fall down and made no attempt to get up. I walked away thinking he was acting. A doctor was brought to him and you know the rest, your honour," said the Tangler in explanation.

The judge just looked down at the Tangler for a minute or two and then addressed him.

"Mr Casey, I do believe that you acted in self-defence and that you showed a certain amount of restraint, but the sad fact is that you hit a man who has a very thin skull on the side of the head, causing him to be hospitalised. Why did you do that?"

"Your honour," answered the Tangler, "how could I possibly know that that man had a thin skull? And another thing, your honour, what business had a man with a thin skull going to these sports days and starting a fight over a little medal? Wouldn't you think he would stay at home and be saying his prayers for himself, and not getting the likes of me into trouble over his thin skull," said the Tangler.

"That's his own business, Mr Casey," said the judge, "what I have to adjudicate on is your guilt or otherwise in the affair."

"I understand that, your honour," responded the Tangler.

"Thank you, Mr Casey, you may step down. I'll give my verdict in thirty minutes," said the judge in a low voice.

"All rise," shouted the court clerk as the judge left the courtroom.

It was the longest thirty minutes the Tangler ever spent, wondering what would be his fate when the court resumed. The sight of Cartwell swaggering around the courtroom as if he owned the place during the interval didn't help. Suddenly, the court clerk said "All rise", announcing the return of the judge and the resumption of the court. The judge sat on the bench and the Tangler was shivering with fear at the back of the courtroom while Mossie Cartwell was oozing confidence as if he was at a birthday party. The judge opened proceedings by outlining the case of Cartwell V Casey. In his summing up he recalled how the man with the thin skull had been hit and hurt. Then he questioned how this came about and, to the delight of the Tangler, the judge laid responsibility for the altercation squarely at the feet of Mossie Cartwell and fined him fifteen pounds for disturbing the peace at the sports day. Cartwell lost his cool and shouted at the judge about his thin skull having been cracked and what he suffered and what he didn't suffer. Finally the judge ordered the police to remove Mossie Cartwell from the courtroom and added another five pounds to the fine for the disturbance he caused. When normality was restored, the judge turned his attention to the Tangler.

"Mr Casey," he said, "I feel you showed great self control and indeed restraint, against great provocation. You told the court that you gave Mr Cartwell 'a tip on the side of the head', isn't that right?"

"That's right, your honour," said the Tangler.

"I believe that to be true because the medical reports show that if you had hit him with all your strength you would probably have killed him, so in a sense you are a very lucky man," said the judge, adding, "you are free to go Mr Casey."

In amazement, the Tangler looked up at the judge. In spite of all his 'tangling' he knew his place and thanked the judge sincerely. He walked out the door of the courtroom a free man, hardly able to believe his luck.

Wakes

One thing about the people of long ago is that they always respected their dead. They would wake them, often for a couple of days and nights, and no matter how poor they were they always did their best to bury them 'dacent'. The scene then when a death occurred in a family was much different than nowadays. There were no funeral parlours, for one thing, or no embalming. Most old people died at home, lovingly cared for by their family, with the local priest attending to their spiritual needs. Neighbours would gather immediately after the occurrence to give any help they could to the bereaved family. A neighbour or a distant relative would be asked to organise the procuring of the timber to make the coffin. This would entail going to town with a horse and cart to collect the wood, and also the lining and mountings. These would be delivered to a carpenter's workshop and in Ballymachad this was usually to the Chipper Kelly's place.

His real name was Bat Kelly but he was nicknamed the 'Chipper' because when anyone would say, "How's Bat?" to him, he would reply, "Yerra, chipping away". It was easy to earn a nickname in those days. When the wood and all the necessary items were delivered, the Chipper would arrange a time for the collection of the coffin on the following day. An excellent tradesman, he had the reputation of been the best around to make coffins so he was the obvious choice to get the order. A neighbour would also collect a habit, a long garment, usually brown in colour, which the dead were laid out in at the time. The neighbour would also collect the priest's dress. This was a white, linen garment worn diagonally across the shoulders by the priest during the burial ceremony.

Three or four neighbouring men would be asked to dig the grave. A grave would never be dug on a Monday, so if the burial were to be on a Monday, it would be dug on Sunday. For a Tuesday burial, the grave would be dug on Tuesday morning. The same men would close the grave at the burial. The average wake would continue for two days and a night, and then the remains would be taken to the church, if the church happened to be near. As there were no hearses at the time, the remains would be shouldered to the church. There was never a shortage of volunteers to shoulder a remains. Young men, and indeed the not so young, would line up to take their turn and some would be very disappointed if they didn't get the opportunity, as sometimes happened if the journey was short.

Some corpses were taken to the church in the morning for Mass and buried immediately afterwards. In the majority of cases the funeral cortege would go direct from the house to the graveyard with the priest officiating at the graveside. Although it often happened that a corpse would be shouldered over a distance of several miles to its last resting place, the majority would be taken by horse and cart. The cortege would consist mostly of ponies and horses with common carts, but there would also be a number of sidecars and perhaps a few traps as well as a good number of saddle horses.

Big Nell Courtney was the woman who used to lay out the dead in Ballymachad. Reputed to have been an army nurse in her youth, she was tall in stature and, dressed in black, she looked the part, a commanding figure of the sergeant major type. When called upon, she would immediately set forth at any hour of the day or night. Big Nell knew all the shortcuts across the fields and, whether it was broad daylight or the darkest night, she'd go by the shortest shortcut possible. Arriving at the house she'd immediately take control and shout orders of what she needed, to which she expected an immediate response. The response would be forthcoming with haste, as her 'fame' had spread and everyone knew what to expect and what was needed. Once the job was completed and whatever the hour of the night, Big Nell would sally forth alone, refusing any company to see her home. On one occasion when she had finished her task at about two o'clock in the morning and was about to leave for home, Paddy the Quack, a low-sized, elderly man who was a neighbour of the dead person, remarked to Big Nell that it wasn't right for her to be going home alone at that hour of the night, and he offered to convey her home.

She looked down at him with disdain and placed her blackthorn stick on his shoulder. Pressing the stick with all her considerable weight and might until she had him almost bent in two, she bellowed, "No man ever conveyed me home". As she released the stick, poor Paddy tried to straighten himself and Big Nell said with venom, "I'm afraid of no one, living or dead, day or night. Do you see that blackthorn stick and the knob at the end of it?" Paddy blinked and acknowledged that he did.

"Anyone," Big Nell continued, "that tries any caper with me will get that down on the top of the head and he'll never know what struck him."

With her hand on the latch of the door, she turned and said, "Good night all and may the Lord have mercy on the dead". To which all present answered "Amen". In a moment she was out in the dark, making her way home by the shortcut.

As there were several people present, the news soon spread about how badly Big Nell had treated the Quack (he was called the 'Quack' because he was good at treating cattle and especially good at delivering calves when cows had difficulty). Paddy was a very popular and well-known man in the area and many people didn't like what had happened and some vowed to take revenge. A few conspired to frighten Big Nell. Paddy the Lad said he knew where there was a huge statue. It was a very old statue of some patriot and it was a valued heirloom. The Lad believed he'd have no trouble getting the loan of it as he was good friends with Johnny, a son of the owner. So Paddy and a few others, who had taken exception to Big Nell's treatment of the Quack, decided that if they could get the loan of the statue, they would teach her a lesson. They planned to wait until she was called out some night and then they would watch out to see what shortcut she took. As there were stiles at every shortcut, they would place the statue on a stile facing Big Nell as she made her way home. A stile consisted of two wooden poles driven into the top of a fence with a couple of spars nailed across them. They were designed to stop cattle crossing the fence at that point while allowing people to do so.

For two months they waited and when an old woman died about a mile across the fields, the conspirators struck! Carefully monitoring Big Nell's movements and having already made arrangements with Johnny for the loan of the statue, they waited patiently. She left her house as it was getting dusk, so they figured that she should be returning around midnight. That gave them plenty time to get the statue in place. Soon after dark they made their move. Johnny had the statue ready for them and decided to join them for the craic. The statue proved to be heavier than they anticipated and they had to get an ass and cart to transport it. But this wasn't a problem as there was a stile reasonably close on the particular shortcut used and they could take the ass and cart right up to it.

Arriving at the stile, they took the statue and carefully placed it on top of the fence at the far side of the wooden spars. Then they tied it with a rope to the spars and also to the poles at either side to make it secure. White in colour and almost man-size, with one arm raised over the head as if giving a speech, the statue looked very impressive standing on the fence. Just below the stile was a gap into another field, so the lads took the donkey down there and tethered him to a furze bush, while they waited for events to unfold. Waiting patiently and rather nervously for a frightened roar from Big Nell as she fainted and fell at the other side of the stile, they jokingly discussed how would they lift her across the stile in such a condition. Mickeen Seán said he hoped she'd stay in that condition until she got home because if she woke up and saw the statue stretched beside her in the ass's cart, she'd collapse again anyway.

Soon the moon began to peep across the wood, causing the Lad to remark, "That's a good job. At least now we will see what we are doing with her". Surmising all the possible eventualities and enjoying the banter, the lads were suddenly stunned into silence when they heard a rat-tat-tat sound coming from the direction of the stile. It would stop for a few seconds and then start up again. This continued for what appeared to them a considerable length of time. Eventually it ceased and, to their amazement, out from the stile walked the indomitable Big Nell. She continued on her way home across the field at a leisurely pace as unperturbed as if nothing had happened. Shocked and disappointed, they hurriedly made their way to the stile. They found desolation!

The statue was destroyed – the raised arm was broken off, the head was split in two, the second hand was also broken and all the body was cracked and severely pockmarked from blows of the blackthorn. As they picked up the pieces by the light of the moon, Johnny was crying. What would his father say if he found out? After all, it was a valued heirloom. Mickeen Seán consoled him by promising that he would get a man he knew who was handy at that kind of work to repair it. And there ended their 'defence' of the Quack.

There were at least three different types of wakes. There were good wakes, there were fair wakes, and then there were bad wakes. Also popular at the time was the American wake which had only one thing in common with the ordinary wake – tears were shed. The wake was considered good or otherwise by the giving out. The 'giving out' was the amount of tea and currant cake, plus porter, snuff and clay pipes full of tobacco, that would be distributed. The old women generally favoured the clay pipes and the snuff. They would go to the wake, dressed mostly in their black shawls. On entering the wake-house they would 'olagone' and shed tears, and offer their condolences on meeting the bereaved in the kitchen. They would then be shown into the room where the dead person was laid out. Here they would kneel down around the bed and offer prayers for the deceased, mostly out loud. From the prayers they would break into their caoineadh. This would continue for a considerable length of time as each person would give their own lament. Some women were well-known for their capacity to caoin or lament and their presence was much appreciated by the bereaved family.

The caoineadh over, they would then be offered a glass of porter or a drop of poitín. On a table nearby would be an array of snuff boxes and clay pipes already filled with tobacco. The women would be invited to try both. Soon the smoke would be curling around the ceiling. During the drinking and the snuffing the conversation would turn to the deceased person. If it was a man, all his mighty deeds would be recalled, such as the great slean's man he was and the almighty amount of turf he'd cut in a day. They'd mention all the hay he mowed and all the wynds of hay he piked on the day making the rick. As this was the usual scene at wakes, some wit once remarked that 'no lazy person ever died!' If the deceased was a woman, the talk would be about the early riser she was and how the smoke would be seen from her chimney at five o'clock every morning. She'd have her line of washing out at seven o'clock every Monday morning, and that would be after milking the cows and having some of the butter made, as well as getting the children ready for school. Her husband would probably be castigated as a no-gooder. He, too, would have to wait until he died to get his due.

In the meantime, the men would call in to pay their respects and offer their condolences, and after saying a short prayer, generally on one knee, they would duck out the back door and congregate in groups in the haggard where they would discuss the deceased and all the topics of the day, and be treated to mugs of porter. The porter would usually be distributed from white, enamelled buckets, but if the enamelled ones were not available the ordinary milking bucket would be used. In those days when money was a scarce commodity, and many a man couldn't afford the luxury of going to a pub even though he had a tooth for porter, a good wake was like manna in the desert.

Usually the crowd of men would be big so there would be two buckets in use. Two men would man each bucket. They were usually relatives or near neighbours and one would hold the bucket while the other one would hand out the mugs of porter. Each man would have at least two mugs, handing out the second and taking back the first and dipping it into the bucket to fill it again for the next man. That routine would be continued until every man got a drink and, after a short break, it would be repeated. Some would often get two drinks per round, as they were known to ramble around on the pretext of chatting with neighbours, thereby getting ahead of the bucket and then slyly move back again to be first for the next round.

One such character was Mickeen Muldoon, a nice, pleasant type of fellow, but with an unquenchable thirst for porter. He'd travel miles to a wake and, on one occasion, he took in two of them on the same day. At the first wake he knelt down on his two knees in the midst of all the women and prayed his heart out. He soon found that praying was thirsty work, so he got up off his knees and slipped out the back door to the haggard. And then, as far as he was concerned, disaster struck – there was no giving out. Licking his lips, he had nothing better to do than to set out for the other wake where he hoped there would be something doing. Arriving at Biddy Mackey's wake, he could see that here the scene was different and the giving out was already in progress. In fairness to Mickeen, in spite of the thirst he went through the same procedure. He went into the house, knelt down, said his prayers and shook hands with all the bereaved, down to the third and fourth cousins, and only then did he make his way out to the haggard.

On this occasion he was lucky because, at that very time, the late Biddy's husband, Mike, was out checking that everyone was getting a drink and, knowing Mickeen, the very minute he saw him, he filled a mug of porter and handed it to him. Still smarting from the disappointment of the previous wake and full of gratitude to Mike Mackey, as he took the mug of porter and without realising what he was saying, Mickeen looked him straight in the eye and said, "May God increase wakes to you, Mike, and I hope that lousy so-and-so below in the valley will never again have a wake". All Mike could do, even in spite of his bereavement, was laugh as he told the story to all the men in the haggard.

Wakes would go on all night and many of the neighbours and cousins would arrive around midnight, prepared to stay the night and give the family the chance to sleep for a few hours. Many yarns would be told during the night about the deceased and their characters would improve with each telling! Many other things would also be discussed, such as the prices asked for animals at the last cattle or horse fair. According to the time of year, the hay or the corn would come up for analysis and such would be the discussions that the night would swiftly run its course. Of course a drop of the 'cratur' would be handed around at various times during the night and it has happened that around six o'clock in the morning, oblivious to where he was, an intoxicated man would start singing a song. Naturally, he'd be quickly restrained and conveyed home.

But there was one wake that would be forever remembered. It was the wake of Nora Tobin, known as Small Nora to distinguish her from another much bigger woman of the same name. Small Nora and her husband Mike worked very hard to eke out a living on their small farm where they reared a big family. Many of the children emigrated to America and the dollars they sent their parents were a considerable help to them in their later years. But the help was too late for Nora as she was bent almost in two from the hard work and the large family. When she died, this created a problem as she couldn't lay flat on the bed to be laid out properly. Big Nell, in charge of operations as usual, decided that she would place a rope across her hips and tie it firmly to the bed and then, with another rope across her chest, they would force the body down as flat as possible. This worked reasonably well and, surrounded by pillows and wreaths of flowers, the camouflage was complete. All the mourners expressed satisfaction at how well Small Nora looked and how she straightened out so well in death.

As she was a popular woman in the community, the wake was well-attended by all the well-known caoiners and the giving out was good. All the women in their black shawls came and did their praying and their crying, and were treated to plenty of snuff and clay pipes and, of course, the drop of the cratur. Paddy the Lad and several more men arrived and, ignoring, the pall of smoke that pervaded the room, they knelt down around the bed and were praying silently when, all of a sudden, Small Nora sat up on the bed. There was consternation! The women that were smoking let the pipes fall out of their mouths to the floor where they smashed on the flags and the snuff went with the breath of all the women snuffing. Coughing and choking and crying, some of them fell on the floor in a faint. The men, some visibly shaken, came to the aid of the women and, lifting them up, took them out to the kitchen where they seated them on súgán chairs. Someone shouted, "Get Big Nell!"

Paddy the Lad took the hint and went out and tackled the jennet. He galloped for Big Nell, arriving back with her in record time. Jumping out of the car, she made a beeline for the door as she shouted back at the Lad, "Bring in the jennet's reins". Making her way through the kitchen and passing by the still-shaken women, she entered the room to find Small Nora sitting up as if she was serenely surveying the scene. The Lad arrived in with the jennet's reins and soon Small Nora was laid out again, surrounded by pillows and flowers, looking more serene than ever. Cajoled by the Lad, the men were the first to venture back into the room and were soon to be followed by the women, still in a very sombre mood. The cause of the problem was that, under constant pressure the iron of the bed cut the rope, but Big Nell and Paddy the Lad engineered something to prevent that happening again.

All in all, the people of Ballymachad were a very caring people who would respond wholeheartedly to the bereaved in their midst. But there was one occasion when the community let itself down badly. Living alone in a small hut in a very isolated part of the parish was a very old woman. For many years she had not been seen out, but a neighbour took care of her food and other basic needs, while the priest would take the sacraments to her. Otherwise, she was a recluse who didn't want any visitors. Then one day she was found dead. With no money or relatives that could be traced, the priest asked some people what he should do. One shopkeeper in the village volunteered to get a coffin and to pay all funeral expenses. The Chipper made the coffin and, to his credit, he waived his fee. Big Nell also played her part with distinction. The shopkeeper had the remains brought to the church in the morning by horse and cart. The priest celebrated Mass and immediately afterwards the corpse was taken for burial. The sad thing was, that apart from the priest, only three people, all men, attended the funeral. When they arrived at the graveyard the priest had to shoulder the coffin with them and when the burial service was over and the woman buried, he thanked the three men and said, "I never knew what it was to be poor until today".

Eviction and Emigration

The great fear of farmers during the reign of the landlords, and indeed for a considerable time after the three Fs were accomplished, was the fear of eviction. Times were bad and it was a real struggle to make ends meet. A lot depended on how the cattle would perform – would the cows milk well and, even if they did, would there be a fair price for the butter? Would there be a demand and a good price for calves and fat pigs and spuds? These were the main worries for farmers. The performance of the cattle and the price obtained for their produce determined their income. Even with things going right for them, their income would still be very meagre, but it paid the rent and kept the bailiffs away – the arrival of the bailiffs was the last straw. It must be remembered that there were no animal remedies in those days. Many of the animal diseases that were fatal at that time are easily cured, or even preventable, today.

However, in olden days, the fatality rate among the cattle population was extremely high especially on heavy land – the farmer farming natural dry land had a better chance of survival and avoiding the bailiff. Fluke in cattle was a big killer and the reason why animals became infected with it was unknown. Every animal was a big loss. But farmers would try to cut their losses by skinning the animal and selling the skin for approximately two or three shillings. It took many years of research to pinpoint the cause. And the cause of fluke was simple – a snail picked up in the drinking water. That is why cattle grazing on wet, heavy land were more susceptible to the disease. The snail was prevalent there and it would be almost impossible for the animals to avoid infection.

Yet there was always a percentage that escaped infection but even if a small number of animals got ill, it would be considered a disaster as it might result in the bailiffs coming to the farm. "The bailiffs went back the road this morning" was a dreaded statement to hear. It put a chill down the spine of many a hardworking breadwinner, a man with a big family to support who dreaded that it could be his turn next. The bailiffs were known to be a heartless crew from the stories relayed by some of their victims – everyone knew that there was no compassion and no mercy to be expected.

There were many stories like that of Billy and his wife, Molly. They were the parents of five children, the youngest of whom was just a baby. Early one morning the bailiffs arrived – they always travelled very early in the morning. The family was just out of bed when they were confronted by three bailiffs who pushed in their door. A third man stayed outside. Billy and Molly soon found out that he was a cattle drover. The bailiffs grumpily explained who they were and what they intended to do. They were not going to evict the family as their debt wasn't big enough to warrant it but they were taking all the cows and whatever cattle were on the land. Overcome with shock and disbelief, Molly begged them to leave one cow for milk for the baby. The reply was a curt no, as far as the bailiffs were concerned she could get milk wherever she liked, all the cows are going, end of story. Looking out the window, Billy saw two peelers arriving. They would provide protection for the bailiffs. With broken hearts, the family watched their six fine cows and two yearling heifers being driven across their front door and up the boreen. Their only means of making a bit of money was gone and they could do nothing about it. There was another worry – would eviction be next?

Evictions by bailiffs and the seizing of cattle and any chattels that were saleable was a daily occurrence that put terror into the hearts of the peasant farmers. Accompanied by Royal Irish Constabulary (RIC) constables and hired cattle drovers, the bailiffs' *modus operandi* was brutal. They would arrive with a 'battering ram' with which they would demolish the dwelling house of their victim, a simple job as the building was often a mud-walled cabin. This left the family no option but to leave the little farm so that it could be rented to another tenant. This, in turn, created a movement among the tenant farmers by which they would organise a boycott of anyone taking possession of an evicted farm. This meant that no one would have anything to do, whatsoever, with the new tenant. No one would talk to him or to any member of his family. The walls of buildings would be painted with slogans such as 'Boycott so and so, the Grabber'.

That family would soon find themselves completely isolated. For starters, with no one speaking to them, they couldn't organise a meitheal for cutting the turf or saving the hay. When they would take cattle to the fair to sell, a group would appear with makeshift banners saying 'Boycott so and so the Grabber', and isolate them by circling round them. The RIC would attempt to catch the boycotters but they would be seen coming, the banners would be dropped on the ground, and those involved would get lost in the crowded fair. No one would dare identify them for fear of reprisals and no dealer would buy 'boycotted' cattle, again for fear of reprisals, as one cattle dealer who ignored the boycott had his hay burned. The boycott also hit the landlords hard, as in a short space of time no one would take possession of an evicted farm for fear of their lives. Some of the so-called 'grabbers' had been tarred and feathered and threatened with more serious consequences if they didn't vacate the land, which a number of them did.

The landlords then installed what they termed 'emergency men' on the evicted farms in a caretaker capacity when no tenant could be found and they appealed to the government for help and protection. Being the planters of the government, help was immediately forthcoming and the RIC was instructed to crack down on the militant farmers. Order was quickly enforced and nightly raids resulted in the arrest of many farmers. Held in custody for a few days, no witnesses could be found to swear on them. It was reported to the farmers that one grabber tenant was prepared to testify against them. That night he had a visit from five hooded men, one of whom carried a shotgun, and was told in no uncertain terms what would happen him if he opened his mouth to the police. It came to the point where selected landlords were threatened with serious consequences if they didn't stop the practice of the battering ram and give more favourable terms to their tenants. Their agents were being molested and threatened and some were killed.

With a few murders committed on a national basis, the situation was getting dangerous for all involved and some landlords responded by lowering the rent for their tenants, while others went to live in England, leaving their agents in charge. Some of those agents were considered reasonable enough but others were very harsh, showing no mercy for the tenants under their thumb. But as some poet wrote, "A people's will is mightier than the sea", so, with constant pressure from the tenant farmers, pressure was mounting on the government to settle this problem of what was known as 'land agitation'. As history has recorded, over a number of years, the landlords saw the writing on the wall. Over time, albeit a long time and compensated by the government, they abdicated their estates and many of them left Ireland's shores. Some of them stayed and became very respected members of their local communities where they farmed extensively on the land they retained.

The tenant farmers had won a famous victory with the three Fs, but for those men who fought so hard to own the land they farmed there was still a long hard road ahead and for many years the bailiffs were still a threat. And it must be recorded that the bailiffs were still very active during the tenure of the first Free State government. Many officials and systems were still in place from the earlier regime and this system of collecting arrears was so endemic in Irish culture that no one looked for a better way. After a lot of hardship inflicted on an honest, decent people, a better way was found but it took some time. In spite of the bad times, the hard work for poor returns and the danger of the bailiff, men were prepared to fight and even die for the land which they perceived as their rightful God-given heritage.

In spite of their hard work, however, they soon found the going tough. The rent had still to be met, rates came on stream, children had to be fed and clothed and farm commodity prices were high. In time, this triggered a new wave of emigration which became a sad feature of rural Ireland for many generations. It was looked upon as an escape hatch by many young boys and girls of the era who could see no future at home. They still shed bitter tears as they said goodbye to their families and friends. Their parents also felt a deep sorrow and prayed many rosaries for the safe arrival of their children in England or America and that they would find suitable work. To alleviate some of that great sorrow the 'American wake' came into being. It was an attempt by the local community to dispel the sorrow of the impending departures, at least until the final parting.

The American wake could be described as a 'hooley' and it was held in the home of the boy or girl about to emigrate. It was the community's response to create some bit of fun and excitement to take their minds off the impending emigration. It often happened that there would be four or five boys and girls from a community booked to sail on the same liner. In this situation, there would be only the one wake. To accommodate the expected big crowd, the house with the biggest kitchen would be chosen. The floor space was necessary for the dancing of reels, sets and hornpipes. All the girls due to travel would be kept on the floor all night as the boys – often their partners at the crossroads dancing on Sunday evenings – would be anxious to have a last dance with them before they departed.

Songs would be sung and they would be mostly lively airs in an attempt to dispel the gloom. Some smart fellow would have a bit of a rhyme about America – the land of the free! There would be a degree of hilarity in the night, especially when some of the older men, with a few drinks in, would take to the floor for a reel or a set and pull out their wives for a dance, a thing they hadn't done since they got married. Now stiff and bent from hard work, their attempts at dancing would add to the gaiety of the night. Of course, the older men didn't think that their dancing had deteriorated since their younger days at the crossroads. On leaving the floor they would invariably remark that the youngsters didn't know how to dance at all. The wake would continue until it was time for the travellers to go home and get dressed. They would then be taken to the train station for their journey to the port. Not much time for tears, but there was bound to be some. At least during the four or five days on the liner they could reminisce on their American wake.

Indeed, it often happened that boyfriends and girlfriends would respond to the love-letters they were receiving by emigrating to the States. The majority of those got married and settled down there and many of them never came home to Ireland again until their children were reared. During and after the Famine people emigrated en masse. This was the period of the so-called 'coffin ships'. It would be impossible to quantify the number of Irish men and women, in what should have been their prime of life, who died on the ship that was taking them to what they looked upon as their 'Promised Land'. Those who died were buried at sea as they fled from the hunger and poverty of their land, a poverty and a hunger that could have been eliminated if the powers that be at that time had had the will to do it. Alas, they were found to be seriously ambiguous in their treatment of their Irish subjects. Still, the majority survived the Atlantic crossing, and though quarantined on Ellis Island for a period, they subsequently helped build America – its roads, railroads and skyscrapers.

To those Irish, America was the Land of Freedom, freedom from hunger, freedom from poverty, freedom from oppression, freedom to earn a decent living.

Known at that time as the 'New World', to many Irish it was a new life. Alas, the vast majority of them never had the opportunity to return to their native land. But they never forgot their families at home in 'dear old Ireland'. In their letters home, especially at Christmas and Easter, they always enclosed dollars with their greetings. As the holy feast days approached, the postman would be monitored and watched, as in those times, those dollars were badly needed by the families back home – they would mean what it said on the enclosed card, a Happy Christmas or a Happy Easter as the case may be. Thrifty and hard-working, many of the emigrant Irish saved as much money as they could and dreamed of coming home and buying a farm or a shop or a house.

Some of them did succeed in doing that while, for others, it remained a dream. And then disaster struck – the US banks went bust and innumerable people were left penniless. This was a cruel blow that caused many suicides. Some of the elderly Irish returned to Ireland as soon as they were able to put the fare together, with very little money in their pockets. Others stuck it out and many of them became very wealthy. Some Irish became involved in politics and that involvement culminated in an Irish-American, the late John Fitzgerald Kennedy, becoming the president of the United States to the acclaim of Irish people everywhere.

One thing that the early Irish emigrants did was to relate a knowledge of Ireland to their children, along with a love for the land of their forebears. They told them of its beauty-spots, its valleys, its lakes and dells. They told them in detail about all these beauty spots that they themselves had never the pleasure of seeing or enjoying, but had heard about them in song and story. Subsequently, wealthy Irish-Americans made Ireland their holiday destination and became very welcome visitors. They came to visit the country's famous beauty-spots that they probably first heard about at their mother's, or perhaps their grandmother's, knee.

A Memorable Match

Sporting Beginnings

At a time when hard work was the norm and the rewards were small, the people still had great heart for living and when the opportunity arose, they would let themselves go and really enjoy themselves. The good thing about entertainment at the time was that it was mostly free, consisting as it did of sports, crossroad dancing, the rambling house or a football match. A match would be arranged between two teams from the parish – a team from west of a given point and a team from east of that point. Great rivalry would be created for the build-up to the big day and bets of a shilling, or a maximum of half a crown, would be the norm. The biggest challenge was to get the use of a field. Tom Redden would be approached and he would usually oblige. Preparing the field entailed a lot of work for the organisers. For starters, the rushes would have to be cut, collected and burned. Jimeen the Man or Small Peter, the two local mowers in Ballymachad, would come on board and do the needful if they weren't too busy. They were the favoured duo to do the job as they would really skin the rushes. There was no pay but they would be treated to a gallon of porter afterwards – if a few bob was collected at the gap going in.

Four or five lads would be detailed to go to the wood for four goalposts while a pick and shovel brigade would be digging four holes for them. A rope between the posts would be the crossbar and there would be no such thing back then as a net. The field would then have to be rolled to close the cow-tracks insofar as was practical. Cow-tracks were very undesirable on a playing pitch, but it was impossible to get a field that was free of them. Few games were played where some player didn't get a máchail of a twisted ankle or a disjointed knee from landing in a cow track after fielding a high ball. Cow-tracks were also very undesirable when it came to the hop of the ball. Many a good player was left clutching fresh air as, beating all opposition, he considered an incoming ball well within his grasp, only to see it land on the verge of a cow-track and hop away from his outstretched hands. Yet they were never a deterrent to young men playing football – the sound of the kicked ball would erase the memory of cow-tracks from their minds and they would gallop onto the field with the same enthusiasm as if it were Croke Park itself.

Mick 'the Whistler' Kelly was an avid supporter of football. He actually derived his nickname from the fact that, if he spotted any foul play watching the young fellows kicking a ball on the summer evenings, he'd give a whistle through a division in his two front teeth that would reverberate around the field and stop play instantly. When asked if he would referee a friendly match between teams from neighbouring townlands, it was a natural progression for him and eventually launched him as a very popular referee and a unique one at that, as he never used a whistle, just his own natural whistling ability. Small in stature, the Whistler made up for it with an edgy temper that was feared by the young players of the area. Paudeen McGurk arrived into a field one evening where a few lads were having a kick around. It was his first introduction to football and he took to it like a duck to water. An hour later the Whistler arrived and, sizing up the number of players, he decided that he would start a game of eight aside, figuring that it would be better training for them. Blowing his unique whistle, he brought proceedings to a halt.

Paudeen looked around and wondered who was the small little man that had the power to stop everyone playing just by a whistle. He turned to the boy next to him and asked, "Who's the small man?" When told he was the Whistler Kelly, the referee, Paudeen just muttered "Is he", and walked over near the Whistler to size him up. The fact that he was the referee meant nothing to Paudeen. Calling all the players to the centre of the field, where they made a circle around him, the Whistler soon had the teams arranged. The Whistler then went to the fence and cut four lengths of sally to act as goalposts. Paudeen was assigned midfield for one team and his opposite number was the 'Doll', a man of six foot two and built accordingly, he was nicknamed the 'Doll' (a name he hated) just because he had the smallest head ever seen on a man. The two had never met before and it was Paudeen's first time playing a football match. However, lining out in a long, baggy pants and size eleven nailed boots against the more experienced Doll didn't cost him a thought.

Straight after the throw-in, in the first encounter between the two midfielders, Paudeen got a few hefty jabs of the elbow in the ribs from the more experienced Doll. Frustrated and under great pressure, Paudeen's temper soared to boiling point and, when the ball came his way again, he picked it straight off the ground and raced down the field with it. He raced right towards the Whistler, who was whistling for all he was worth, and, as he came near, the ref shouted, "Drop that ball you brute". But Paudeen roared back at him, "Come out of my way or I'll walk down on you". Followed by the Doll, the now berserk Paudeen, with the ball clutched firmly against his chest with one hand and hitting out at anyone that came near him with the other, never stopped until he put the ball between the two sallies. Turning as if to resume his position, he came face to face with the Doll who had followed him.

"You bloody big head," said Paudeen as he walked passed him.

The Doll was overjoyed. To be called 'a big head' made his day. He overtook Paudeen and, reaching out the hand of friendship to him, he said, "I'll meet you tonight in the Shanty. I must buy you a few pints". Thereafter a friendship developed between the two but whenever they met on the football field, as they often did, no quarter would be given. Stressed by the events of the first fifteen minutes, the Whistler decided to abandon the match, but it was the beginning of better games to come and of many memorable duels between the Doll and Paudeen.

Over the course of time the game of football grew increasingly popular in Ballymachad. On long summer evenings, the young men of the parish would go to a local field and have a kick about until dusk. This field, in time, became known as 'the football field'. It was owned by the genial Tom Redden who always claimed that he never gave anyone permission to use it but that it had been 'taken off him'. This came about when Santa Claus brought a football to the young Reddens one Christmas. Immediately they stuck two sticks into the ground as goalposts in a field not far from the house. Here they played at every opportunity, and were always joined by their dog Paddy. Paddy was a big, strong, playful collie that soon got a liking for football! A great cattle dog, it wasn't long until the boys had him trained to stand in the goals and they would take turns taking shots at him.

An unusual dog, Paddy would stand up to their hardest kicks and seemed to revel in stopping them. After every 'save' he would push the ball with his nose out the field again and, like any good goalie, would run back and take up his position once more. In ones and twos youngsters started to join them and it was only a matter of time until the adults arrived. Big goalposts were soon erected at both ends of the field – it was now 'the football field'. A man with a keen interest in all things Gaelic, Tom Redden didn't object. On the contrary, he encouraged his own sons and, indeed, all the youth of the place to play Gaelic football and was prepared to play his part by supplying the amenity to do so.

With no shortage of potential players, Mick the Whistler Kelly suggested that a team should be put together.

"I'm talking about a right team," stressed the Whistler, "a team that we can go places with."

"What places are you going to?" shouted some fellow.

Looking at him with a scornful scowl, the Whistler retorted with bitterness in his voice, "What I mean by going places is that we would have a team that would win matches. Do you understand that, brainless?"

The questioner just hung his head.

"I think Mick is right," said Tom Redden (no one would never call him the 'Whistler' to his face). "I propose that we appoint three or four selectors who, in consultation with Mick, will pick the best possible team to represent Ballymachad," added Redden.

"Here, here! Here, here!" shouted a bunch of young fellows from the back.

The Whistler put the ball rolling by immediately proposing Tom Redden himself. A busy man, Tom wasn't anxious for the job but, having made the initial suggestion, he agreed to play his part. The next name mentioned was Gerry Muldoon, an astute middle-aged man with a big, bushy moustache and well-groomed sidelocks. Reluctantly, he accepted the 'honour' as he called it and, having accepted, he stressed that their main aim should be to bring honour to the parish and put Ballymachad on the map.

"Here, here!" again from the lads at the back, eager for the fray.

The Whistler suggested that someone from the west of the parish would be desirable. Immediately someone shouted, "What about Mickey the Dug?"

"What about him?" asked the Whistler.

"He's a knowledgeable auld lad about football, maybe ye could stick him in. I'll guarantee you he's no daw," was the reply. "Is he present?" asked the Whistler."

"No," came the answer, "But I'm certain he will take the job and be mad for it. He trains us at the west and is right good."

"We'll take your word for it," said the Whistler, "tell him be here tomorrow evening at eight o'clock."

The New Club

Mickey the Dug, whose real was Mickey Duggan, duly presented himself the following evening, arriving on the stroke of eight. A good sign of him to be so punctual, thought Redden, and the others though the same. Later they learned it was characteristic of the man and that he was a very good choice who would prove an asset to team training. The scene was now set to bring footballing glory to Ballymachad. In the shade of a friendly furze bush, highly motivated and with great ambition, the new football club met in session for the first time. Awareness of the fact that they had nothing but the name, not even a proper ball, didn't dampen their enthusiasm. The question of the ball was the first to be tackled and there was unanimous agreement that, as it would cost five shillings, they would have to have a collection among the members. They also agreed that it should be made known that donations from anyone who cared to contribute would be most welcome.

The consensus of the meeting was that they would invite all the young men of the parish to come to the field two evenings a week and, by putting them through their paces, they would pick the nucleus of a team – perhaps twenty five to thirty – for special training. It was also agreed that the parish priest would be asked to say a few words from the altar about the new club and encourage the youth of the parish to support it. As it happened it was a labour of love for the priest as he was delighted that something was being done for the youth of the place. The five shillings was duly collected and, as Gerry Muldoon was taking calves to the fair the following Thursday, he was given the money and ordered to search the town for a proper sized football. It proved to be a hard assignment and he searched every shop in town to no avail.

But as he was leaving the last shop, a man tipped him on the shoulder and, excusing himself, said, "I couldn't help overhearing you asking about a football. May I ask if you tried Moloney the harness maker?"

"Never heard of him, what part of the town is he in?" queried Muldoon.

"Go out the door there now and turn to your right," directed the stranger, "continue up the street and go in the second laneway to your right. You can't miss him, you'll see the harness hanging on the door."

"Sound man," said Gerry, laying his hand on the man's shoulder as he made for the door. Following the instructions, in five minutes Gerry was inside in Moloney's workshop.

A tall, bearded man, with pipe in hand, Moloney looked the picture of relaxation, with a smile on his face and a twinkle in his eye. Gerry ventured, "Good day, sir".

"And good day to you too, sir," was the polite reply, "can I help you?"

Gerry felt extremely foolish at that moment, asking a harness maker for a football. He wondered if the stranger who directed him here was a joker. At that moment, to his amazement, the stranger walked in the door.

"I see you made him out," he said.

"Oh, I did, sir," blurted Gerry.

"So ye have met before," remarked the smiling harness maker.

"Well, yes," answered the stranger, "I hope you were able to help him,"

"We didn't talk any business as yet," said the harness maker.

Just then Gerry spotted a football hanging off the ceiling – the stranger was right after all. Now, with confidence, he explained his mission to the harness maker, he wanted a football. Moloney looked him up and down and asked, "How did you think I would have a football?"

"That man told me," said Gerry, pointing to the stranger.

They both laughed, as if it were a big joke.

"You're lucky," smiled Moloney, pointing to the ceiling, "There is just one left."

Standing on a box, he took down the ball and handed it to Gerry, saying, "Here it is complete with bladder". Gerry took it and, looking up at Moloney, remarked, "It isn't pumped at all?"

"No," said the genial Moloney, "do you want me to pump it for you?"

"If you would, please," said a mannerly Gerry.

"Very well so, I'll get it pumped for you," responded Moloney, walking out the door with the ball cradled in his arm.

Alone now with the stranger, Gerry asked him, "How come the harness maker is dealing in footballs?"

"He is not actually," replied the man, "he just makes one now and again for the local lads. You were just lucky that he had one made. I'll guarantee you it will be a good one."

Moloney returned with the ball pumped as hard as a rock and hopped it on the floor so hard that it hit the ceiling.

"What's the damage?" asked Gerry.

"Give me six shillings," said Moloney.

"Would five do you? We are just trying to start a club," said Gerry and, with the poor mouth, added, "money is scarce."

"Well, fair play to ye for trying," said Moloney, "take away the ball with you and if you, or any of your neighbours, ever want harness made, give me the turn."

"We will to be sure. I'll spread the word and thank you very much and may the Lord increase business to you," said a delighted Gerry.

"Where are you from?" asked Moloney, as he handed the ball to Gerry.

"I'm from Ballymachad," Gerry proudly answered.

He was taken aback when Moloney remarked, "I never heard of it". Gerry looked at him incredulously, hopped the ball on the floor and said with conviction, "You'll hear a lot about it soon". Tucking the ball under his arm and again thanking the harness maker, a proud Gerry left for home.

A meeting had been arranged in the shade of the same big, friendly furze bush for that evening, more or less to learn how Gerry got on in his search for a ball. Gerry was the last to arrive. As proud as punch, he hopped the ball before him as he approached. All the members examined it in turn and thought it was a mighty ball. What had it cost was the next question. With a roughish smile Gerry said, "Well now, I must explain that it is a handmade ball so it was dear".

"How much is dear?" questioned the Dug.

"Very dear, the price of at least two calves – ten shillings," joked Gerry.

'Ten shillings!" they all roared in unison, "we'll have to have another collection."

Each of them had to inspect it again and the joker Gerry gave a running commentary on how it had been handmade with the most expensive leather, to note the beautiful stitching and how hard it was, and the lively hop that was in it. He kept extolling its virtues to such an extent that one of them actually said that it sounded cheap. When he told them the truth they were flabbergasted and delighted. The Ballymachad football team had the best ball that could be bought – for nothing.

The word went out that training would commence the next evening and that all aspiring footballers should attend at half past seven at the latest. Early next evening Paudeen McGurk and the Doll arrived and tried out the new ball with a kick about. They declared it a "beauty". Soon there was about thirty of the "cream of the parish", as the Whistler called them, all kicking to and fro, anxious to get the feel of the new ball. They were soon brought to attention by the unique blast of a whistle from the man himself, the Whistler. Calling them one by one, he directed the first player to his right and the second one to his left, and continued this process until he had fifteen on either side. Leading them to centre-field and aided by the selectors, they were each given their respective positions. All eager to be stars, they took up their positions, the ball was thrown in, and the first training session was on. These training sessions continued two, and sometimes three, evenings a week during the summer and eventually the selectors and the Whistler felt that it was time to pick a team from among the forty or so who were training.

Meeting as usual under the furze bush, they made a commitment to pick the team after the next training session which was scheduled for a Monday night. "They're picking the team on Monday night" was the comment on everyone's lips over the weekend. It generated fierce interest among young and old alike and it was the topic of conversation in the forge all day Saturday and again after Mass on Sunday, the priest's support for the club adding to its status. Nothing else was discussed in the Shanty among the drinking fraternity and, as many of them had sons aspiring to football glory, with a few pints of porter on board, arguments were the order of the day as to who should, or should not, be picked. On a few occasions arguments went as far as men offering each other out to settle the issue with fisticuffs. But, in the vast majority of cases, it was nothing more than lively banter with all wishing the club well.

Picking the Team
Monday evening arrived cloudless and sunny and by half past eight the crowd on the sideline was unusually big. An air of anticipation and expectancy prevailed. Two teams were picked, the ball was thrown in and every player knew that

this was their time to impress. Stripped to the shirt and trousers, the latter held up with wide braces across their shoulders, and with strong, nailed boots, they fought a battle royal, knowing that they were under the eagle eyes of the selectors. Every fifteen minutes four were called to the sideline and four others were put on. This was to give all the boys who were regulars at training a chance to show their skill. The atmosphere was electric and it continued for about eighty minutes until everyone had got their chance. Then the Whistler blew full-time.

Now it was in the hands of the selectors who, in pensive mood, adjourned to the furze bush for their deliberations. Gerry Muldoon sat on his grug, chewing a blade of grass, as was his wont. The others knelt down on one knee around him, as if praying to him for enlightenment. Some of the crowd dispersed while others walked aimlessly around the pitch, anxiously awaiting the result of the deliberations of the selectors. The selectors found it a difficult call and, after deliberating for an hour, they decided that they wouldn't name the team until Tuesday night. Muldoon, throwing out a big green spit from the blade of grass he was chewing, said it was better to sleep on it. The smart alecs had a field evening saying, among other things, "Our selectors will go down in history as the men that picked a team in their sleep".

Clever enough, in order to avoid a crowd pestering them, the selectors rendevouzed on Tuesday in Jack Mulligan's grove at three o'clock in the afternoon. It was a quiet, isolated place where there would be no one to bother them. At four o'clock they had their team picked – somehow it seemed a lot easier in the afternoon – maybe it was the solitude of the place. When they arrived at the football field at eight o'clock that evening, they were glad they had the business done because the place was thronged. All the players were kicking the ball aimlessly around the field – the crowd of onlookers seemed more interested in finding out the make-up of the team than the players.

As there was no such thing as a public address system at the time, the selectors walked onto centre-field. Surrounded in a circle formed by the crowd in an instant, they felt isolated and hoped their selection would be acceptable to all. If not, the situation could become very volatile and they had no escape route. As Tom Redden was a man that people in general looked up to, he got the onerous task of reading the names and positions of the selected team. Being the affable man that he was, he spoke as follows:

"First of all, my friends, I would like to put things in perspective. As you all know there are almost forty young men who have come to this field two or three nights a week and taken part in the training sessions. You also know that fifteen is a team, plus five substitutes. Therefore you will realise how hard a task it was for us to choose. Our mandate was to pick, what we believe, is the best team of players to represent Ballymachad. We believe we have done that. We sincerely hope we have done that."

A few men clapped and then a burst of applause.

"Name 'em," shouted some fellow from the back of the crowd.

"I'm just about to do that," replied Redden, "but first let me explain that the team I'm about to name is a provisional team which means we are still free to experiment with other players. Our promise is that we will do just that – so now for the team – in goals is Paddy Mike."

"Great, sure he'd stop a bullet," shouted a curly brown-haired, young fellow. A big, grey-haired man waved a blackthorn stick in the air and said in a commanding voice, "No more interruptions now until Tom is finished. We want to know the team as quickly as possible, that's why we're here".

Tom continued: "Full back is Patcheen Cronin, on his right is the Spider Hayes and on his left is Curly Casey. In the next line of defence we have the Butcher Roche, with Mickeen Óg on his left and Tommy Short on his right."

Not a tittle from the crowd.

"In the centre of the field we have the two great rivals, the Doll and Paudeen McGurk," Tom said.

That drew a favourable chuckle.

"Now to the forwards," continued Redden. "At full forward we have Billeen Mike, on his left is the Pedler Lacy and on his right we have Dandy Jim."

That put a smirk on a lot of faces.

"Outside them, we have Baby Jack Quirke in the centre, with Mickey Jer on his left and the Snuffler Kirby on his right. The captain will be Spider Hayes and we will pick subs as the need arises to suit different positions," concluded Tom Redden.

Slow to show any emotion, favourable or otherwise, the crowd fell into little groups, all of them having their own discussions, and, presumably, their own ideas. The first to comment was the grey-haired man with the blackthorn stick. His remarks were short and to the point. "I congratulate ye. I'm convinced he have done a great job and I'm sure the team will do Ballymachad proud."

"Here, here!" came the shouts from around the circle. The silence was broken and there were calls for the members of the team to come together and march into the circle. A section of the circle parted and the new team, led by Spider, proudly marched in. The reaction was spontaneous as caps were waved and some thrown up in the air. In the deafening roar, old men cried tears of joy and the poor creatures hadn't even a handkerchief to wipe their tears. But that didn't matter, they had lived to see this day, a new dawn, a step forward in the fight for their Gaelic culture and who knew what it might lead to. There were calls for Spider to say something and, after repeated calls, he responded, saying, "I'm proud to captain this team and I can assure you we will do our level best to bring honour to Ballymachad". He got great applause but refused to say another word.

Suddenly there was silence. Two constables were standing at the gap viewing the proceedings. In legal terms at the time it could be deemed an offence for large groups to congregate. There was a big sigh of relief when the two policemen left the scene. The Whistler was delighted with the response from the crowd and his promise was that they would now seek a suitable team to play. Training would continue unabated, and he predicted that they would give any team a run for their money. The crowd slowly dispersed, and the mood was great, expectations were high and the whole community felt uplifted as never before. But there was still a lot of work to be done.

The Build-up

Retiring to their usual meeting place at the furze bush after the team was announced, the members pondered where they would go from there. The consensus of opinion was that they should search for a team to play a real game to give the boys experience at that level. Gerry Muldoon said he would be going to town on Wednesday and that he would make inquiries if he came across anyone interested in football. He added that he would call to Moloney, the harness maker, as he seemed to be either involved with a club or with people who were running clubs. Arriving in town on Wednesday, Muldoon made a beeline for Moloney who was delighted to see him and made inquiries about the club. Gerry filled him in on the happenings, putting great emphasis on the formation of the team.

Then he broached the question, "Do you know any team suitable for a match with us?" Moloney looked down at the floor in thoughtful pose. Then he looked up at the ceiling with a faraway look in his eyes. Gerry couldn't understand how he had to put so much thought into a simple question. Finally Moloney spoke. "I have now made a mental assessment of all the teams I know and I have come to the conclusion that there is one team that would suit your purpose. Now, tell me, would ye prefer to play at home or to travel?"

"Oh, we would have to play at home as it is our first match," answered Gerry, "and furthermore, all the local supporters would go stone mad out of their heads if it wasn't played at home because they would have no way of travelling and the thought of missing their first match would cause a riot."

"I can appreciate that," said a considerate Moloney. "I'm sure the team I have in mind to play you would be prepared to travel. They have a lot of supporters with sidecars, back-to-back traps, horses and common cars, so travelling should be no problem to them."

"Who are they or where are they from?" inquired Gerry.

"They are from Ballyhooley, a place on the Limerick border. The most of them are Limerick lads," explained the harness maker.

"We won't hold that against them," joked Muldoon. "When, do you think, would they come to play us?"

"When would ye be ready?" asked Moloney.

"Well now, that's a good question," answered Muldoon. "You see, I'm only one member of the club so I'll have to think about it."

After a thoughtful pause, thinking out loud, he said, "today is Wednesday, what about Sunday week, would that suit?"

"'Tis your call. I'm sure it could be arranged for that day. There is a neighbour of yours, Mick Sullivan, calling to me at the weekend for harness, I'll give him a message for you. Would that suit ye?"

"That would be perfect," said Gerry, "tell Mick Seán and he'll deliver it all right, no better man."

Elated with the success of his mission, that evening Gerry met his colleagues at the furze bush as a training session was in progress. He related in detail his agreement with the harness maker and all complimented him on his negotiating skills. They were all looking forward to Sunday week and what promised to be the likes of a day Ballymachad had never seen. Of course, it had to be all hush hush until Mick Seán brought the definite answer on Friday evening, no point in raising hopes and then dashing them.

Arriving home late on Friday evening, Mick Seán met Tom Redden on the road and when Tom asked him had he any news, he said that the harness maker told him to tell Gerry Muldoon that everything was arranged for the match to be played on Sunday week as requested. There was a slight sting in the tail though, they had to make sure the team were properly togged out. The club officers, meeting later that evening at their usual venue, were very upbeat at confirmation that the match was going ahead and decided to make an official announcement, which they did, and threw the whole parish into a fever pitch of excitement! There was some worry, however, over the togs business.

The Dug stated that white togs were coming into fashion lately and a few teams had them.

"And where did they get them?" asked the Whistler.

"They didn't get them any place, they made them," said the Dug.

"Made them!" all shouted in unison.

"Yes. They made them out of flour bags. Any woman handy with the needle would turn out one of them in no time," said the ice-cool Dug.

Flour at the time came in ten-stone, white sacks, but the question was how many in the parish were buying it by the ten-stone. Tom Redden reckoned that anyone that was buying the ten-stone bags would have all the bags saved as they also made bed sheets of them, so he believed it would be feasible to collect twenty or twenty-five of them and one of them should make a togs.

Gerry Muldoon proposed that they put the onus on the players to procure a ten-stone flour bag for the purpose of getting a togs made, if possible by their mothers. Agreeing to this proposal, the officers walked out to centre-field and, after an almighty blast by the Whistler of his unique whistle, they beckoned the players around them and explained that they would have to be togged out properly for their match on Sunday week This entailed each player and sub locating a ten-stone white flour bag and having it made into a togs. The captain, Spider Kelly, on behalf of the players, asked what kind of a thing was a togs. The Dug explained that they are a knee-length, very simple to make – no fly required – just a piece of elastic around the waist to hold it up.

"Any woman good at sewing could make one for ye or of course the tailor could make them or even the dressmaker. I'm sure ye would be embarrassed to go to her," he concluded.

This created great excitement among the players and the most of them scampered off home to procure a togs by hook or by crook for the biggest day of their young lives.

Back again in the shade of the furze bush, the Dug explained that to be properly togged out all the players would have to wear the same ganseys.

"Who could afford that?" complained Muldoon.

"We have the chance of a lifetime to get them for the players," argued the Dug.

"How?" was the curt response.

"Simple out," responded the cool Dug, "Hold a church-gate collection. The people are on a high, they will give what they can afford and we have only next Sunday to do it."

There was silence in the camp.

"I can see your point," said Tom Redden, breaking the silence, "what would you spend the money on?"

Prompt came the reply:

"I would buy at least fifteen green ganseys, one for each player, and if we had enough money, I would buy five for the subs."

A deafening silence reigned. Again it was Redden who broke the silence.

"I propose we do what the Dug has suggested. I have no doubt that the vast majority of the people support the club and I'm sure many would like the opportunity to support it in their own small or big way. If enough money isn't collected, I will give the shortfall," and, looking straight at the Dug, he continued, "I guarantee to you that the players and subs will have their ganseys."

Again silence, this time broken by the Dug. He went over to Tom Redden, shook his hand and said just one word – "Thanks". Nothing was discussed or talked about in the parish for the remainder of that week, and all the next week, only the match. Eager hands that were handy with the needle worked all day, every day of the week, and often into the small hours turning flour bags into short trousers so that their team would be on a par with the opposition. The church-gate collection was well-supported with people dropping their pence and shillings, in accordance of what they could afford, into a tin box placed on top of an upturned tay-chest. Much to their delight, and with the help a small contribution from Tom Redden, the team were fitted out with green ganseys.

In the meantime, the menfolk were busy clearing rushes or any other offending growth from the field. Midweek, after a couple of heavy showers of rain, Tom Redden's servant boy, himself a player, rolled it several times with a horse and heavy roller to eliminate cow-tracks or lumps that might be a danger to players. Handyman Seán Fada was drafted in to put the two crossbars in place. Getting three lads to help him, he went to the wood to procure two saplings of the required length and substance. After a prolonged search, they found exactly what was needed and, shouldering them, they marched back across the fields. A tall man himself, Seán Fada nailed them to the uprights about six inches above his own head. He then cut off the protruding end to make it look professional. Anxious to be helpful, another group of young men were detailed to cut and remove any protruding briars or bushes along the perimeter fence, just for appearance sake, with strict instructions no to interfere with the big furze bush. On the Friday all was set for the big event and the place was agog with excitement.

The Match

On Sunday, Ballymachad woke up to lovely, sunny and warm morning, just what everyone in the parish was hoping for. After all, this was the most important day, ever, in the Ballymachad calendar, and a wet miserable day would have spoiled the occasion. Everything was looking perfect even though the team had no colours as such. But word had spread quickly that the players would be wearing green ganseys. So, displaying great enthusiasm, some supporters made makeshift green flags. It didn't matter a hoot that they were made from discarded clothing. Not at all, they were now flags and they were proudly flown on a few vantage points in the village and also from trees along the road from the village to the field. All the players attended the nine o'clock morning Mass and they all wore their new green ganseys as directed by the Whistler, which made them very conspicuous.

The parish priest gave what could be described as a pep talk – reminding the people, especially the players, of their Gaelic roots. He complimented the players and their mentors for taking the initiative of forming a Gaelic football club and a Gaelic football team. He wished them success in their match, but also emphasised that performing and playing the game was the important thing – winning was just a bonus. However, he urged them to strive to win, but not to be disappointed if they lost, there would always be another day. As the priest turned his back to the congregation to continue the Mass, an unusual thing happened, those present burst into loud and prolonged applause. His comments and words of encouragement were appreciated and gave a great boost at a time when morale was low. After Mass Tom Redden and Gerry Muldoon went to the sacristy and asked the parish priest to do the club the honour of throwing in the ball. Replying in the affirmative, the priest declared that he would be honoured.

Around midday the village began to take on something akin to a carnival atmosphere. A number of local musicians made their appearance. With their instruments half concealed, they congregated in front of the school. Máire Cáit was the first to pull her jew's harp out of the pocket of her bib and to commence playing. Mickeen the Man soon joined her with his concertina and Paddy Joe Mike gave a few belts to his bodhrán. Small Peter pulled a side flute from inside his coat and the music wafted around the village. A crowd commenced to gather and when the band played a reel, a group, in exuberant mood, danced an eight-hand reel in the middle of the road. For over an hour there was craic and gaiety, the likes of which had never happened on a Sunday afternoon in the village before. In the meantime, down on the football field, club members were busy marking the sidelines with a row of small furze bushes at each side. They also marked the end lines with the furze. The goal lines were marked with lime and a small circle of lime marked centre-field.

At one o'clock a sidecar arrived in the village carrying about nine passengers. Soon there was a string of them arriving – back-to-back traps, sidecars, horses and common cars, saddle horses and, to cap it all, two jennets and a mule were the last to arrive, all loaded as tightly as sardines in a box. The club had four or five men appointed to direct the strangers to the field. Many of them complained of an insatiable thirst but were very disappointed to learn that the local constabulary were mighty strict and they very insulted when they were directed to the village pump. Approaching the football field, they were told to take their animals into the field where they could tether them to the hedge. Two young fellows, Mickie Óg and Seánie Thompson, were detailed to stand at the gap with two discarded snuff canisters from Peggy Mike's wake, with orders to collect sixpence per head from men and a truppeny bit from women and to give free entry to children. When the boys asked what they would do if people didn't want to pay them, Tom Redden told them to do the best they could. Soon they were busy as the people started arriving in droves, and the rattle of the money falling into the canisters was music in the ears of the club members.

Scheduled to start at two o'clock, it was a quarter past before the local team raced onto the field to be greeted with tumultuous applause. When the local girls saw the boys in their short, white trousers, they rollicked with laughter on the sideline. They thought it was the funniest thing they ever saw. Two minutes later the men from Ballyhooley took to the field, to more subdued applause it must be said but, nevertheless, a good enough reception for the visitors. Togged out in their white shorts, they wore beautiful, white ganseys with blue hoops. They really looked the part. Redden and company were thanking their lucky stars that they had the white shorts too and, thanks to the Dug, the green ganseys. How bad they would have looked in long baggy trousers in comparison!

Out in the centre of the field Redden, Muldoon, the Dug and the Whistler were in conversation with a number of Ballyhooley officials. They were discussing how the game should be played. Agreement was reached for each team to play half an hour in one direction and then to change over and play for another half hour the opposite way. It was obvious, however, that there was some other problem. When this problem was solved, Redden explained that the visitors had brought their own referee and were insisting on his refereeing the match. When told that the local club had their own referee appointed, there was stalemate. Finally, the Dug proposed that it should be decided on the toss of a coin to which they eventually agreed. Ballymachad won the toss.

"Appoint your referee," said the man from Ballyhooley to Tom Redden.

"That's him there," said Tom, pointing to the Whistler.

"Him!" said the man in sheer amazement.

"Yes, him," confirmed Redden.

"Has he a whistle?" asked the man (their own referee sported a whistle hanging from his neck).

"No," answered Redden, "he never uses one."

"Never uses a whistle!" exclaimed the man.

And, walking away, thinking out loud, he said, to no one in particular, "What brought us to this place?" Of course, to a stranger, the Whistler must have really looked eccentric. Low in stature, with polished leather gaiters (no one ever saw him without gaiters), sporting a goatee beard and wearing a black, hardy hat, he really didn't look the part of a referee. As Gerry Muldoon was accompanying the parish priest to centre-field, Redden gave the nod to the Whistler to start the game. With three loud, shrill whistles that even silenced the crowd, the players went on the alert mode. Paudeen McGurk and the Doll took up their positions in the middle of the field, as did two from the opposition. The Whistler handed the ball to the priest when he arrived and then he gave a whistle to put the players on high alert. The priest turned his back to the players and, after a minute, threw the ball over his head and the game was on.

Jumping high, Paudeen caught the ball in mid air, amid thunderous cheers and ably protected by the Doll who warded off the opposition with what was afterwards described as a spreadeagle manoeuvre. With a powerful kick, Paudeen sent the ball right into the full forward line. Billeen Mike and Baby Jack Quirke went for it together, a thing the were warned not do, and between the two of them it fell into the hands of the full back who cleared it out the field. A good enough start thought Tom Redden, and the rest agreed. The full back's clearance landed centre-field and was quickly picked up by the Doll. Surrounded by Ballyhooley players – no one knew their names – he passed it to the outcoming Dandy Jim who, in turn, sent it to the Snuffler Kirby who sent it across to Mickey Jer. Under pressure he tapped it to full forward Baby Jack Quirke and back again it came to the Snuffler. The Snuffler was about to shoot when he was manhandled by a few players. The Whistler gave the first whistle of the game and, amid abuse from the opposition, awarded a free to Ballymadhad.

Designated the freetaker, the Pedler Lacy, as cool as the gentle zephyr blowing across the field, placed the ball on a small hump in the field and, standing back, amid abusive shouts from Ballyhooley supporters, slowly and deliberately came forward and gave it a powerful lash. But he had hard luck. The ball hit the crossbar. Hard luck it seemed but as it happened the defence lost their cool and in the excitement, blundered, and the ball crossed the line – a goal for Ballymachad! The crowd went wild. The Whistler whistled for the kick-out but no one was listening. The goalie had the ball under his oxter and had no notion of parting with it until his demand that the goal be disallowed was met. Sensing a problem, the Doll and Paudeen, the two strongest men on the field, began running down the field to support what they perceived to be their besieged team-mates. But before they arrived, the Ballyhooley officials intervened and told their players in no uncertain fashion to stop the antics and to play the game. The Whistler whistled and play resumed.

The kick-out landed straight into the arms of the Doll. Surrounded by about five players who were much smaller in stature than him, he punched the ball over their heads into the waiting hands of Paudeen. Now a marked man by the opposition, Paudeen was immediately surrounded by several players but, with sheer strength, he cut himself a gap through them and got his kick-in. A shorter kick than usual, it was beautifully fielded by one of the Ballyhooley lads who sent it straight into his own full forward line. Patcheen Cronin, the full back, went up for it but it slipped from him and was quickly picked up by one of the forwards who, with great flair, sent it over the bar. At this juncture the Ballyhooley mentors changed tactics – they were now kicking the ball out short, hoping they would be able to bypass the Ballymachad centre duo who were fielding every ball and sending it straight back in again.

Spotting the change, the Ballymachad mentors were quick to move. Paudeen was told to go back into the half back line. The Doll was to stay put as such, but if he saw the opportunity he should rove about to collect the short ball coming out. This was a tactic to confuse the opposition and make them wonder where he would be. There was now pressure mounting on the home backs and the next ball was cleanly fielded by corner back, Spider Hayes, who despatched it to the waiting Doll whose high long kick was misjudged by both the backs and the forwards as it hopped between them and went straight over the bar. Ballymachad were steeped in luck with this, their second easy score. The Ballyhooley officials were getting annoyed and shouted at their players from the end line to mark up.

Picking a suitable spot, the Ballyhooley goalie carefully placed the ball for his kick-out. To the annoyance of the Whistler, he took his time and at the third whistle, he gave it everything he had. The ball rose in a beautiful curve, almost straight for the Doll. Majestically, the Doll rose to bring it down, but as he became airborne he was pushed in the back, missed the ball and his opposite number took possession. Sizing up his options, with great self-control, he tapped it neatly to his waiting centre forward who, in spite of the attentions of the Butcher Roche and Mickeen Óg, delivered it into the outstretched hands of his full forward. Surrounded and harassed by Patcheen Cronin and the Spider

Hayes, he managed to pass it to the corner forward who blazed it passed Paddy Mike. A goal! Now the teams were level. The Doll was furious, there had been a blatant foul on him, the Whistler let them get away with it and it had resulted in a goal for Ballyhooley.

To be fair to the Whistler, the antics of the Ballyhooley 'keeper with the kick-out prevented him from running up the field to be in his proper position to spot the foul. Paddy Mike's kick-out was fielded by a Ballyhooley man as the Whistler whistled the end of the first half. The teams retired to their respective corners of the field where they were joined by their mentors and were soon surrounded by enthusiastic supporters. The Doll was still furious and called the Whistler names he was never called before. But he wasn't present to hear them, he stayed neutral from both teams during the interval. Presently, from centre-field the Whistler whistled for the resumption. The visitors reacted immediately and ran to their respective positions. The homeside were still getting instructions and words of encouragement from Redden, the Dug and Muldoon. Finally, after three blasts from the Whistler, they raced onto the pitch and were greeted with great applause.

The Whistler threw in the ball and the second half was on. Ballyhooley were the first to break away and before the local lads had time to settle, the ball was over the bar, putting the visitors a point in front. From the resulting kick-out the ball dropped short of centre-field but, with great anticipation, the Doll brought it down from the clouds, kicked it straight into the hands of Paudeen who, with his dander up, raced forward, throwing lads to the left and right of him. With most of the opposition left in his wake, he took a shot at goal and the ball skimmed over the crossbar. It could easily have been a goal but no harm was done and the sides were level again. For the next twenty minutes it was a ding-dong struggle with both teams exchanging just two points apiece. Into the last five minutes it was still level pegging, still anyone's game. Then it happened!

As if from nowhere, a long ball landed right into the full forward line and was picked up by the visitors' full forward. Tackled by Patcheen Cronin, there was a battle royal and in the panic situation that ensued, Curly Casey shouted at the top of his voice at Paddy Mike, the goalie, "Paddy, Paddy, Paddy! Watch out, watch out I tell you". The full forward sneaked the ball to one of his forwards who fired a rasper of a shot just inside the goalpost. It was stopped just on the line, not by Paddy Mike, the goalie, but by Paddy the Dog, and the ball went harmlessly outside the post and over the end line. Tom Redden's dog had been lying down, sunning himself, behind the goals, but no one took any notice of him. When he heard Curly shouting, "Paddy, Paddy!" he thought that it was his 'call to arms' and responded the only way he knew, as he had been trained by the children.

There was consternation. The Ballyhooley lads claimed it was a goal and Patcheen Cronin, the Spider Hayes and Curly claimed that the ball had never crossed the line, which, of course, it hddn't. The Whistler arrived on the scene to investigate. Surrounded by several highly incensed Ballyhooley players, he first of all called for calm. But he was shouted down by calls of "It was a goal, it was a goal!" When a bit of calm was restored, the Whistler spoke.

"I'll just ask one question and the answer to it is yes or no," he said.

There was a rustle of discontent among the players which he ignored.

"The question is, did the ball cross the line?" asked the Whistler.

"No, but it was a dog that stopped it," came the reply.

"I don't care if 'twas your grandmother that stopped it, if it didn't cross the line it wasn't a goal and that's final," said the Whistler.

He gave a blast of a whistle and shouted, "Kick out that ball".

The ball was kicked out and he blew the full-time whistle. The Ballyhooley players and supporters were unhappy with the result but the local team were delighted not to have lost on their first outing and were looking forward to better times ahead. A local shouted to a Ballyhooley supporter as they left the field, "Ye didn't win!" Prompt came the reply: "How could any team win here, where even the dogs play football."

"True for you man," agreed the local.

Wedding Bells

Making A Match

Despite the poverty of the era, people still got married and it was always a big occasion for the families involved. When the news spread that a match was made it would generate a lot of gossip in the community, and if it happened to be a girl marrying into a farm, the burning question on everyone's lips was how much would she carry there. This would be discussed in every house in the locality. After mass on a Sunday, men would congregate in groups racking their collective brains as to how much she would be likely to take to the farm she was marrying into, in other words, what was her fortune? The farm she was going into would be discussed, whether the land was arable or boggy and what number of cows the farm was capable of carrying. Was it a good farm to produce butter? What kind of a farmer was the boy's father?

All this would be aired and, of course, the groom-to-be would be the subject of a thorough examination. If he had the reputation of being a hard worker the gossipers would say, "She'll have a tough life with that fellow – no day is long enough for him". Another would add, "True for you, I heard for a fact that his father often had to go searching for him in the evenings when he'd be turning bawn in the springtime and found him asleep in the headland, too tired to make the house". This prompted another wag to add, "Ah sure, 'tis how she'll have a great time with him. He'll be a quiet man in bed!" On the other hand, if the groom-to-be was presumed to be the lackadaisical type, they would be very vocal in their sympathy for the poor bride-to-be, declaring that, "That fellow couldn't dig his dinner". That was the worst thing that could be said about a man on the land, that he couldn't even dig a bucket of spuds for the dinner. The wag, taking up the cue, would cap it with the enjoiner, "My heart goes out to the poor girl, she'll see more dinner times than dinners".

The bride-to-be-too would come in for special scrutiny – would she be a capable farmer's wife? The main question would centre around her ability to milk cows and feed calves, but also a big question would be if she was considered well able to feed pigs. Her culinary capabilities would be brought into question – was she a good breadmaker or a good hand at 'turning out' a currant loaf? The women, in their shawls in a huddle after Mass on a Sunday, would go so far as to question her ability to stuff the goose properly for the Christmas dinner. When there was unanimous agreement that the poor girl hadn't a clue, the subject would be changed and the question asked, "How will she be able to handle auld Bessy, her future mother-in-law?" Then poor old Bessy herself would get a rub from a neighbour saying, "It won't be aisy to get on with her. The poor girl will have her work cut out to plaise her". All this was just good-humoured banter, with no vindictive intent. Communities were close knit and many of them were related and inter-married. What was said today about a couple would be said again tomorrow about another couple so the wheel went around with no insult intended.

Some matches were made between a boy and girl who had never met. It happened on numerous occasions that a farmer would arrive home from a cattle fair and, in an intoxicated voice, would proudly declare that he was after making a match for his daughter to a man living maybe twenty miles away. Twenty miles was a considerable distance in those days but, nevertheless, matches were often made for couples at that distance and even further afield. It did happen on numerous occasions that the couple never met or even saw each other until they met at the altar to be married, often at seven o'clock in the morning. If the wedding was during the winter months, considering the bad lighting at the time, they would have to wait until daybreak to have a good look at each other – too late for any change of mind.

Maggie Browne of Ballymachad considered herself lucky – she was friends with a nice boy just down the road named Patsy Óg. His father was Patsy Lynch, hence the Óg, just to distinguish them. Neither Maggie's father, Mickie Joe Browne, nor her mother, Mary Ellen, had ever spotted a thing between the young couple. Maggie played a class act to avoid suspicion and Patsy Óg, too, played his part – at the crossroad dance he would dance with different girls all evening. A beautiful set dancer, he was the type all the girls loved to dance with, as they could be sure that he wouldn't stand on their toes, or spatter their shins if the platform was wet. Maggie was happy with the last dance. Perhaps some of the young dancers knew the score but nobody spilled the beans. Truly they were playing a blinder what with Patsy Óg calling in to Maggie's house, sometimes two or three times a day, for a chat with the family, and Maggie doing likewise, visiting Lynch's and chatting with Patsy Óg's mother, Biddy.

Both families were close friends for as far back as any one of them could remember. Like all neighbours of the era, if any one of them ran short of tea or sugar or any household commodity, they would just run to their neighbour who would be glad to oblige. That was a usual occurrence between the Brownes and the Lynchs, because of their close proximity to each other. As far as Patsy Óg and Maggie were concerned everything in the garden was rosy. Soon, however, and unbeknownst to them, a spanner would soon be thrown into the works.

On a big fair day Mickie Joe took a cow to the fair and, having sold the animal, he was waiting around until three o'clock to be paid, as was the usual custom at the time. Hungry and thirsty and with the price of the cow now safely in his pocket, Mickie Joe made a beeline for Murphy's snug, a favourite haunt of farmers on a fair day when they had their business completed and were in need of sustenance for the journey home. Entering the snug he was surprised to find that there was no one there, but he surmised that many farmers weren't yet paid for their stock. Calling for a pint of porter and a bacon sandwich, he made himself comfortable. He was enjoying his repast when the door opened and in walked a big, burly man, as big as the full width of the door. He was an unusual looking man in that he had a beautiful, well-trimmed moustache, but he had very unkempt sidelocks and a shaggy head of hair. The stranger looked down at Mickie Joe and in a brusque voice he asked, "What are you atin'?"

"A bacon sandwich," said Mickie Joe.

"Is it good?" was the next question.

"Well, I find it all right. At least it keeps the hunger at bay and that's all that matters to me," replied Mickie Joe.

"Well said, man," responded the stranger, clapping him on the shoulder so hard that some of the pint that he held in his hand was spilled.

Mickie Joe wasn't very enamoured with his new snug mate and while sizing him up as he was giving his order, his dislike for the stranger increased. He's too bloody brusque, thought Mickie Joe. Of course, the spilling of some of his porter was a cardinal offence. Having placed his order and taking a small round table with him, the man sat himself down on a stool at the other end of the snug from Mickie Joe who thought, "Thank God for that". Soon the barman arrived with a mighty big bacon sandwich and two pints of porter that barely fit on the little table. The man took the sandwich in both hands and opened his mouth wide, displaying the longest teeth Mickie Joe had ever seen in a man, and bit into the middle of the sandwich. He ate with a ferocious appetite and soon there was fat from the bacon flowing down his jaw. He just wiped it off with the back of his hand as he reached for one of the pints of porter. The stranger downed the pint in record time and then, much to the disgust of Mickie Joe, he let off a belch of gas that reverberated around the little snug. With a look of satisfaction on his face, the stranger reached for the second pint. This he drank in a slow relaxed manner, savouring every drop. He then stood up and, brushing his waistcoat and trousers of any crumbs, he gave another belch of gas. He threw an eye towards Mickie Joe and said, "That auld porter is very gassy". Mickie Joe just nodded.

Sitting down again he commenced to engage Mickie Joe in conversation, starting off by asking him where he was from. Mickie Joe told him Ballymachad.

"Bad auld land around there," was the stranger's instant assessment, much to the disgust of Mickie Joe who had fierce pride and meas on his property.

"Who told you that?" countered Mickie Joe.

"I know it, I was out there," was the reply.

"You must be a bloody bad judge," Mickie Joe replied sarcastically.

Noticing that he had ruffled Mickie Joe, the man backed down and just said, "Maybe I am".

Now there was silence between the two. After minutes of this deafening silence, Mickie Joe, his blood boiling after the bad land insult, went on the offensive.

"Where are you from yourself?" he asked.

"I'm from West Limerick," was the reply.

"A lot of bad land around there too," was Mickie Joe's salvo.

"It isn't all bad. I'm in the eastern side of it and my land is like the Golden Vale, naturally dry, you couldn't wet it," countered the man.

"Bad land to have in a dry summer," suggested Mickie Joe. "A man near me with dry inchy land like yours has to feed hay to his cows in a dry summer."

"My land is different, it can stand up to the sun, no matter how hot it gets," said the man with such conviction that Mickie Joe was inclined to believe him.

"How many cows are you milking?" asked the man.

"Ten cows, right good wans, as good as could be got any place," boasted Mickie Joe, and then added, "what about yourself, how many are you milking?"

"Thirteen great wans and I have heifers as well and a stallion horse," was the reply.

Slightly taken aback, Mickie Joe asked what kind of a stallion horse he had.

"A heavy draught horse breeding great foals. I always parade him at the big spring fair," replied the man.

"Would he be steel grey at all?" asked Mickie Joe.

"Oh, that's his colour all right. Did you see him at the big fair?"

"Would you be Gerry Kelliher by any chance?" inquired Mickie Joe.

"That's me. How did you guess?" asked the man.

"I saw the steel grey horse at the big fair last spring and someone said a Gerry Kelliher owned him and it stuck in my memory," said Mickie Joe.

"I wasn't there at all that day. I have kind of given the place over to the son so I thought that he may as well be getting to know the people," said Gerry.

"Oh, so you have given over your place," said Mickie Joe,

"I have indeed. I don't believe in keeping young fellows from settling down until they are old men. My father never gave me anything until I was nearly fifty years of age and I swore that I wouldn't treat my son like that," said Gerry.

"Ah, sure you're away with it now, with the son married and all, you're a free agent," responded Mickie Joe.

"Ah, but I'm not, I still have the reins and will keep them until he gets married however long or short that will take," Gerry declared solemnly.

"Yerra, sure I thought he was married and all," said Mickie Joe.

"Not at all, I'm doing my best to get a suitable woman for him but so far, I haven't succeeded," mused Gerry, and then, as if an afterthought struck him, he looked Mickie Joe straight in the eye said, " By the way, would there be any girl of mature age and with a good understanding of what it is to be a farmer's wife around your country, that would be interested in getting married?"

Mickie Joe looked at him incredulously and made no reply as his mind was working overtime.

"Well?" said Gerry when Mickie Joe wasn't forthcoming.

Finding his speech, Mickie Joe just asked, "Would he marry a girl that far away?"

"Of course he would, because I'd make him. That is, if everything was above board and the fortune was good," Gerry boldly replied.

Another period of silence ensued and was broken when Mickie Joe asked, "And what size of a fortune would you be expecting?"

"You have someone in mind, you rogue," Gerry cunningly suggested.

"You didn't answer my question," countered Mickie Joe.

"Tell the truth, have you someone in mind?" pleaded Gerry.

"I might have but I have no business going home with half a story. I'll have to know the fortune," argued Mickie Joe.

"Very well, I'll trust you," said Gerry. "The fortune I'm asking is two hundred pounds but now, between me and you, I'd take a bit less if I got the right girl."

There was silence again.

Mickie Joe's mind was now in a muddle – would he take the bull by the horns and say what he was thinking or would he walk out the door and go home? Something inside him said 'stand your ground and don't run'. He was said by the inner voice. Fondling a fresh pint of porter which had been ordered by Kelliher, Mickie Joe raised it to his lips but immediately put it down again without tasting a drop of it.

"Gerry," he said, "business is business and I want to tell you that the girl I have in mind for your son is my own daughter."

It was now Gerry's turn to look incredulous. He quickly snapped out of it and came over and stretched out his hand which Mickie Joe clasped and the two men shook hands.

Both men, now on first name terms, sipped their pints and Gerry was the first to speak.

"I have described the type of woman I want for a daughter-in-law. Let us be frank, would your daughter fit the bill?"

"I can honestly tell you that I have no doubt whatsoever but that she would, and more," said Mickie Joe with great emotion. "That's what I like to hear, and . . . " but Mickie Joe cut in on him, saying, "But there is a big impediment, you are asking too big a fortune, way too big".

Gerry Kelliher was visibly taken aback by this statement. He scratched his head, pulled his nose and twisted his left ear as tension built up within him. Then, as if an interior voice said to him 'Gerry take hold of yourself', he brought himself to his full height and, looking down on Mickie Joe with a frown on his face, he said, "How much too big?"

"A lot," was the curt reply.

"How much is a lot?" inquired Gerry.

"An awful lot," said Mickie Joe.

This angered Gerry and he gave Mickie Joe an ultimatum, "Will you be a man or a mouse and say what you're thinking or forget about it". A hard man to ruffle, Mickie Joe just looked at him with a big smile on his face and calmly asked, "How much less would you take?" Gerry, still in a bit of a titter, answered with another question, "How much are you prepared to give?"

"Half of it," replied Mickie Joe simply.

"I would split the difference if I was sure I was getting the right girl – a hundred and fifty quid – but as I said, that would be for a girl with the proper credentials," declared Gerry.

"That's why I'm offering you just a hundred smackers Gerry, because the likes of the girl you are getting will be hard to find. A woman that can turn her hand to anything, whether 'tis milking cows or feeding calves or pigs, or staying up at night looking after a sow littering, or minding a pet banbh. A woman that would go to the bog and foot a slean of turf in a piece of a day on her own and draw it out with an ass if she was put to it. A woman that would sit down at night with a pair of knitting needles and turn out the finest gansey you ever wore, you wouldn't get the likes of it in any shop – feel the wan I'm wearing, just feel it," he said as he moved over to Gerry.

With a perplexed look on his face Gerry felt the gansey and nodded his approval.

Mickie Joe, now on a high and feeling that he was winning the argument, continued apace.

"Put her into the garden and she'd weed turnips or mangolds with any man and pick spuds as fast as two men could dig 'em. And as well as all that, she is a famous dancer, wan of the best reel and set dancers at the crossroad dance every Sunday evening. God bless the girl, she has energy to burn – the likes of her shouldn't be asked to carry anything into a place, only her clothes," he concluded.

Gerry then handed him another pint of porter, commenting, "You must be thirsty after that". Feeling he was in the driving seat, Mickie Joe just said, "I have told you the truth and the fortune is a hundred pounds, or no marriage". Gerry was mesmerised, he didn't know what to say or do. He gulped his pint and paced around the snug for about fifteen minutes as if in a daze. Finally, he faced towards Mickie Joe, took two steps in his direction and said, "If she's as good a girl as you describe, and I'm inclined to believe you, 'tis a deal".

The two men shook hands and Mickie Joe called for two pints and before evening the two of them were drunk. Mickie Joe confided to Gerry that he would make the announcement when he got home and put the wheels in motion for a wedding as soon as possible. Gerry agreed he would do the same and later on the bride would have the honour of naming the day of her wedding. Both men agreed they had been fortunate to meet and that they had done a great day's work. As was usual in that era, the consent of the couple was irrelevant, with no consideration given to the fact that the couple didn't know each other. The thinking was that they would have a lifetime to do that. While they were rejoicing at the prospect of being future in-laws, Paddy Mike, a neighbour of Mickie Joe's arrived in. Mickie Joe immediately gave a signal to Gerry not to mention their business.

"You'll drink a pint," said Mickie Joe to Paddy Mike.

"I will not. I have enough of it drank and so have you," said Paddy Mike and, with a bit of temper in his voice, he continued, "I'm waiting for you for the last two hours. You told me you'd meet me in the Square. I'd never have found you only someone saw you going in here hours ago. Come on home," he ordered.

With a knowing look at Gerry, Mickie Joe took his leave and went out the door with Paddy Mike who was still giving out. He was lucky, because he had walked to the fair with his cow and if Paddy Mike wasn't such a good neighbour, he'd have to walk home again. Paddy Mike found Mickie Joe highly elated but put it down to the fact that he seemed to have a lot of drink on board which was unusual for him, so he asked no questions.

The Announcement

Paddy Mike dropped Mickie Joe off within a hundred yards of his house and with the excessive drop of drink taking its toll, he staggered the last few steps home. He opened the half door and arrived into the kitchen and, if it hadn't been for the table in the middle of the kitchen floor, he would have fallen, as he tripped over an old pan on the floor that was used to feed the dog. Luckily for Mickie Joe there was no one there as they were all out milking the cows. Settling himself into a big súgán chair, he soon fell fast asleep and that was the condition Mary Ellen and Maggie found him in when they returned from milking the cows.

Mary Ellen went over to him and gave him a few nudges, but the response was just a few grunts.

"Glory be to God, but he's flaming drunk, whoever he met," she declared.

Maggie broke into uncontrollable laughter. She had never before seen her Dada drunk, as usually he would only drink a pint or two at the very most. But as far as Mary Ellen was concerned, it was no laughing matter and she told Maggie to stop her laughing, explaining that her father could be full of contrariness when drunk. Still in a laughing mode, Maggie decided to give him a few nudges herself, hoping to wake him as she wanted to hear him talking when drunk. Her mother cautioned her to leave him alone and let him sleep it off. Mary Ellen then hung the kettle on the crane and Maggie set the table for their supper.

Throughout the meal, every time her father gave a loud snore Maggie burst into renewed laughter, much to the annoyance of her mother. Mary Ellen knew what to expect from him in his present condition and told Maggie that he would wake up after about two hours – which he did, almost to the minute. He was a bit groggy and mildly disorientated and he asked for a drink. Maggie quickly gave him a drink of water. Tasting it, he looked up at her with bleary eyes and said, "What's wrong? Are ye out of porter?"

"Where do you think you are?" asked Maggie with laughing eyes, "we don't stock any porter here," she joked.

Her mother beckoned her to stop the joking and leave him alone, adding, "He'll be all right in a short time".

Presently Mickie Joe stood up and went out the back door. Maggie decided to follow him but Mary Ellen, understanding what he went out for, stopped her saying, "He'll be back again in a minute and the fresh air will do him good. He'll be grand after it". Her words were prophetic because when he came in he was as sober as a judge. Well, almost. Maggie couldn't understand the transformation. Sitting himself down in the same chair, Mickie Joe appeared to be in a great mood with a smile on his face. He seesawed on the chair and was the very picture of happiness. Suddenly he spoke, in a tone that was definitely an attempt to sweeten the pill for Maggie.

Feigning a cough, he cleared his throat and, with great gusto, said, "I've done a great day's work today", and then stretched in the chair with a big smile.

"You have. You've just sold a cow and drank a belly full of porter," Mary Ellen retorted sarcastically.

"Ha! Ha! That's what you think but you don't know what I went through today. I'm telling you 'twas a hard bargain but I won it though," he boasted, slapping his knee with the palm of his hand.

"He's still drunk," whispered Maggie.

"And tell us now what else did you do today, apart from selling the cow and drinking?" inquired Mary Ellen.

"Maggie, listen girl," Mickie Joe commenced in a still semi-blurred voice, "you'll be proud of me and I'll be proud of you, settled in a fine farm of the best of land. You'll be driving out in your fancy pony and trap like all the gentry and they'll be all admiring you driving along and saying to each other, 'That's the new Mrs Kelliher – wasn't she the lucky girl to get into that fine place.' Ha! Ha! Won't you be the proud girl, waving at them with gloves on your hands."

"What are you talking about?" questioned Maggie.

"You must be gone out of your head from the drink," declared Mary Ellen.

"'Tis ye that's drunk when ye don't understand plain English," Mickie Joe declared arrogantly.

"Maybe we would if we heard it spoken," angrily replied Mary Ellen.

"Well, if that's the case with ye, I'll spell it out for ye in plain language," retorted an angry Mickie Joe, "what I'm after telling ye is that I have a match made for Maggie here with a young Kelliher boy from beyond West Limerick."

"You have what?" shouted Maggie.

"I'm after telling you. I have a match made for you. You're going into a fine farm of the best land in Ireland, with thirteen fine cows and breeding heifers and a stallion horse – the stallion is a big earner of money you know – and sows and pigs and what more would you want?" said Mickie Joe.

Maggie, perplexed, looked at him with eyes of wonder. But Mickie Joe continued, "I have fixed the fortune and all. You're carrying a hundred pounds there," he declared.

"A hundred pounds," shouted Mary Ellen in disbelief, "where would we get a hundred pounds to give anyone?"

"Well, he was looking for two hundred," explained Mickie Joe, "but I broke him down when I told him the great girl she is, so I said to myself that we might be able to scrape up a hundred pounds over a few months and throw it to him. Maggie has the honour of naming the day of her wedding, so she can delay it until we have the bit of money together."

Mary Ellen was speechless, but if she was, Maggie wasn't.

"Dada," she said, "how would you ever think of expecting me to marry a man I never saw?"

Looking her straight in the eye, he advised, "Look around you, aren't there several matches made like that, all happily married."

"Are they though?" questioned Maggie.

"They are, of course, girl," her father replied. "Don't you know that marriages are made in heaven, Maggie?"

"Are they?" questioned Maggie.

"They are, without a doubt," Mickie Joe confidently said.

"That's great news altogether," remarked Maggie, "because if that is the case, mine couldn't be made in Murphy's snug."

Mickie Joe threw an unbelievably dirty look at her and all he could say was, "Stop your smart-alecing and do what you're told".

"For a change, now Dada," charged Maggie, with sincerity in her voice, "let you do what you are told."

"What's that?" inquired a surprised Mickie Joe.

"Scrape up that hundred pounds as quick as you can, because I might need it if my boyfriend proposes," declared Maggie.

This admission brought back Mary Ellen's voice and she exclaimed, "What! You have a boyfriend."

"Of many years," Maggie said confidently and, with a roguish smile, she declared, "He could pop the question at any minute and that hundred pounds might be needed so Dada, keeping scrapin', all is not lost."

"But what will I say to Kelliher? I have an agreement made with him," Mickie Joe said.

"Tell him the truth," advised a delighted Mary Ellen, 'tell him that your daughter has a secret boyfriend and she will not budge."

It was a sobering thought for him, in more ways than one. Mary Ellen looked at the clock and saw it was ten o'clock and time for the rosary. "Down on yer knees," she declared, and this was as good a way as any to bring the subject to a close, at least for the night. Mary Ellen gave out the rosary and when Maggie's turn came to give out her decade, Mickie Joe, still smarting from the take-down of not getting his own way with the match, intervened to say, "Maggie you have no business praying, girl, unless you do what you father tells you". Maggie, as quick as wink, replied, "And what business have you praying, Dada, trying to force your daughter to marry a man she never saw and that you didn't see either".

A very upset Mary Ellen intervened, imploring, "Will ye shut up and stop it? Do ye want to draw the wrath of God down on top of ye!"

"Right," said Mickie Joe, "pray away Maggie", and the rosary continued to its conclusion.

Mickie Joe promptly got up off his knees but knelt down again at Mary Ellen's promptings, remarking, "You'll keep us all night on our knees" as she commenced to say the trimmings. Maggie prepared a nightcap of three mugs of hot milk, as was usual, prior to retiring for the night. So ended an unusual day in the lives of the Browne Family. But there was more excitement to come.

The Secret Boyfriend

First up out of bed the next morning was a very craw-sick Mickie Joe. He went out to the field at the west of the boreen and drove in the cows to be milked, an hour or so earlier than usual. Maggie and her brother, Seamus, who was a year her junior, soon joined him as he stalled up the cows to be milked. When they asked why he got up so early, he angrily told them that he couldn't sleep a wink all night and squarely put the blame on Maggie for what he called her 'rebellious disobedience'. Maggie defended herself angrily.

"It's my life you're dealing with, my whole life. 'Tis I who would have to live with that fellow in West Limerick – not you! I'll marry who I like. I told you that I am friends with a local and that's who I hope to marry when the time comes," she said defiantly, a girl generations before her time.

"You'd better think fast, you're no chicken you know," Mickie Joe said nastily.

Standing in the doorway of the stall, unobserved, was Mary Ellen, tears running down her cheeks. She was a very amiable person and listening to Maggie and her father arguing caused her a lot of pain. But still, when the chips were down, she was on Maggie's side. Apart from the fact that she wanted her only daughter to be near her and in Mary Ellen's opinion West Limerick was light years away, she honestly believed that when it comes to marriage, a life-long commitment, a girl should be allowed to make up her own mind. And that was her earnest wish for her daughter.

Over breakfast there were further skirmishes between father and daughter with Mickie Joe finally declaring that he wouldn't believe that Maggie ever had a boyfriend, but that if she had one, it was her duty to let her family know who he was. Maggie immediately took up the challenge.

"Right," she declared, "I will not tell you his name, but I'll do better, I'll bring him to the house to ye and ye can have a good look at him."

"When?" asked an excited Mary Ellen.

"Any day, or night, for that matter, ye like, I'll land him into the kitchen to ye. Ye can have a good look at him and check him up-side-down, because he's going to be yer son-in-law, whether ye like him or not."

Such defiance left the couple speechless.

After about five minutes Mickie Joe opened his mouth to say something, but forgot that he had the pipe in his mouth so it fell to the floor and got smashed on one of the stone flags. Strangely enough, he took no notice of it and never even mentioned it again. Mary Ellen thought that it was the shock of Maggie's onslaught and the thought of bringing her man to the house, a thing that no girl ever did before. Mickie Joe stood motionless, with his two hands in the pockets of his bawneen, looking down at his broken pipe for about fifteen minutes. The two women retreated to the fireplace and sat themselves down in a corner each. Mary Ellen felt the tension very much and, looking across at Maggie, she felt that she still looked defiant. Mickie Joe eventually turned and, half looking towards the women, he said in a loud whisper, "What is the world coming to at all?", and walked out the back door.

"Maggie," said Mary Ellen in a plaintive voice, "your father is very upset."

"I'm upset too, you know, Mama, how could he expect me to do what he wanted? Answer me that, Mama," said Maggie.

"He thought he was doing the best he could for you. Every father wants to do the best they can for their daughters and he was thinking of Mary Seán Rua from west the road whose match was made like that and she's happy out," her mother answered.

"Mama, no one knows who's happy or not happy, when a person is caught in a life-long arrangement they just have to make the best of it and if they are not happy they will just cover up their predicament and suffer on. How many eloped when matches were made for them, when they were been pressurised to marry a stranger?" Maggie said.

Mary Ellen just changed the subject.

"Tell me the truth," she coaxed, "have you really a boyfriend?"

"Didn't I tell you that I would land him into the house to you, seeing is believing," laughed Maggie. "As a matter of fact I could bring him this Friday evening."

"Oh, glory be to God, you can't bring him that soon. We would have to whitewash the kitchen. Don't you see the state of the walls after the sow and the litter of banbhs being in here?" Mary Ellen said with a note of panic in her voice.

"Yerra, he wouldn't take much notice of things like that, he'll be only looking at me," Maggie joked.

But that wouldn't do Mary Ellen who insisted that first impressions are best.

In the meantime, Mickie Joe wandered aimlessly about the yard and the cowhouse until, eventually, he rambled in home as disgruntled as ever.

"Have ye any notion of cooking a bite?" he asked.

The porter sickness was now healed and his appetite had come back

"Your sense of smell must be gone. There is a pan of bacon on the brand and a skillet of spuds on the crane and they will be up on the table in ten minutes. That should heal your craw sickness," remarked Mary Ellen who was now on a bit of a high at thought of meeting her future son-in-law.

After the dinner, Mickie Joe was making for the door again, but Mary Ellen called him back.

"Come back here," she said, "the house has to be whitewashed inside and outside because you future son-in-law is coming next Friday and surely you would like to make a good impression."

Mickie Joe was reluctant at first but the women finally got him to row in with their wishes and soon he was working enthusiastically in the big clean-up. Donning worn old trousers and as just as worn old coat, he tied a rope around his waist and commenced whitewashing, outside first as the day was dry. He could work inside of a wet day with the light of the lamp, if all went to all.

Maggie and her mother were delighted that Mickie Joe had stopped sulking and seemed to be resigned to the inevitable. Both Mickie Joe and Mary Ellen had great pride in their little place, hence their desire to work to have everything spic and span before the stranger who was seeking their daughter's hand in marriage. Having whitewashed the dwelling house inside and outside, Mickie Joe proceeded to whitewash the outside walls of the cowhouse and then got the loan of a ladder from the Lynchs to do the two gable ends. Enthusiastically he trimmed the hedge in front of the house as well as a fir tree that was growing in the yard – a thing he never did before.

Next day he brushed the yard and even tidied up the dung heaps in front of the cowhouse. He cleaned out the henhouse and washed and scrubbed the floor of it until it was spotless. Then he whitewashed it inside and outside, actually giving it two coats as it was never whitewashed before. He was working so hard at the clean-up job that Mary Ellen was getting worried about him, confiding to Maggie that he might be overdoing it. Maggie just laughed and said, "'Tis his own fault. He had a right to keep away from his West Limerick friend".

Finally Friday dawned, a nice brisk day with a clear sky and lots of sunshine. Mary Ellen found it the longest day she ever remembered. He, "whoever he is", as Mickie Joe always referred to him, wasn't due to arrive until about eight o'clock in the evening. But they were well prepared to receive him – Mary Ellen had a feast ready consisting of choice slices of homecured bacon, turnips and pandy which could be washed down with the best of buttermilk. On top of that, she had pancakes, an apple pie and a specially baked currant loaf (her speciality) for afters. As eight o'clock approached, tension was running high with Mickie Joe and Mary Ellen. Maggie didn't seem to be the least bit excited, which Mary Ellen couldn't understand. At five minutes to eight the back door opened and in walked Patsy Óg. Mary Ellen nearly lost her head and took Maggie up to the room and asked her to try and get him out of the house, by hook or by crook, before 'himself' would come.

"You wouldn't want to give it to say to the neighbours, you know Maggie, for fear nothing would come of it and then they would be all saying you were let down," Mary Ellen said.

Maggie smothered a smile and said she would do her best. Mary Ellen urged that her best mightn't be good enough and said she had to make sure to get rid of him.

"Come on so," said Maggie, "we'll see what happens."

Her mother was about to say something, but Maggie literally pushed her out the room door in front of her and into the kitchen. Mickie Joe and Patsy Óg were serenely engaged in conversation when the women re-entered, much to the disgust of Mary Ellen who commenced winking and grimacing at Mickie Joe, intending to attract his attention in the hope of getting Patsy Óg to go home.

Eight o'clock passed and no knock on the door. He isn't very punctual anyway, thought Mary Ellen. About half past eight, Maggie decided to put the kettle on. Mary Ellen was very disappointed but she couldn't say a word.

"Come on Mama, we'll lay the table," Maggie said.

Mama gave a look at her that would stop a clock but she had no better to do, but oblige. Soon Maggie had all the food on the table and told them to sit out.

"Dada, you sit at your usual place, the head of the table. Mama, you sit inside the table next to him and Patsy Óg, you sit at the other end of the table," she ordered.

Mary Ellen thought she was gone mad, that she had been let down and didn't know what she was doing with temper and frustration. As Patsy Óg walked towards the table, Maggie took him by the hand and said, "Dada and Mama, meet your future son-in-law". There was shock and there were tear, followed by a great outburst of joy. With tears in her eyes, Mary Ellen jumped up and threw her arms around Patsy Óg and kissed him. She then gave the same treatment to Maggie.

Mickie Joe didn't even stand up but called over the young couple and, taking the hand of Patsy Óg in his right hand and his daughter's hand in his left hand, he said with great emotion, "You are as welcome here as the flowers in May, Patsy Óg, and from the bottom of my heart I wish ye a long and happy life together". He added, with a knowing look at Maggie, "I didn't know a thing, you know". He tried to say something else but, overcome with emotion and with tears in his eyes, he just couldn't. Maggie came over and kissed his forehead. In the excitement, the meal was forgotten. It was several minutes later when ice-cool Maggie – she was the only one of them that kept her head – urged them to sit out again and partake of the meal, which they did with great enthusiasm.

Patsy Óg cleared his plate in quick time and wasn't a bit shy in taking a second helping. Mickie Joe also ate with an appetite and, licking his lips, he ordered Mary Ellen to go up to the loft and bring down a bottle of poitín, saying, "This calls for a celebration". Mary Ellen passed the bottle on to Maggie, saying, "You would be the fastest up the ladder". Taking every second step, Maggie was up and down in quick time and Mickie Joe uncorked the bottle with his teeth. He had the entire contents to himself as Patsy Óg was a teetotaller and the women never indulged either. Fearing he would go too far on the bottle and get knocked out, Maggie slapped the cork back on the bottle and, in spite of her father's pleadings, returned it to its hiding place. Mickie Joe and Patsy Óg chatted all night about cattle and horses and at midnight they were in deep conversation about greyhounds.

When the conversation turned to cutting turf, Maggie got impatient and beckoned to Patsy Óg as she went out the back door. He was a mannerly fellow and so, after a respectable length of time, he thanked Mickie Joe and Mary Ellen for the lovely night and slipped out the back door. Maggie conveyed him about a hundred yards down the boreen and told him she feared that their relationship would now be in the public eye in a matter of days. But it wasn't, as both families were very private people, so the engagement was kept under wraps for the most part of a year until there came another twist to the saga. This was when the news trickled through that Maggie's brother, Seamus, was friends with Patsy Óg's sister, Maureen, so now the possibility was to double the match and there would be no fortune involved – it would be just status quo. After a wait of about two years that's what happened, Maggie went down to Lynchs and Maureen came up to Brownes after an unforgettable double wedding.

The Double Wedding
When news of the double wedding broke it was greeted with great excitement. That two popular families were joining in wedlock was fantastic news, something

that had never happened before in Ballymachad. It certainly gave the gossipers something to talk about, something to distract their minds the reality of life and the opportunity to delve into – as they saw it – the good and the bad attributes of both families. They really rose to the occasion and gave it wind. They started by wondering how the priest would handle the occasion. The surmising started – would he marry the four of them together or would he do "wan after the other?" Maybe marrying two couples in one go might be too much for the "poor man as he's moving on you know" was one of their worries. Then they wondered would the one bridesmaid and the one best man do the two of them? No one knew because it had never happened before.

Their next big worry was whether the chapel was big enough to hold the crowd. They genuinely felt that all frail type of men or women with bad chests should stay away for fear of suffocation. Another question to be pondered on was who would be asked. As the day of the weddings loomed closer, that changed to "who was asked?" especially by those who had not yet received an invitation. Another imponderable was in which house the wedding breakfast would be held. The custom at the time was that the wedding feast would be held in the bride's home, but again no one knew – because the likes of this had never happened before and the families involved were keeping their cards close to their chests. It must be remembered that at that time the rite of marriage was usually celebrated, often without Mass, at seven or eight o'clock in the morning, hence the term 'wedding breakfast'.

After Mass on the two Sundays before the date of the wedding, the only thing talked about was the weddings. As usual, the two farms were discussed from all angles, some saying that Brownes was the better farm for butter and others adamant that Lynchs was a better farm overall, having a lot of inchy land along the river and the advantage of the river was for watering the cattle. Others pointed out that parts of Lynch's land were subject to flooding, which prompted another man to suggest that flooding was as good as manure to land. While the menfolk were discussing land issues, the women were concentrating on the style that would be on view on the big day, especially what the brides would wear and also what their bridesmaids would show up in.

"The sooner that these weddings are over the better, there isn't a dacent dinner cooked or a day's work done in the parish since the news broke," declared Paddy Tom, an astute middle-aged man who was a couple of hours waiting for his wife after Mass every Sunday since the news broke as she gossiped with women who she hardly ever spoke to before.

At last, the big day dawned, bright and sunny – an ideal day for a wedding. The first was scheduled for seven o'clock in the morning and the second to take place immediately afterwards. The parish priest, Fr Tom Dunn, an athletic type of man belying his years, was a stickler for early weddings so that they wouldn't interfere with his daily schedule. At six o'clock in the morning the crowd commenced gathering and when the grooms arrived in a pony and trap, accompanied by their two best men, they were greeted with mighty applause. Mickie Joe was on the reins and he steered his pony right up to the church gate. The four boys jumped out before the pony came to a stop and scampered into the church as fast as they could, to be greeted at the door by the priest just as he opened it.

At ten to seven the brides arrived in a sidecar, accompanied by their bridesmaids, to a thunderous reception from the waiting crowd. Poised and smiling they waved to the crowd, disembarked and with slow and deliberate steps entered the church, to be followed by the crowd who had patiently awaited their arrival. The Brown and Lynch families occupied the two front seats on either side of the centre aisle. In a matter of minutes the church was packed and late arrivals had to stand in the porch on the tops of their toes to get a peep. Presently, a smiling Fr Dunn emerged from the sacristy and the crowd stood, as did the wedding party. A very able man, he soon put the crowd at ease by asking them to be seated. He then welcomed the brides and grooms and proceeded to give an excellent explanation of the sacrament of matrimony. In spite of the packed church the proverbial pin would be heard dropping.

The first couple to be married was Maggie and Patsy Óg and afterwards they returned to their seat, the same seat this time. Seamus and Maureen then got the beck from Fr Dunn and, with their bridesmaid and best man, proceeded to the sanctuary. In quick time Fr Dunn declared them husband and wife. A relaxed Fr Dunn invited both couples with the bridesmaids and best men to join him in the sacristy to sign the register. Coming out onto the sanctuary after the signing, both couples made their way down the centre aisle, closely followed by their parents and close relatives, to loud applause from the packed church. Outside the two couples stood side by side and were congratulated by their friends and neighbours as they exited.

Out on the road a surprise awaited them! Just outside the church gate was a big four-wheeled covered wagon, beautifully painted, pulled by two black steeds all decked out in harness to match. Sitting in the driver's seat was a distinguished-looking, bearded man, dressed in a black tailored suit and wearing the tallest black hat ever seen in Ballymachad. At his right hand side a long whip stood erect, which he was constantly rubbed with his white-gloved hand. He spoke to no one. To add to the mystery, two men exited from the wagon. Dressed in swallow-tailed coats, hardy hats and buttoned waistcoats, they approached the newly-weds as soon as the congratulations were over, and with impeccable manners invited them, with few words, to board the wagon for the trip home.

Reluctant at first, the newly-weds appealed to their parents for advice as to what to do. After a short discussion, the parents said, "Why not? Ye'll never get the chance again". The couples boarded the wagon by steps at the rear. They found a really luxurious interior with seats along both sides adorned with beautiful cushions while in the centre were tables with gleaming tops. The two 'ushers' were also on board and just as the wagon commenced to move, they opened a built-in press from which the took bottles of mineral water and glasses and served the wedding party with drinks. The mood in the wagon was subdued as all aboard were enthralled with their surroundings and the 'ushers' didn't speak, which was the most enthralling thing of all.

Leading the drag, the covered wagon was soon followed by dozens of sidecars, traps and saddle horses, all jockeying for position to be as near as possible to the wagon. Tempers flared on a few occasions as traps and sidecars collided in the jostling for a place in the line-up. However, someone had to be last and the more level-headed men stayed put, enjoying the melee and waiting until all crackpots were sorted out. Arriving at Lynch's house, the newly-weds and their party disembarked. Everyone wondered who the driver of the wagon was and how he knew which house to take them to.

"He must be a local, otherwise how would he know, sitting up there in his perch," declared Mickeen Seán, an inquisitive man who would go to any extreme to find out the secrets of others.

"Do you know what you should do?" said Tom the Thatcher, priming Mickeen Seán, "go up the steps and have a close look at him, be by the way interested in the horses, and then give a kind of a stagger and let on you are falling off, and grab his beard."

"Pon my word, 'twould be wan way of doing it," agreed Mickeen Seán, taking the bait.

He immediately made a beeline for the covered wagon which was caught in traffic and couldn't move. When he was beside of the wagon, he moved along towards the step and found that there were two steps to climb. The driver was looking the other way and seemed to be engrossed in what he was watching, and when he turned around Mickeen Seán was standing alongside him. The driver showed a certain amount of panic which he quickly controlled. Mickeen Seán commenced by admiring the team of horses, but he got no reply, just a nod. Being tall and lanky, Mickeen Seán was looking down on the driver and thought about lifting off his big hat, but on closer examination saw that there was a strap under his jaw.

Just then he got the break he was waiting for – the horses made an involuntary movement for some reason and he actually got a genuine stagger and automatically grabbed at the man's head, pulling at his beard so whole thing came off. He very nearly fell to the ground but the man caught him by the arm and who was he looking at but Paddy the Lad! The Lad gave a despised look at him and said, "Mickeen, why didn't you mind your own business and I'd have pulled it off". The two 'ushers' were two local young men, promised money for the day by the Lad and ordered to keep their mouths shut which, in fairness to them, they did. Disgusted that he hadn't escaped detection, the Lad was very vexed with Mickeen Seán and let him know it, calling him all sorts of names. Mickeen Seán didn't care what he was called, he was over the moon that he had cracked the secret.

Invited into Lynchs for the breakfast, the Lad got the two ushers to take care of the horses while he was eating. After a stiff glass of poitín, he sat down to the meal and in a short time he was being questioned about the wagon and where he got it.

"'Tis a long story," he commenced. "The wagon and the horses belong to Mortimer, the retired judge that was on the stepping match committee. I was often out at his place doing odd jobs for him, so one day I hopped the ball to him and asked would he give me the wagon and horses for the double wedding. No problem, he said, but advised me to put a bit of thought into it and create a surprise. It was Mortimer's idea to dress up and he supplied the attire and actually made me up with the beard. He also supplied the mineral water that the ushers gave the wedding party. The ushers were also the judge's idea and he also supplied their attire."

It was all only a bit of fun the Lad said, explaining that he would have to return the horses and come back again to enjoy the wedding party. He then took his leave to do just that.

As the two houses were in close proximity and as the number guests was big, the wedding breakfast was served in both houses so all were accommodated in quick time which was considered a great feat for the women involved. When the meal was over they sang and danced and drank all day. The majority of the guests kept the momentum gong into the small hours. All the local musicians played their hearts out and vied with each other as to who would play the longest. All kinds of songs were sung with great gusto, many by men who had never been heard singing before.

"The power of poitín and porter is mighty to loosen the vocal cords," declared Mickeen the Mouse Casey, himself adding to the festivities with his rendition of several old ballads.

Considered the greatest bash at any wedding in living memory, the double wedding was fondly remembered for many years by all who had the pleasure of being part of it and all future weddings were judged by its standard. But time doesn't stand still and just a month later, there were rumours of another wedding that really tickled the imagination of the locals. Was it true or was it just that – a rumour?

The Other Wedding

'Twas Paddy the Lad who broke the news and no one believed him. Ballymachad locals were sceptical about believing the Lad. Yet some close neighbours were of the opinion that there could be some grain of truth in what he said. On close observation, the couple involved were doing unusual things. The man was observed on several occasions picking up the woman in his ass and car and taking her to town. His ass was spotted tethered to the railing of the presbytery and, after about an hour, the two of them were seen walking out the small gate accompanied by the parish priest. So the general opinion by close neighbours was that something was afoot.

"Well, 'tis no shame for them anyway', said Mickie Tom Pat and then asked the question, "How long are they going together?"

The reply came quick from Paddy Joe Hurley – "Always."

"How long is 'always'?" asked Mickie Tom Pat with a smile on his face.

"As long as I can remember and I can remember back to the night of the big storm that knocked all the wynds of hay," declared Paddy Joe.

"Yerra, sure that's fifty years ago," said Mickie Tom Pat.

"'Tis all that," agreed Paddy Joe, "and you can start counting from there, fifty wan, fifty two. I don't know where could you stop."

As they were talking, along strolled the Colonel, a man of great age himself who had served in the British Army, hence the name. Joining in the conversation, he was asked his opinion as to the age of Bessie Muldoon and Peter MacRory, the couple in question.

"What do ye want to know that for?" inquired the Colonel.

"Because there are talks that they are getting married," said Mickie Tom Pat.

"Getting married!" exclaimed the Colonel and gave a scart of a laugh, "I'd suggest that it is doting they are."

"But seriously, though," suggested Paddy Joe, "what age do you think they are?"

"Well," said the Colonel, "I think he is supposed to be one age with me and I have just turned eighty so he is that age anyway." Pressed to say what age he thought Bessie was, he replied that she wasn't much younger and could be seventy-eight or even seventy-nine.

"They were friends when I joined the army and now they are getting married, you say," said the Colonel.

"Well, 'tis rumoured anyway," said Mickie Tom Pat, "we are not sure but the signs are ominous."

If the double wedding caused excitement – which it did – this one, as the saying goes, 'took the biscuit'. Old Biddy Muldoon, looking out over her half-door, beckoned everyone she saw passing in for a chat and without saying, "How are you, or how aren't you?" would just say, "Did you hear the news about the auld couple?" One morning she called in Mary Malone, an elderly woman on her way to the shop, who lived not too far from the couple in question. She excitedly commenced her cross-examination by saying, "I suppose you know all about the wedding". Disappointingly, Mary just said, "Whisha, I only heard the rumour that's going around".

"We heard that rumour too," said Biddy.

"Did you?" Mary innocently replied.

"We did and when I heard it first, I nearly died and Mickeen fainted. Did ye die above?" asked Biddy.

Mary's first inclination was to laugh, an inclination she miraculously controlled. She was anxious to get away so, with great presence of mind and knowing it was something they would like to hear, she changed the subject by saying, "Did ye hear that old Molly Quilter died?"

"No, never heard it," said Biddy, "did you hear that, Mickeen? Old Molly Quilter kicked the bucket."

"Never heard a word of it," replied Mickeen, "isn't it time for her though, sure she's there always."

"That will make a great wake," said Biddy, "we'll have to go to that Mickeen."

"Oh, we will of course, we will have to go there. Sure there will be great giving out there, God rest her," said Mickeen.

"Amen to that," prayed Biddy.

Mary promptly made her escape. As she walked out to the road, Biddy shouted at her from across the half-door, "If you hear anything about the auld couple let me know".

"Right-o," said Mary, half turning towards her but delighted to be out of Biddy's clutches.

The rumour lived on and after a couple of weeks there was a breakthrough. Peter asked Tom Seán's son, Timmy, to stand with him and a couple of days later, Bessie approached young Jane Morrison and asked her to be her bridesmaid. The wedding was now official. And that led to a deluge of questions being asked. A question that baffled the locals was why old-stagers like them would ask youngsters to stand with them. No one could give a categorical answer to that question, though several attempted to explain it. Some said that it must be that they were half doting, while others said that maybe with youngsters with them they felt young themselves – if they had an auld lad and an auld woman of their own age, every time they would look at them they would be reminded of their own age, and maybe be the cause of them turning back from the altar. Whatever their thinking, the wedding went ahead as planned. Paddy the Lad, who was just after buying a second-hand sidecar for hire, was hired to take the happy couple to the church. He was ordered to take in Peter first and drop him off and then go out and collect Bessie.

He duly arrived at Peter's house at about six thirty in the morning and found the groom washing his face in a basin of cold water outside the door. Lathering his face well with soap, Peter produced an open razor and, holding a bit of a broken mirror in his left hand, he removed his overgrown beard with great dexterity. He then spilled the basin of water which a few ducks went to drink but, on tasting the soap, they changed their minds and waddled to the pond in the haggard for fresher water. Peter went indoors and in about ten minutes emerged dressed in a navy blue suit, a fancy hat, white shirt and flashy tie. With the aid of a blackthorn stick he made his way to the sidecar and the Lad helped him to board. Apart from having to use the blackthorn, the Lad said Peter looked as good as new. When they arrived at the church, the Lad gently helped him alight and conveyed him to the door where they found the best man, Timmy, already there and chatting with the jovial Fr Dunn.

The Lad then made an about-turn to pick up Bessie. When he arrived at her home he found her ready and waiting, accompanied by her bridesmaid, Jane. The Lad invited them to get on board immediately, explaining that the priest was waiting. Bessie was wearing a multi-coloured short coat and a long skirt of homespun material. With her hair rolled in a cuck at the top of her head, she belied her years. She linked arms with Jane and, with the aid of a stick, she walked out the door and it gave the Lad all he could do to lift her onto the sidecar. He asked Jane to sit alongside the bride for fear she'd fall off if he hit a pothole in the road. When the arrived at the church they were surprised to see a good many of the neighbours gathered, especially as no invitations had been issued.

Fr Dunn didn't delay proceedings once the bride arrived. He welcomed the couple and gave a nice talk to suit the age group of those involved, having first made sure they were comfortably seated inside the rails. He proceeded with the marriage ceremony and, after searching several pockets, Peter eventually pulled a ring from his waistcoat pocket and placed it on Bessie's finger. She complained that it was a bit tight but when he succeeded in pushing it up a bit further she said it was grand. As there was a series of steps on the entrance to the sacristy, the ever-thoughtful Fr Dunn brought a small table in to the sanctuary for the signing of the register. Peter just made his mark, an X, as he couldn't write his name. Bessie, on the other hand, had no problem on that score. Taking the pen, she slowly and carefully wrote her name. The priest then gave those present a sign to clap, which they did with great gusto to the surprise of the newly-weds.

When the register was signed, the couple stood up and, with aid of their sticks and linking arms, they proceeded to leave the sanctuary and walk down the aisle. They were again greeted with great applause and were clapped and cheered all the way out to the church grounds. Paddy the Lad was waiting with his sidecar and looked for help to put the couple on board. Peter and Bessie sat at one side and the bridesmaid and best man sat on the other side. The Lad soon had his steel grey cob jogging along at a steady pace and all the neighbours, despite not being invited, followed on with their horses and cars and saddle horses, making it a very respectable drag indeed.

When Peter and Bessie arrived home they were greeted with a mighty big surprise. Outside Bessie's house was a green patch all the way out to the road. This was now covered with tables, all of them draped with a motley selection of coloured cloths. All the neighbouring women had come together and put up a meal fit for a king. Every woman in the locality brought cups and saucers and plates and jugs and kettles, and most of them also brought tea and sugar and food. The food consisted of currant loaves and plain loaves. Someone brought a cooked goose, while others brought cooked chickens and there were also a few cooked ducks on the menu. The Reddens didn't come because Tom was sick but they sent milk and butter and a skelp of cooked bacon. It was a beautiful, bright, sunny day and all was set for a great welcome home for the bride and groom. More people were arriving all the time and every family from a wide radius was represented. Three musicians arrived and shortly afterwards young Patsy Mike arrived belting a bodhrán for all he was worth.

Paddy Tom Kelly took charge of organising the men into a welcome-home party. He got them all to move onto the road and lined them up on both sides of the road to form a guard of honour. He then directed the musicians to be prepared to line up in the middle of the road when the horse and sidecar would come into view at the bend of the road. With everything in readiness, the clip-clop of a horse was heard. Paddy Tom shouted "All ready" and some smart-alec replied, "All ready and correct, sir", bringing a smile to Paddy Tom's face. Imagine their disappointment when around the bend sailed old Billy the Kid Sugrue, standing up in the car on his way to the bog for a rail of turf.

Twenty minutes passed and some were getting tired of standing and were about to disperse when the clip-clop of a horse was heard again.

Paddy Tom addressed the crowd saying, "Men, have patience now, this could be them. Ye all know what to do if it is". The clip-clop came closer, adding to the tension and excitement, which was running high by now. Suddenly, around the bend on the road, a horse came into view. Eyes were strained to identify the driver.

"'Tis them all right. I can see the Lad on his perch," shouted Paddy Tom. "All get into line," he ordered.

The musicians took to the centre of the road, as directed, with Patsy Mike bringing up the rear with his bodhrán.

The couple were mesmerised as they were driven through the guard of honour. Bessie said afterwards that she thought she had died and gone to heaven when she heard the music. Peter was sure he was dreaming and as he alighted from the sidecar he was so disorientated when he saw the whole lawn covered with tables, he couldn't figure out where he was and wanted to board the sidecar again to go to Bessie's house. It took great persuasion to get him to walk through the array of tables and into the house. On entering, he saw Bessie chatting with a few neighbours and asked her, "What are you doing here? I thought we were going to your house". Paddy Tom handed him a good throw of whiskey laced with a drop of poitín to put a bit of giz in him and told him to sit down near his wife at the fire.

After about half an hour chatting with the neighbours Peter was back to normal. Paddy Tom remarked that he knew the drop of strong drink would do the trick and straighten Peter out. In the meantime the local women were busy catering outside on the lawn. Great credit was due to the neighbours who had so generously contributed to a lovely homecoming to a couple that wouldn't be able to organise anything themselves. When the meal was over, the lawn was cleared and the jamboree began with a vengeance. The musicians, having had a good meal and a few drinks, were rearing to go. They played with great gusto and soon they had the crowd doing all kinds of figure dancing on the lawn, with young and old joining in the fun.

Hearing all the music, Peter and Bessie, now recovered from their hallucinations, appeared in the doorway. It took very little to persuade them to join in the fun.

They were known for having been good dancers in their youth and they took to the lawn as the band struck up a waltz to cheers from all the assembly. The lawn didn't lend itself to good dancing, especially to dancers of their age. However, they managed to support each other for a couple of rounds and it could truthfully be said that they danced at their own wedding. The fun continued unabated and there wasn't a blade of grass left on the lawn by three o'clock in the afternoon. Then the singing started. Mickeen Joe stood in the doorway and sang a song called 'The Man from Faraway', a rendition that was never heard before by anyone present. When he finished there was great applause which tempted him to say, "That was a hard song to sing". Some joker in the middle of the lawn replied, "'Twas a way harder to listen to it". Poor Mickeen Joe jumped up on his ass' back and went home in a temper.

But there were plenty more singers who kept the show going and in the middle of all the merriment someone called for a step dancer.

"Sure we have no place to dance," replied a little slip of a girl.

"I'll soon get a stage for you," said a foxy-haired man and, true to his word, in a few minutes he wheeled a horse's car onto the lawn.

He placed the shafts up on the ditch and said to the girl, "There is your stage for you, don't let us down". The girl had a chat with the musicians and then she got a crow's lift onto the stage and danced a beautiful hornpipe. The crowd formed a semi-circle around the stage and when she finished they shouted up at her, "Give us a reel". The band struck up a reel and the girl obliged with another beautiful performance. Urged on by the crowd, she finished her act with a slip-jig to thundering applause.

The craic was great and everyone was enjoying themselves when, alas, it came to a sudden end – the honeymooners appeared in the doorway, dressed in their working clothes! Peter announced that they had to go and milk their cows.

"Bessie and myself would like to thank ye all for what ye done today for us. We enjoyed it great but we have to milk the cows now and we wouldn't like to stop ye of milking yers," he added.

Paddy Tom went to them and volunteered to milk their cows, encouraging them to stay and enjoy their wedding, but to no avail.

"Ah, not at all, Paddy. Some of them are cross and they might kick ye and hurt ye," said Peter.

Supported by blackthorn sticks in one hand and a milking bucket in the other, they slowly made their way to the cowhouse. And so the festivities came to an end. This was a shock for all the young people of the place who had planned on coming late that evening, expecting a great night's entertainment. Disappointed, Paddy Tom gave his verdict, "I didn't think it before, but that pair must be doting".

The McGurks

The McGurks

The McGurks were a family whose great great grandparents were evicted from a large farm of good land and forced to settle in a small, rundown house on a couple of acres of land on the banks of the Shannon. Here, their lifestyle changed dramatically. No more the fine herd of cows or the big gardens of wheat, barley and oats. Surely they must have missed the lovely team of horses and perhaps a dashing hunter or two, and the sound of the hunt Master's bugle. It must have been a real heartbreak for them to be forced to walk away from their fine home with just a few belongings packed into a donkey and cart which was given to them by a friendly neighbour. But they weren't the first to be dispossessed and they were not the last. That, however, was poor consolation.

But that was several generations back and the present generation of McGurks were happy with their lot. They made a living fishing on the Shannon and working with local farmers. They would go out at night in their canoe and fish for herring until dawn. They had a pot on board half full of turf and during the night they would start a fire and place their frying pan on top of it, adding plenty of lard and an onion or two. Then they would cook the fresh herring and eat the meal along with plenty of homemade bread, well plastered with salty farmers' butter, washing it all down with bottles of goats' milk. Thus fed, their energy levels would zoom upwards and they would row that boat for hours on end.

Once the catch was landed as dawn broke, Maggie McGurk would get breakfast ready while her husband Dan sorted out the fish, getting them ready for sale throughout the local villages. Selling was Maggie's job and their son, Paudeen, took responsibility for tackling the ass and putting him under the cart. Together Dan and Paudeen would load the fish onto the cart and all was then ready for Maggie to do her selling, first in the villages and afterwards from house to house throughout the countryside. She was reputed to be an excellent sales person and rarely came home until she had sold the last fish. In the meantime, Dan and Paudeen went to bed to get a few hours sleep after their night at sea. The length of their slumbers was governed by whether or not they had been hired to work for farmers and if they had, their rest would be short.

Paudeen was the elder son, aged fifteen years, and he was a tall, muscular, strapping young fellow who had always seemed bigger than his years. He had little education as he quit school at a very young age, under, it could be said, unusual circumstances. School at that time was not compulsory. It was a place of strict discipline that was enforced with the cane at the Master's discretion. Paudeen often incurred the Master's displeasure for failure at lessons and was a regular recipient of punishment with the cane, which usually consisted of one, or sometimes, several, slaps on the hands. In certain cases it could include a few on the posterior. At ten years of age, and big and strong for his age, Paudeen was already rowing the canoe with his father at every opportunity.

He was getting fed-up with the school business which was restricting his liberty and, what was worse, he was getting beaten with a stick by an old, grey-haired teacher with a big, white whisker and this sometimes made his hands too sore for rowing. Paudeen often thought of catching him by the whisker while he was being punished, but he never got up enough courage. Then one day the bubble burst during geography lesson. The Master shouted at Paudeen to stand up. The boy stood up.

"What is the capital city of England?" the Master asked.

"Dublin, sir," said young McGurk.

"Did you not hear me?" said the Master, "I said England."

"And I said Dublin," said Paudeen.

"Well, you're wrong," said the Master going for the cane, "come up here and I'll warm your hands for you and you'll remember it the next time."

"I will not," said Paudeen.

"What do you mean 'you will not'?" said the Master.

"It manes that I will not go up," repeated Paudeen.

"Well, if you will not come up then I will go down," said the Master, brandishing the cane.

All the other pupils were seated while Paudeen stood there like a statue as the Master slowly moved towards him. When he was within two steps of Paudeen, the boy bolted. He jumped up on the desk and then jumped from desk to desk until he reached the one nearest the door. With a mighty jump he landed at the door, opened it in a flash and ran into the hall picking his cap off the peg as he went and then out through the schoolyard. The Master gave chase but by the time he reached the schoolyard, the barefoot McGurk was jumping the school wall without even putting a hand on it. Down across Mickie Seán's field he raced and when he felt safe he looked back and there he saw the Master standing inside the school wall looking after him. Paudeen decided he'd give him a big wave and then raced on home. That was his last day at school.

Many years later there was an unusual sequel to his sudden exit from the educational system. One warm Sunday afternoon Paudeen was stretched out in his canoe sunning himself. There was a spring tide and the water was almost level with the bank. All of a sudden, Paudeen saw a person walking, more or less in his direction, in the second field up from the shore. He watched him closely, because he thought it was unusual for a person to be taking that route to the sea as there was no stile or pathway through those fields and the pathway to the shore was two fields to the west. However, he kept his eye on the stranger as he felt that no local would be traveling via those fields to get to the sea. As he watched he could see that it was a man who seemed to be wearing a straw hat and that he was picking wild flowers as he walked. When the man came to the fence of the field next to the sea, he had great difficulty getting over it. He had to traverse almost the length of it to find an opening to get through. Finally he did get through and continued to walk on, still picking the wild flowers.

As the man got closer, Paudeen couldn't believe his eyes – in spite of the straw hat and bunch of flowers, he recognized his old school Master. The Master hit the seashore about one hundred yards to the west of where Paudeen was relaxing in his boat. He was hoping the old man wouldn't come towards him and that he'd walk away to the west. The two had not met since that fateful last day at school and even though five years had passed and the Master had by now retired, the happenings of that day came back to Paudeen and his temper began to rise. Thinking these thoughts, he turned to give a look to see where the Master had gone and his heart started to pound – the Master was within twenty yards of him and was walking towards him. There he was, looking down at him in the boat, with his straw hat and his bunch of flowers and the same long, white whisker that Paudeen had so often felt like pulling.

"Hello," said the Master.

"Hello," said Paudeen.

"You're McGurk, are you not?" asked the Master.

"That's me all right," was his answer.

"All your family are very good oarsmen I'm told, is that correct?"

"Correct," said Paudeen.

"Ye used to be fishermen?" questioned the Master.

"We still are. You mustn't be buying our fish," said Paudeen, with a bit of temper in his voice.

"What makes you say that?" asked the Master.

"If you were buying our fish you'd know we were still fishing, wouldn't you?" retorted Paudeen.

"Good thinking, my boy, good thinking. Tell me, would you take me for a row, just about five paces from the shore, nothing further?" asked the Master.

Paudeen looked up at him in amazement without saying a word.

"Well?" said the Master, "will you take me?"

Paudeen was like someone in a trance and when he found his speech he said, "I suppose I will," and after a second or two he added, "Sir". Paudeen tidied up the boat a bit and then said, "Hop in so, sir". The Master stepped onto the boat and as his weight swayed the canoe, he almost fell overboard but he recovered and seated himself in the stern. He still was clutching his bunch of flowers and the straw hat was at a crazy angle on his head.

"Make yourself comfortable now, sir," said Paudeen as he put out the oars and started to row.

"Remember now, McGurk, just five paces from the shore," said the Master.

"Sound out," said Paudeen, rowing his best.

Silence reigned supreme between the two men for a while and the Master seemed to be enjoying the experience, that was until he took a look back and saw that he was about half a mile from the shore. Then he panicked and attempted to stand up, but as he did so, Paudeen gave a sudden mighty pull on the oars and he fell back onto the seat.

"McGurk turn back, turn back quick I say," said the Master, "I said just five paces and it looks that we are out a mile. Turn back now I say."

Paudeen never answered him but kept rowing and after a short while the Master, this time in a pleading tone of voice, said, "Please, McGurk, please turn back. I don't want to go to Clare". McGurk still said nothing, but kept rowing until he reached the marker buoy in the middle of the Shannon. Then he pulled in the oars and, catching the gunwale of the canoe to the left and the right of him, he rocked the boat from side to side.

He looked the Master straight in the eye and, with all the venom he could muster in his voice, he said, "Do you remember the last day that I was at school? Do you?" The Master was dumbfounded and after the boat got a few more rocks, he muttered fearfully, "I don't remember anything".

"Well," said McGurk, "if you have a bad memory I have a good one and I remember it well. You chased me out of the room with a stick so say your prayers because I'm going to drown you right now."

He rocked the boat again and the straw hat fell off the Master's head into the water. The bunch of flowers also fell from his trembling hands into the Shannon and, as the Master saw them both float away with the current, he felt doomed.

He again appealed to Paudeen to bring him ashore and said, "What do you want to bring me home?"

"How much have you in your pockets?" said Paudeen.

"I don't know," said the Master.

"Empty them," ordered Paudeen.

The poor Master emptied his pockets there and then. Paudeen was amazed at what he saw and agreed to bring him ashore. How much money, no one ever knew. In fact, no one locally ever knew of the episode until Paudeen himself told the story many years later one night in the Shanty, when he had more porter drank than he should have. Whenever he was pressed to tell how much the Master had in his pocket, he'd just smile and say, "A good lot".

The years rolled on and the McGurk children grew up. The two daughters went into service to farmers for eleven months, as was usual for girls at the time. The younger boy would go fishing with either his father or brother Paudeen. But Dan was getting worried as he saw a serious threat of coastal erosion coming, slowly but surely. He could see that every year the sea was moving closer and closer to his house and it worried him. Where would he get a home if the unthinkable happened and they had to vacate their house. It was a small house, but Maggie was very house proud and she kept it neat and whitewashed inside and outside. Some time later, the unthinkable did happen and the sea came within a few feet of the wall of the house. Dan was faced with the task of finding alternative accommodation and he had to find it fast.

But he was lucky when someone told him the whereabouts of an unoccupied house that might suit. It was owned by Tom Redden, a strong farmer and who was known to be a decent sort of man. Dan decided that he would approach Mr Redden even though he had never spoken to the man in his life. But, as he said to Maggie, "Sure I have nothing to lose and everything to gain". In response Maggie said, "Isn't it a pity that you haven't someone to go with you, someone that knows Tom Redden".

"That would be a great help," mused Dan, "maybe I'll ask Seán Fada. He works with the Reddens now and again, he'd know Tom well and I think he gets on well with him."

Seán Fada was a handyman and was well-known locally. On the morning Dan when went to see him, Seán was sitting in the corner, half asleep, with the pipe in his mouth. When Dan entered and said, "God bless all here" he woke up with a start.

"Yerra, how's Dan? 'Pon my word you gave me a fright. I was dozin' so I was," said Seán.

"Nothing wrong with that," said Dan, "but 'twas a pity to disturb you though."

"No harm done me man. You're as welcome as the flowers in May," said Seán, "shove in and take a chair."

Dan sat down and they chatted about the weather and the fishing. The conversation even drifted back to old times when they were young and the house dances they frequented, the girlfriends they had, their 'old flames' as they called them. The reminiscences of the old flames came to an abrupt end when Mrs Seán Fada entered. The chat stopped completely and as the two stayed silent longer than usual, Madge, after putting her bag of messages on the table, put her hands on her hips and looked straight at the two men saying, "Did ye lose yer tongues or what? Ye must have been talking bad about me or talking about something very private". That observation seemed to give them their voices back, as they shouted in unison that they never mentioned her name, high or holy, which was true, but they didn't volunteer to say about whom they were talking.

It wasn't long before Madge had the kettle hanging on the crane over a blazing turf fire and the tay made for Dan, Seán and herself. Dan was very shy in drawing down the reason for his visit, especially in the presence of Madge who was well-known to be a gossiper. He didn't want anyone to know that he was looking for a house, for the present anyhow. So after they had eaten Dan said to Seán, "Will we give a ramble out?"

"Why not," answered Seán, as Dan turned to Madge and thanked her for her hospitality saying, "Thanks for the tay, Madge, and may God increase your store". In the meantime, Seán Fada, being a very shrewd man, was thinking in his own mind that Dan was in some kind of trouble so, as they moved away from the house, he broke the ice and said, "Dan is there something bothering you?"

"Well, now as you said it, there is," said Dan.

With his voice breaking with emotion, he told Seán the whole story of his predicament and he finished by saying that a couple of more spring tides could leave him without a home and no where to go. Seán Fada had great sympathy for Dan and his family and asked, "Can I do anything to help you?"

These words were like music to Dan's ears. He now had a listening ear which made it easier for him to ask for the favour. He opened his heart to Seán on the spot and said, "I know that you are on good terms with Tom Redden and I was told that he has a small house empty. Is that true?"

"Oh, he has a house all right and 'tis not very small. 'Tis a slate house," said Seán.

"A slate house, did you say?" interjected Dan, "I'd never be able to pay the rent of that. What would he be charging?"

"How would I know what he'd be charging," said Seán, "sure we don't even know would he rent it but I'll tell you one thing, if he does rent it, he wouldn't be the hardest man in the world to pay."

"Even so," said Dan, "'tis a slate house so it would have to be dear."

"Well," said Seán, "there is only one way to find out. We'll go up to him this minute."

Taking the shortcut through the fields, they made their way to the Redden homestead. On their way they came upon the 'slate house' as Dan called it and that's what it was called for evermore. They didn't enter it but had a good look and Dan was thrilled with what he saw, especially as there seemed to be a strong acre of ground going with it which would be ideal for his five goats and puck. However, he still had this great fear that it was so good that he'd never be able to meet the rent. He said as much to Seán again and Seán, a born optimist, said, "Never say die man until you're dead. Redden is a good old sort and you'd never know your luck".

They finally arrived at Tom Redden's and as they were walking through the yard, they were met by two big, barking collie dogs. Dan thought they were in trouble and said, "Seán, let us run for it," but Seán, who knew the dogs, just said, "Come here, Shep, oh poor Sally," and the barking stopped. The dogs came forward with wagging tails to be rubbed and petted by Seán, and in turn by Dan who was, by instinct, a dog lover. Tom Redden strolled out from the back of the house and continued down to meet the two visitors. Dan took stock of him as he approached. He saw that Redden was a very big man, a bit obese he thought, and he sported a huge, bushy moustache and well-groomed sidelocks. He looked to Dan to be in his mid-fifties and as Redden got nearer, he formed the opinion that he seemed to be a pleasant type. Later he was to know that his first impressions of Tom Redden were not too far off the mark.

Tom Redden saluted the men in his big bellowing voice, and asked Seán Fada who was the man with him.

"This is Dan McGurk, he's a fisherman," said Seán, and he was just about to say the nature of their visit when Tom blurted out, "Ah, sure we know his wife well. We buy fish regularly from her, lovely fish too, always very fresh". He shook hands with Dan saying, "You're very welcome indeed". This, along with the praise of the fish, put Dan somewhat at ease. This would be the first news he'd have for Maggie when he'd get home. As Tom was very interested in fish, including the different species, the different nets used and the life and work of fishermen in general, the conversation continued in this vein long after he had brought the two men into the kitchen where he produced a bottle of poitín. Now, there are times when both of them would indulge, but this wasn't one of them.

They still didn't like to refuse his hospitality outright, so they both said, almost together, "Just a very small drop so," because they both knew that if they had a drop too much they would get so drunk that they would have forgotten what they came for. How then would they face home or how would they come back to Tom Redden again? They had their chance now and with these thoughts in mind, Seán Fada opened the proceedings saying, "Now Tom, I must tell you that this is not a social visit".

"I was thinking as much," said Tom, "what can I do for ye?"

"Well, 'tis Dan here that is in a big spot of bother but I'll let him spake for himself. Spake up Dan, don't be shy or ashamed, tell out your sad story and I know in my heart and soul that Tom Redden here will do the best he can for you," said Seán.

The poitín was having an effect on Seán, just enough to give him the courage to say what he said and set the ball rolling. Redden was well-known to always have the strongest of poitín and even a small drop had an effect. The drink also had an effect on Dan, because, although a shy individual, he rose to the occasion and, in a voice full of emotion, explained his problem with great clarity, stressing the urgency of the situation and ending with the plea, "Please, Mr Redden, in God's name, help me if you can". Redden, for his part, had listened very attentively to all of what Dan had to say and when Dan finished there was complete silence for several minutes. Tom Redden was the first to break the silence saying, "I must say that I'm very sorry to hear of your sad situation. Have you seen the house, the slate house, as you call it?" 'Twas Seán who answered.

"I showed it to him on the way over. We didn't go in though, but he liked what he saw."

"Well," said Redden, "as you have seen it you know that it is a bit run-down and the plot of ground with it needs tidying up. Have you a cow, Dan?"

"No," replied Dan, "but I have five goats and a puck."

He was half afraid to mention the puck, fearing that Tom Redden might not like the idea of a puck around the place. However, in case he'd be getting the house, he wanted to be on the straight with Tom to avoid any problems afterwards. He was soon to find out that his fears about the puck were unfounded.

"Well," said Tom, "fair enough, you can have the house. You'll have to do a bit of work on the acre of ground of course – clear the briars and bushes that have almost taken over the place and 'twill feed your goats and puck. It will be great to have a puck around the place. I'm told it's very good to have one with cattle as they protect them from brucellosis."

Dan couldn't believe his luck, but still he worried about the burning question of the rent. No one had mentioned it yet. He decided to take the bull by the horns and ask Tom Redden straight. So he spoke up.

"Now Mr Redden, I must say that I'm deeply grateful and thankful to you for giving me the use of your house and I think that I'll never be able to thank you enough. That said, I'd like to talk to you about the rent – what would it be by the week?"

Tom looked at him and said, "Oh, yes, the rent".

"That's right, the rent, sir," said Dan.

Redden thought for a minute, as if he was doing mental arithmetic, and it was a minute that felt like an hour to Dan. Finally he spoke.

"The house needs a lot of doing up and, as I said, the land attached also needs to be taken care of. So, taking everything into consideration, I have decided that there will be no weekly rent. What I would like you to agree to is this, that you would work with us for a few weeks every summer saving the hay as the need arises. Do you agree to that?" asked Redden.

Dan's eyes filled with tears of happiness and, with deep emotion, he said, "It couldn't be better, sir, I agree to every bit of it, sir". The two shook hands and Seán Fada, also deeply moved, laid his hand on Dan's shoulder and said, "Cheer up man, for you a new day has dawned". His words were to prove prophetic. When Dan got his emotions under control, he asked Tom Redden when could he move in and was told whenever he liked. After some more chat about local happenings and again refusing a 'drop of the cratur', the two men took their leave of Tom Redden and rambled home across the fields.

The Move

Seán and Dan chatted about the success of their mission as they made their way home. Dan was delighted with the outcome and talked about the great reception they had received from Tom Redden – how he was so nice to them, stood them the drop of poitín and was so easy to deal with as regards the house, especially the way he arranged the payment of the rent. Dan considered that very significant as he wouldn't have to be trying to have hard cash every week to pay out, which would have made things very hard what with money being so scarce. The availability of work was very unpredictable in those times and was also badly rewarded, but if a man had no work he'd have no income at all, hence Dan's jubilation regarding the method of paying the rent for the slate house. Dan knew only too well what it was like to have no income, because in bad stormy weather, often for weeks on end, he couldn't venture out fishing, but then, at least, he had no rent to pay. As they approached Seán Fada's house, Seán insisted on Dan going in with him just to break the journey.

When they entered, Madge was knitting in the corner beside a blazing fire. She looked the pair of them up and down and then asked where they had been all day. She stood up and walked up to Seán to smell his breath and then she proceeded to do the same to Dan.

"Wherever we were," said Seán, "it wasn't where you think we were."

Thinking that there might be an argument between Seán and his wife, for which he himself would feel responsible. Dan moved to forestall the event.

"Well, now, Madge, I must tell you that, today, your husband Seán did me a mighty good turn," he said.

"Did he now?" said Madge, rather sarcastically.

"He did indeed then. He found me a house," said Dan.

"What do you mean by a house?" Madge asked in bewilderment.

"I must tell you the facts of the matter," explained Seán. "You see, Dan is in a great spot of bother so he came here today looking for help. As you know he lives down near the sea, too near it in fact, and that's the problem because in a very short time his house will be washed away by the tide. So someone told him that Tom Redden had an empty house on his land, and, knowing that I knew Redden, he came here to ask me to put in a word for him with Tom. I felt that the best way to do the business was for Dan and myself to go straight up to Tom Redden and get an answer, win or lose. And that's what we did, and that's where we were all day."

"Dan, I'm awful sorry," said Madge, "I didn't know you were in such trouble. How did ye get on with Redden? They say that he isn't the worst of 'em. I hope ye got on well."

In fairness to Madge, she had a big heart and was very charitable under a somewhat frosty exterior.

'Twas Dan who spoke next.

"We got on famous, Madge. That Tom Redden is a dacent man. He landed down with a bottle of poitín first thing – he'd make us drunk if we took it – but we watched ourselves. When Tom's back was turned Seán said to me that we'd better be careful or we'd forget what we came for. Tom does have the strongest poitín brewed. But, that said, we had no trouble at all. He gave the house to me with a heart and a half and said I could take possession any time I liked. But I was very straight with him too. I told him that I had a puck, just for fear he'd have any objection, and sure he was only delighted. He said that pucks were great with cows, who'd ever think that?"

"Well, Dan," said Madge, "I must say that I'm delighted for you and I wish you and Maggie and all your childer a century of happiness in it. The kettle is just boiling, so sit down and we'll have the tay."

"Oh, no tay for me Madge," Dan protested, "I must be making tracks. Herself will be anxious to know what happened as she thought I was just coming as far as here to talk to Seán and now 'tis evening. Thanks just the same."

With these words he moved towards the door and as he did so, he clapped a hand on Seán Fada's shoulder, a silent thank you, and went out the door and turned for home across the fields.

On arriving home, he found the house empty. Maggie was milking the goats in the haggard and he could see their sons below at the canoe mending the nets. Alone in the familiar kitchen, Dan suddenly became very nostalgic. He had been born and reared in this house and it was to this house he brought Maggie as his bride, it was in this house all his children were born and reared too. It might be small and have mud walls, it might be thatched with gilcock, but it had a lifetime of memories and it was his castle – it was home. And now he had to leave it and let it fall into the sea, just walk away from it and leave it to its fate. These thoughts overwhelmed Dan and tears flowed down his cheeks. Hearing the rattle of buckets as Maggie washed them outside the door, he tried to pull himself together. The door opened and Maggie came and said, "You were a long day out, what did Seán Fada say?"

"Seán Fada said that the best thing to do was to go right up to Tom Redden and ask him straight out," answered Dan, "and that's what we did."

"Well?" said Maggie.

"Well, the long and the short of it is, but first I must tell you that Tom Redden said that he knows you well and that they often bought fish from you. He said that they were always lovely and fresh. When I heard that I knew it was a good start," said Dan.

"I often called there all right if I had fish left coming home as they were always good for a half dozen," said Maggie, "but what I want to hear now is the long and the short of it."

"Well, 'twas like this," commenced Dan.

"I don't care what 'twas like," Maggie interrupted, "all I want to know is did you or did you not get the house?"

"I got the house Maggie, with a heart and a half and 'tis a lovely slate house. It needs a bit of a doing up, you know what I mean, a tidying up, shall we say. And what's more, there is a fine straik of ground going with it so there'll be plenty to ate for the goats so we're steeped in luck," said Dan.

"That's all right now and it sounds great," said the astute Maggie, "but you said 'twas a slate house and slate houses do be dear you know, so what about the cost? I mean the rent – will we be able to meet it?"

"Don't be wan bit bothered, Maggie, all that is fixed up. We'll have no rent to pay," said Dan joyfully.

"No rent!" shouted Maggie, "what makes you think that? Isn't it well-known we'll have to pay rent?"

"Can't you listen to me," retorted Dan, "Tom Redden said there'd be no weekly rent. We just have to give him time saving the hay in the summer. Now, what do you think of that?"

"Thanks be to God and His blessed mother, 'tis great," said a relieved Maggie.

A type of uneasy silence seemed to descend on them for a time, as they both struggled with their emotions. 'Twas Maggie who eventually broke the silence. In a breaking voice, she asked, "Do we really have to go?"

"We have no choice, Maggie," Dan said sadly, "I wish we had, but don't you see where the tide is?"

"What about the fishing?" asked Maggie, holding back the tears.

"The fishing," mused Dan, "I don't honestly know, we're moving a good bit inland to different country and different people. It won't be easy. Maybe we'll find different work. God is good and fishing isn't all sunshine either."

"I know, sure," said Maggie, "and it's dangerous too. Ye'll never know all the rosaries I said for ye when ye were out there at night."

They were both overcome with emotion and, as the tears came, they consoled each other in an embrace.

"Pull yourself together, Maggie," whispered Dan, "the lads are coming in."

At that, the latch lifted and Paudeen and Donal came in.

Paudeen and Donal immediately sensed something was happening. Paudeen asked if there was something wrong. His mother answered, "We're leaving this place. Your father got a house from Tom Redden".

"And a fine slate house it is too," cut in Dan, "and there's a fine patch of ground going with plenty to ate for the goats and the puck."

"Is it far away from here?" asked Donal.

"'Tis a far journey all right if you go by the road but 'tis a good bit shorter across the fields," answered Dan.

"And when are we moving?" asked Paudeen,

"Anytime at all we like," said Dan, "the sooner the better I suppose. If there's another high tide we'll be in big trouble."

"And what are we carrying with us – are we carrying the spuds and the turf, as well as the goats and puck?" asked Donal. "We're carrying everything that can be carried," said Dan, "haven't we all the birds in the cages and your mother will want to take the hens and the cock, and the hen turkey of course. And sure we'll have to take the ducks – wouldn't we feel lost without a duck egg for the breakfast? See now, we have a lot of things to carry and that's not counting the table and the chairs and the beds and the skillet and the oven and the brand, not to mention the tongs and the kettle and the big pot and the small pot and the couple of pos."

At this point Maggie gave a smirk.

"'Tis no laughing matter," said Dan, "everything will have to go, they'll be all needed and won't all the bed clothes have to go, and the cups and saucers and the plates and the pannies. I know I'm forgetting something, but sure it will be all sorted out as we load up. We might even carry the crane if there is no crane in the slate house. The big question is, how we will get them all shifted?"

"'Twill take us days," said Paudeen, "all that will fit in the ass's cart and rail is two goats at the most."

"And the puck would fill it himself," volunteered Donal.

"Ah, we could tie the puck behind the cart and he'd follow on and that would solve that," suggested Dan. "You'd want a good rope, he's a strong old bugger you know," said Donal, "if he broke lose we'd never catch him."

"We'll cross all them bridges when we come to them," Dan replied, "anyhow we haven't decided when we're going. I suppose it will be someday next week. What do you think Maggie? Name a day Maggie – we'll let it be your call – what day would you choose?"

"Well, if 'tis my call, as you say, I'll go by what the old people used to say," replied Maggie, "'Monday for health, Tuesday for wealth, Wednesday the best day of all, Thursday for losses, Friday for crosses and Saturday no day at all'."

"And what about Sunday – you never mentioned Sunday?" Donal joked.

"Isn't Sunday a day of rest, you pagan. We'll move on Wednesday," declared Maggie, "but I'd like to see the house before then."

"If you say so," said Dan, "we'll pay a visit there tomorrow."

So Wednesday was agreed upon as the day on which they'd cut their ties with their old homestead, for better or worse, but hoping it would be for the better and at least they wouldn't have the danger of the tide flooding them in the slate house.

In the meantime, and unknown to Dan and Maggie, Seán Fada had organized a gang of their neighbours-to-be to work on the slate house. Tom Redden sent over a man with a bag of lime and he whitewashed the house, inside and outside. Seán himself repaired a few of the windows that were broken and replaced some of the flags on the kitchen floor that were out of place. Paddy the Lad arrived with a tin of brown paint and painted the front and back doors as well as the window frames. Mickeen Seán brought two of his sons, armed with slashers and a hatchet, and they started clearing the briars and bushes from the front and then the back of the house. Even the Briar did his part – he spent the most of a day drawing gravel from the river with his jennet and filling the sloughs on the boreen leading up to the house.

As he had promised Maggie, early next morning Dan tackled the ass and put him under the cart and the pair of them set out to visit their new home. It took them over an hour to get there and when they did arrive, Dan almost fainted. It happened to be the very day that all the neighbours were working on the house to have it clean and tidy for Dan and Maggie but the first thing that struck Dan was that Tom Redden had reneged on his promise and had given the house to someone else. He thought they had already moved in and were doing it up. A terrible disappointment overcame him and then anger took over and he hit the poor ass a belt of the ash plant he had in his hand as he turned him around in the yard to get out of there as quickly as possible. Luckily enough, Seán Fada was washing his trowel down near the well and he spotted the cart coming into the yard. When he saw Dan turning around to leave, he rushed over to talk to himself and Maggie.

"Hello, you're both very welcome," shouted Seán, with a big smile on his face.

As he got closer, he heard Dan angrily say, "I never thought he'd do it. I thought he was a man of his word". At this stage, Seán was right beside the cart, and he caught the reins and pulled the ass to a halt.

"What are you talking about?" said Seán.

"You know well what I'm talking about," shouted Dan, on the verge of tears, "you were there and you heard him, I never thought he'd do this to me. I took him at his word. I thought him to be a straight dacent man and look at what he done to me." "Yerra cool down," said Maggie, "sure we'll get a house some other place. There is as good a fish in the sea as ever was caught."

"What are ye talking about?" said Seán, perplexed at Dan's attitude, "didn't Tom Redden give you this house. Is it how Maggie don't like it?"

"Ah, come on now and stop joking, do you think I'm a fool altogether. He gave it to me all right, but can't I see that he has now given it to some other one and that they have moved in," said Dan bitterly, "look at it all whitewashed and aren't you working at it – what else are you doing with a trowel in your hand?"

'Twas then that Seán Fada realized what was wrong with Dan and, with a big scart of a laugh, he said, "So you think Redden gave away the house on you? Not at all – 'tis how your new neighbours are getting it ready for you. When are you moving in? Come on in Maggie and meet your new neighbours and have a look around".

Maggie jumped out of the cart like a shot. Seán Fada put his hand on her shoulder and conveyed her into the kitchen. Poor Dan was so perplexed he stayed sitting in the cart for a few minutes until he realized he was alone. All of a sudden he jumped out the cart, caught the ass by the head and guided him over to the fence where he tied him to a bush. He then straightened the cap on his head and walked like a soldier on parade towards the door where he stood for a few seconds as if between two minds what to do next. All of a sudden the door opened and Seán Fada appeared. He got a bit of a start on seeing Dan standing there and said, "Oh, Dan, I was just going out looking for you. What happened you?"

"I had to tie the ass, I was just coming in," and in a whisper he asked, "how does she like it?"

"Come on in and ask her yourself, or is it how ye aren't on talking terms," joked Seán Fada.

In the meantime, Maggie was being shown around by Mary Kate, a neighbour who was doing some painting and giving the house a general tidying up. Seán did the introductions.

"This is Mary Kate Black, a neighbour and a good one. And now Mary Kate, this is Dan McGurk, you have already met his wife Maggie – they're your new neighbours and I'm sure ye'll get on well together," he said.

"Yerra, why wouldn't we get on. We'll get on like a cow and a cock of hay, won't we Maggie?" said Mary Kate.

"We will of course, what's to stop us," Maggie answered, "I'm so glad we came today to see the house and met you, Mary Kate. It's nice to know where we are coming to."

"What do you think of it?" asked Dan.

"I think 'tis out of this world. It isn't a house at all, 'tis a mansion," Maggie said glowingly.

"'Tis all that," added Dan, "and a lot more. What a fine kitchen for an eight-hand reel!"

Both Dan and Maggie had been great set dancers in their youth, as a matter of fact it was through their love of dancing they first met.

"Yes indeed, and still plenty of room for the hens' coop," said Maggie.

"That's a fact. You're dead right Maggie, that's the one thing I forgot when I was figuring out what we had to move, the hens' coop," replied Dan.

They were on such a high about the house that they carried on this conversation oblivious to the presence of Seán Fada and Mary Kate, who, it must be said, had the good manners to discreetly leave the kitchen. Coming down to earth, Dan and Maggie decided that they had better be starting for home. Mary Kate said she had tay ready and insisted that they sit down on a form that was along the wall. She handed them cups of tay and a couple of slices of homemade currant cake she had brought with her to give to the men helping in the doing up of the slate house. Having had the tay and cake and highly elated, Dan and Maggie thanked Mary Kate and took leave of their hosts. They found that the ass had eaten all the grass off the fence as far as the rope tethering him would allow, so they felt that he too was ready for the road home. Dan soon drove the ass into a steady trot and the pair exchanged very few words on the journey home, both reflecting on the new life that lay ahead.

Arriving home Dan unhitched the ass and let him off in the plot with the goats. Immediately, the ass rolled over several times, as was his wont, to refresh himself. Paudeen and Donal were waiting for their parents in the kitchen, all keyed up to hear the news. Maggie excitedly described their new home – the fine kitchen and the lovely rooms and how all the neighbours had turned out and done the whole place up.

"And there's a fine loft too," Dan cut in, "did you go up to the loft at all, Maggie?"

"Indeed I did not, what do you think I am to climb up that ladder and Seán Fada there!" she said.

"'Tis a fine airy loft then with plenty room for two beds and three if you were stuck," Dan said with a chuckle.

"Do you know, I'd love to see it myself," said Paudeen.

"And so would I," murmured Donal.

"Ye'll see it now on Wednesday, that isn't too long to wait sure," said Maggie as she filled the kettle and hung it on the crane. "Well, now, lads," said Dan, clearing his throat, "we'd better put our heads together and consider how we're going to do the moving. I think that we should take all the house stuff first.

That'd be the beds, bedclothes, pots, pans, cups and saucers and the pannies. The brand and the griddle and the oven and, of course, a handful of turf. That house would need a fire."

"Is there a crane there?" Paudeen inquired.

"There is to be sure," answered Dan, "and a fine one."

The next few days were filled with making plans for shifting their belongings, then changing them again. After hours of talking and many arguments, they usually found themselves back at square one. The talking and the arguments continued over the weekend and through Monday and Tuesday and still they had no firm plans made. The fact of the matter was that they had only one ass and cart and whatever way they would twist it and turn it, they could only carry a small amount in a load. Because they had never before had to do the likes of this job, it was driving them crazy. On Wednesday morning they were up at five o'clock but they still hadn't decided what to load first. As dawn was breaking they were tackling the ass and Paudeen said that it would take them a week to shift everything. Suddenly Dan said, "Stop talking a minute, do ye hear some noise?" They all listened and after a few seconds Paudeen said, "That's like the sound of a horse and cart coming along the strand".

"Yerra, who'd be coming along the strand at this hour? asked Dan, "it must be traveling above on the road and just an echo from the strand."

"Whatever you say about an echo," cut in Donal, "that noise is from the strand and 'tis coming closer."

He was right. Minutes later, through the dawn haze, they saw the outline of a horse and cart with a rail and a man standing inside guiding the horse, coming towards them.

"Where in the name of goodness is that fellow going this hour of the morning?" Paudeen asked.

"Some poor fellow going astray I suppose, whatever brought him this way," replied Dan.

But he wasn't going astray. When he drove up to where Dan and the boys were, the driver jumped out of the rail and asked, "Is this Dan McGurk's place?"

"It is," said Dan, "and who are you, may I ask?"

"My name is Tommy. I work with Tom Redden and he sent me here to collect stuff you want to take to the slate house. Aren't you moving today?"

"I am," said Dan, rather dumbfounded, and before he could say another word, Tommy blurted out, "I'm supposed to come back again for a second load and as there is another horse coming, we'd better start loading". Dan realized it was make his mind up time so he asked, "Will you carry turf?"

"Anything at all, no problem," was the cheerful answer.

At that moment they heard the second horse coming along the strand. Tommy pulled up to the rick of turf and, with the three McGurks and himself, they filled the rail in a short time, then Tommy climbed on top of the wheel and clamped it. As he pulled away with his load, the second horse arrived and Dan asked the driver would he take turf, as all that was left was a load and that would be one item gone. Again, a cheery "No problem" and that secured the turf. Tommy wouldn't be back for at least a couple of hours so they had a bit of time to consider what load to give him.

Dan thought that it would be best to give Tommy all the bulky stuff, such as the beds, mattresses and bedclothes and maybe even the oven. Donal asked about the birds in the cages.

"I was wondering about them," remarked Dan, "and what I think we might do is hang them on to the side of the rail, three at each side and one off the back gate with the load of the beds."

Dan was a great bird fancier all his life and he was determined to continue the pastime in his new surroundings. There was also a small pit of spuds to be taken, but they could wait if all went to all. However, shortly after that, there was another unexpected arrival when Seán Fada drove in with the Briar's jennet. The McGurks were flabbergasted.

They had spent days and nights worrying and wondering how to get their belongings moved and now, in a few hours, they would have moved lock, stock and barrel. They couldn't have imagined it in their wildest dreams. Paudeen suggested that three goats would fit in the jennet's cart and two would fit in their own ass's cart and that would take care of the goats.

"What about the puck?" Donal queried.

"Didn't I say that we would tie him on behind the ass's cart and he would follow the smell of the goats. We'll tie him short and there will be no problem," counseled Dan.

So they loaded the goats and then, after a few failed attempts, succeeded in catching the puck. Having never been caught since he was a kid, he went berserk. Dan was the first to catch him by the horns and Paudeen and Seán Fada moved in to tie the rope around his horns. They had just succeeded in tying it on one horn when the puck seemed to realize that he was being captured and, with a jerk of his head, he threw Dan, who was a bit light in body-weight, up in the air like a football. Luckily for Dan, he landed on his feet without a scratch and Paudeen and Seán Fada, the two strongest men in the place, were being pulled around the haggard by the puck. But they held on to him and when Dan recovered from his sojourn in space, he went to their assistance but by then the puck, now covered in sweat, was winded and they had him under control. They succeeded in putting the rope around both horns and walked the quietened puck over to the carts loaded with the goats.

The next dilemma was how would they tie him to the cart. Paudeen said to tie him to the inside rider so as to keep him walking along the side of the road. Seán Fada said no because if he was tied to the rider, he could easily capsize the cart, goats and all. He suggested that the best place to tie him was to the axle. Dan agreed that it was the most sensible place to tie him and without further ado, Donal took the rope and went on his hands and knees under the cart and tied the rope with a running knot to the axle. They were now all set now for the road and Maggie called out for them to come in for tay, the last to be brewed in the house. While they were having the meal, Tommy arrived for his second load. When asked if he'd like a cup of tay, he said no, that he'd wait until they had finished eating and they he could take the household furniture, including the utensils if they fit.

When the meal was over, Dan decided that they all would help to load Tommy's cart and then they would all leave together – the two horses, the jennet and the ass. He noticed the puck was getting very uneasy, so he exhorted the men to load up as quickly as possible. Dan himself took charge of the birds by tying the cages onto the side of the rail and one onto the back gate, as he had said he would. In quick time the beds were dismantled and loaded and Maggie, for her part, had all the bedclothes folded and packed in old boxes that were once used to take fish. When all was loaded, they found that there was very little room left for the utensils, but they did manage to fit an oven, a kettle and a few saucepans. Just then Dan had a brain wave.

"Wouldn't it be handy if the dresser was laid on top of the rail and it would be one big item out of the way," he suggested.

All agreed it would be worth a chance and immediately Maggie was ordered to take all the delft off the dresser. The dresser was duly taken out and it fit snugly on top of the rail, even though it extended out one foot at each side of it.

Now they were ready for the road and the cortege took off, the horses led followed by the jennet and the ass brought up the rear with the puck in tow. It was a strange sight surely and there were many onlookers along the route. Old Nell Tade was looking out over her half-door and she called out to her husband, "Come out quick 'till you see the menagerie crossing". All was going well – the horses had pulled away, as was to be expected, leaving the jennet and the ass together and the puck, although straining the rope now and again, was obliging enough, that is until they were crossing by Máire Cáit's cottage. Máire Cáit had a black and white fox-terrier that was known to be vicious, and he happened to be stretched out sunning himself in front of the house as the jennet and the ass passed by. It is to be presumed that he smelt the puck, because he raced, barking, down the very short driveway and bit the puck in the heel. The puck went mad and, roaring his own unique roar, he jumped, and pulled and reared up on his hind legs. Still the dog kept up the barking and finally the rope snapped. Then the trouble started – the puck attacked the dog and the dog ran up the little driveway with the puck in hot pursuit and jumped in over the half-door. The puck tried to do the same but only succeeded in getting his front legs up on the half-door. He stuck in his head as far as he could but the horns stopping him going any further.

Poor old Máire Cáit was dozing in the corner when the commotion woke her. When she saw the apparition, as she later called it, with the big horns and the terrible smell, she thought 'twas the 'old boy' and she gave a fierce roar and fell to the floor in a faint. She said afterwards that she was sure she saw fire coming from his eyes! Her husband, Tom, who was out at the back of the house, heard his wife's roar and ran in the back door. When he saw the face and the horns in the doorway he rushed over, presumably to get him out, but never saw his wife on the floor and stumbled across her, hitting his forehead off the wall. By the time he had recovered, Dan, Paudeen and Seán Fada had arrived, having left Donal to take care of the jennet and the ass. They were able to control the puck and lead him away, after apologizing to Tom and explaining to him that his dog was the whole cause of it, which he accepted, still never realizing that poor Maire Cáit was in a faint.

They tied the rope to the axle again, it was a bit shorter but not much, and continued on their journey. The menagerie kept moving and without further incident they arrived at the slate house.

"First things first," said Dan, "we'll have to untie the puck and hold on to him with the rope until we have the goats unloaded for fear he'd gallop away."

This is what they did and when the goats were safely inside in the field, they marched the puck in after them and let him go. Free again, he ran towards the flock and smelled each of them in turn, just to make sure they were his own. In the meantime, all the household stuff, including the birds and cages, was taken into the house and the turf was put in a tidy rick at the east gable end. Without further ado Dan and Donal steered their ass back towards the old homestead, followed by Seán Fada and Paudeen with the Briar's jennet.

Back home Maggie wasn't idle. She had all the spuds bagged and ready, as well as the remainder of the contents of the house packed and outside in the yard so the men quickly loaded the donkey and jennet. Maggie found space for herself in the ass's cart where she could be alone with her thoughts and emotions and 'twas left to Dan to close the door for the last time. This was a chore he'd rather have avoided and the emotion of the move got to him and he broke down. Pulling himself together, he walked towards the ass and, catching the reins and without looking back, he started for his new home, walking beside the cart, and closely followed by Seán Fada and the two boys with the jennet. They were all walking as the rail was packed tight and the hens' coop, with all the hens, ducks and the turkey packed into it, was stretched on top, leaving no room whatsoever for passengers. Without incident on the journey and with very few words, they arrived at the slate house as it was getting dusk.

First things first, they helped Maggie out over the rail and she went straight into the house. Mary Kate Black was there again, and she had a fine fire blazing in the hob. Maggie was delighted because it took the cold, bare look out of the place. Soon they were busy sorting out the beds, deciding which way to turn them – they never before had so much room. Mary Kate gave great advice and assistance in this, and, indeed, in all matters related to setting up their new home. The hens' coop was the biggest item to be taken in, but first they had to decide on how to manage the fowl inside in it. Dan decided that the ass's rail would be unloaded first and then all the fowl transferred to that rail while the coop was been taken into the kitchen and fixed up.

This worked like a dream, the coop fitted snugly under the loft and the fowl were soon installed in their new surroundings. The ducks and the drake were housed in a small outhouse that was attached to the north side of the house, while the hen turkey got her own compartment in the coop. Seán Fada warned

Dan to secure the door well in the duck's house as there were foxes in the locality that would love a duck for breakfast. In a short time most things were fairly shipshape and the kettle was singing on the crane. Mary Kate laid the table, the tay was made and it was a very hungry crew that sat down to their first meal in the slate house. There was a lot more to be done – the birdcages were just thrown up in the loft out of the way for the present and other odds and ends were scattered here and there, but all that could wait until tomorrow.

The Housewarming

Settling in on the first night in their new home, the McGurks burned the midnight oil. For the sheer novelty of it, the twoboys opted to sleep in the loft. They had to take up their beds and dress them themselves, as there was no way Maggie would climb the ladder. They pushed the birdcages aside and after a few arguments about whose bed would go where and who'd sleep in the single bed, they finally settled down for the night. In the meantime, Maggie decided that she'd take all her plates and cups and saucers out of the fish boxes and put them back on their rightful place on the dresser. This she proceeded to do, but to her amazement she couldn't find the dresser.

Dan was sitting half asleep by the fire so she called out to him, "Dan, where is the dresser?"

What dresser?" said Dan, only half waking.

"The dresser! Surely you know the dresser," retorted Maggie.

"Sure it must be there someplace, maybe we forgot to bring it in," Dan said sleepily, "I'll go out."

In a minute or two he was back.

"Well?" said Maggie.

"'Tis outside up against the gable end of the house, that's how we missed it," Dan explained.

"You'll have to bring it in this minute," ordered Maggie, "because I want all the ware up on it for the morning."

"I'll have to call one of the lads so," said Dan.

He immediately went up a few steps of the ladder and shouted at Paudeen to come down quick because the dresser had to be brought in.

Paudeen was not in the best of form when he arrived down.

"Couldn't that auld dresser wait 'till morning," he grumbled.

"'Tis your mother wants it in," explained Dan, "she wants to have all the crockery up on it for the morning."

"Ah, that's her all right," said Paudeen, "come on so and we'll bring it in for quietness sake."

They went out immediately and soon found that the dresser was heavier than they thought, but what with Paudeen's strength and his temper at been called out of his bed, they managed to get it in.

"Where do you want to put it?" asked an impatient Paudeen.

"Maybe it would fit there to the left of the hen's coop," suggested Maggie.

So they pushed and shoved until they got it fitting neatly next to the hen's coop under the protruding floor of the loft. Paudeen immediately scampered up the ladder and in a few minutes he was enjoying his slumber again. Maggie worked happily until the small hours to get her ware back on the dresser. For her it was a labour of love.

Bright and early next morning Dan was up and about, and after he had the fire blazing and the kettle hanging on the crane, he went to the ducks' house to collect the duck-eggs and to leave the door open for the ducks to ramble out. Himself and Paudeen would always have two apiece for the breakfast and the others would have one each. Maggie, after a night of fitful sleep, got out of bed not feeling great. She was wondering what she would have for breakfast when she looked out the window and, to her shock, saw Mary Kate and Seán Fada arriving. It soon transpired that Mary Kate had brought a supply of food with her, just in case, she said, that Maggie couldn't get around to cooking. To Maggie it was like manna in the desert. Soon they were all sitting down to a meal including Seán Fada who had brought porter. Maggie wouldn't have any as she preferred to drink a drop only at night and for it to be mulled. The mulling procedure involved placing a leg of the tongs in the fire until it was red and then sticking it into a mug of porter and leaving it there for a short time. Some liked to add a spoon of sugar and others preferred it without according to their taste.

After a while and a good few mugs of the porter, Seán Fada stood up and said he had an announcement to make.

"It isn't a natural thing," he declared, "that a family should come into a cold damp house that wasn't inhabited for years, as a matter of fact I'd go so far as to say that it is a dangerous thing to do. So to dispel the said cold and damp I declare here and now that we will have a housewarming."

"Here! Here!" shouted Dan in the corner, the heat of the fire and the porter having combined to elate him to the extent that he was ready for anything.

Maggie wasn't as impressed.

"Will you shut up, Dan," she said in a kind of whisper, "don't you know we couldn't afford a housewarming."

She was about to say more but Seán Fada, having overheard her, cut in, "There is no one asking anyone to afford anything. I'm saying we will have a housewarming and the sooner the better before the spring work starts in earnest. As they say, hit the iron while it's red. Isn't that right, Dan?"

"Right you are, you're a sound man, Seán Fada, a man in a million," said Dan in a slurred voice, "we'll have the housewarming, why not, Maggie, do you hear me Maggie? Be getting your dancing shoes ready girl, because we are going to dance. 'Twill be like auld times."

Maggie made no reply, but Dan, although a bit tipsy from the porter, was cute enough to hit her soft spot. He knew that dancing was her passion and that it was the one thing that would get her to agree to the housewarming.

But Seán Fada wasn't in the mood for waiting for agreements.

"We'll hold it on Friday night week," he declared. "That will give ye time to settle in and give me time to round up musicians and dancers and singers and all kind of entertainers. We'll have music to raise the rafters, we'll have dancers throwing their legs in all directions and yourself and Dan will have to join them, Maggie. We'll have singers to sing songs of our patriots, living and dead. We'll have three-hand reels and four-hand reels and eight-hand reels and for good measure we'll have a sixteen-hand reel thrown in. I'm telling you we'll knock sparks off the flags with reels and hornpipes and slip-jigs and I'll guarantee you that by the time the cock crows at day-break, the damp and the cold will be gone and this will be the warmest house in the barony."

There he stopped and sat down just inside the back door, as if he had suddenly run out of words, as if he had just finished a prepared script. There was a deafening silence for a few minutes, then Mary Kate turned to Maggie saying, "That was porter talking. It must be great stuff". The next minute Seán Fada was on his feet again, as if an afterthought struck him, and so it had. Clearing his throat he said, "I forgot to say something and 'tis that this housewarming is, above all, a party to welcome our friends, the McGurks, into our community and we wish them many happy years here". Then he sat down again, and wiped the sweat from his brow with his cap, which made Mary

Kate remark, "I think the house is getting very hot already". Dan then stood up, very unsteady on his feet, and in a very slurred voice said "I" and said no more for a few minutes, but then continued: "My, my, my, self and Mary Ka, I mean Maggie, thank you very much for the porter and the party, and I… I… I want to sa…say some something and I… I don't know what it is."

Maggie was very embarrassed and went over to him and showed her annoyance by saying, "Will you shut up and sit down before you fall down". Dan obliged and as she turned towards Mary Kate, a loud snore from the direction of the back door told Maggie that Seán Fada had fallen under what the women described as the relaxing power of porter. In a short time Dan was in slumber land at the head of the table.

Maggie looked at the two of them and said to Mary Kate, "What will we do with the two babies?" Mary Kate replied, "The same as you would do with any babies – wait until they wake up". After sleeping sound for a half hour or so, the two of them amazingly woke up at the very same time and both men seemed to have a problem realizing where they were.

"Dan, was I saying something?" asked Seán Fada.

"Well, do you know, Seán, 'tis like a dream to me that you were saying something about warming a house," said Dan.

"Oh, you're dead right," said Seán, "'twas about the housewarming. Everything is okay Maggie, everything is in order, prepare your steps, isn't that right Dan?"

"As right as rain," answered Dan, "we'll have a hula-hula."

"What's that, Dan?" asked a perplexed Seán.

"I don't know what 'tis, but whatever it is, that's what we're going to have," said Dan.

"Well, now, that sounds, I dunno how it sounds, but at any rate I'd better make tracks or herself will be on the warpath," said Seán. "Would you have an onion handy Maggie? I must ate an onion so that she won't smell the porter."

Maggie peeled an onion and gave it to him and, munching on it, Seán Fada left for home.

With Seán Fada gone and Dan still groggy, Maggie and Mary Kate had their own chat.

"Do you think that Seán Fada is serious about the housewarming, or will he forget about it when he sobers up?" Maggie asked.

"You can be certain and sure," replied Mary Kate, "that he will not forget about it. He will be thinking and planning and asking this one and that one, day and night, especially anyone who can dance a step, or rasp a fiddle, or sing a song, or do the idiot in any form and, guaranteed, the house will be packed."

"And what in God's name will we be able to give them? We have hardly any money," groaned Maggie.

"Don't worry wan bit about it," advised Mary Kate. "There will be more here in the line of food that would be put out at the biggest wedding, or even the best wake, or even the two of them put together because no wan will come empty-handed and Seán Fada will have them all touched up and they will all by trying to best each other in what they'll bring. The women will be showing off their cooking and throwing spars at each other about their respective cakes and scones and buns. They'll be things like, 'Did you see Nell's cake and the way it sunk in the middle?' Or they'll be saying to each other something like, 'Did you try Mary Bessies' scones?' If the answer is no, she'll be told, 'You're as well off, there wasn't taste nor flavour from them, she must have made them with sour milk.' Or someone might say, 'Did you see the currant cake the Briar's wife brought? She must be up in the loft when she threw the currants at it, and the few that were there sank to the bottom.' And then, for the drink, the men will have a join – that means that each of them will throw a bit of money into the kitty – and Seán Fada and some other one will do the buying. So now, Maggie, stop worrying, and as well as enjoying the dancing, the singing and the music, listen in to the women and you'll learn a lot about your new neighbours, wait and see. But having said that, always remember that it is more or less friendly banter, say a word against any of them and you would see how quickly they'll close ranks."

"Well now, Mary Kate, I must ask you this," said Maggie, "can you tell me why Tom Redden gave us the house on such good terms and then sent the horses to shift our belongings?"

"Well," replied Mary Kate, "I don't know about the house, he probably figured that the house was idle and that this way it would earn him something in kind, as they say. As regards sending the horses, I would put that down to his wife, Rebecca, as she is a very charitable woman and she's known to often push Tom in that direction, not but that Tom is good too in his own right."

By now Dan was beginning to straighten himself and stretch like a cat in the morning. He got up and took a mug from the dresser and went to the white, enamel bucket for a drink of water, but it was empty.

"You'll have to go to the well," said Maggie, "if you want a drink."

Without a word, he picked up the bucket and went out the back door to the well.

"The puff of fresh air will do him good," remarked Maggie, "I didn't see him as drunk for years, I hope he won't be making a habit of it."

"Ah, take no notice of that," urged Mary Kate, "when the housewarming is over it will be back to the grinding stone and there won't be time for drinking porter."

"That's for sure," agreed Maggie, "and what's more, the price of it won't be there either."

Mary Kate soon took her leave, promising to come again to help Maggie prepare for the big night. In the meantime there was little Maggie or Dan could do, only wait, as Maggie said, "in fear and trepidation". But she soon forgot about it, at least for the present when Paudeen came in the back door and announced that one of the goats had given birth to a lovely kid.

"Which wan of them?" asked Dan.

"'Tis the maol," was the answer.

"Is it a he or a she?" asked Maggie.

"It's a she," said Paudeen.

"Oh, great," chuckled Maggie, "she's a great goat. It will be great to have her breed because she used to always have he-goats."

The days rolled on and none of them could settle down to do any work with the worry and the excitement of what was to the McGurk family an unknown event, a housewarming. They wondered what would happen when all these people, who were complete strangers to them, started arriving. The tension was really getting to Maggie and to cool off, she washed the kitchen floor every day and after collecting the eggs, she tidied up the hens' coop several times daily.

At last the big day dawned. All the family were up early – the goats were milked, the ducks were let out for the day and the duck eggs collected. Maggie washed the flags on the kitchen floor again and Dan filled a couple of bags of turf, to be ready to keep the kettle boiling. In case he'd forget it, Donal got strict orders from his father to be sure to put in the ducks early for fear the fox might have a party too. Around three o'clock the two McGurk daughters arrived, all excited about seeing the slate house for the first time and, of course, looking forward to the party. Maggie was by now a nervous wreck and when the cock gave out his unique crow for no apparent reason, she got such a start that she jumped a foot high off the floor, much to the amusement of Dan and the girls.

Shortly afterwards, Seán Fada arrived with the Briar's jennet, loaded down with jars of porter and several different types of mineral drinks. He also had on board an unknown quantity of wine and a certain amount of whiskey, again the amount was top secret. And he had, apparently, already stated that poitín would not be allowed on the night and that the jennet wasn't carrying any of the contraband. Seán's real reason for the ban was that the men would get too drunk too quickly and might spoil the night's entertainment. As a matter of fact, he intended to apply strict control to the giving out of the drink, so that no one would get drunk and make a nuisance of themselves and spoil it for others. Here was a man who would drink more than he should at times, but when the occasion demanded it, he could – and would – discipline himself, and would push that discipline on others if circumstances warranted it. He felt that this particular function did warrant it and he was prepared for it.

At six o'clock Mary Kate arrived, loaded down with two kettles and a big tin can of milk. She told Maggie that Tom Redden was bringing more milk and a supply of butter. Soon the guests started to arrive. Mickeen the Fiddler was one of the first to arrive with the fiddle case under his arm. An excellent musician, he loved house parties and obviously loved his music as he would play until broad daylight in the morning. Máire Cáit arrived with a jew's harp in her fist, mad for the night out, and armed with some goodies to eat as well. The Reddens came, Tom and Rebecca with their son in a pony and trap. The son came to take home the pony and was under orders to come again for his parents at some hour of the night, but not too early though. As Mary Kate had predicted, they brought a big supply of milk and butter and a few cakes, as well as a jar of porter for Tom. Jimeen the Man and Small Peter came together. Small Peter sported a long wooden side flute that he always claimed he made himself. No one knew whether or not he had and it didn't matter, because he could play the finest jigs reels and hornpipes as well as slow airs that would rise the cockles of your heart.

Mickeen the Man had a concertina under his oxter. A shy man, he stayed near the door until Small Peter commenced playing a rousing reel, and then he nervously moved up alongside him, sat down and took the concertina from inside his coat and joined in the reel. But if he did, Máire Cáit planked herself down between the two of them, pulled out her jew's harp and joined in the music. Just then, as if it was timed, Paddy Joe Mike came in the door with a bodhrán which he really had made himself from a goat's skin. He gave it a few rattles just inside the door, as if to announce his arrival, and he kept hammering it as he walked up through the kitchen to where the three were playing. Heating it at the fire so that it would have the proper sound, he then moved over near the musicians, and with expert timing joined them and the hooley was on.

In the meantime, Dan and Maggie were welcoming the people, with Seán Fada and Mary Kate doing the introductions. The women were all dressed up in their colourful homespuns while some of the older men were in their Sunday bawneens. As soon as all the guests had arrived, Dan, who was delighted with the music, moved over near the players. The musicians moved from reels to jigs and then to hornpipes and when they did, Dan could stick it no longer. He hopped out on the floor and, picking a nice clean flag, he gave a beautiful exhibition of a hornpipe. The crowd cheered spontaneously and for whatever reason, the cock in the coop crowed, some said he was just cheering his master. As the applause died down, Mickie Mike Jer arrived with a melodeon in a bag across his shoulder. A popular character, he was applauded as he made his way across the floor to join the musicians. Taking out the melodeon, he folded the bag, placed it on the form and sat down on it. Just then Máire Cáit put the jew's harp to her lips and gave out some kind of a sound that was anything but musical.

At that exact moment, the band started playing a reel in perfect unison and partners were on the floor in a shot, the men knocking sparks off the flags with their boots and the girls dancing at arms length, afraid that their toes might be pounded into pulp by the big, nailed boots if they dared move too close. It was a well-known fact that many a girl got a lasting *máchail*, that not only finished her dancing career but also her marriage prospects, by dancing too close to a fellow with size eleven or twelve nailed boots. Still, it was a risk most girls were prepared to take and they became adept at keeping their dancing partners at a safe distance. When the reel was over someone suggested that Tom Redden sing 'Boulavogue', his favourite party piece. Happy to oblige, Tom stood up and in his lovely tenor voice started to sing.

> *At Boulavogue as the sun was setting,*
> *O'er the bright May meadows of Shelmalier,*
> *A rebel hand set the heather blazing*
> *And brought the neighbours from far and near.*
> *Then Father Murphy, from old Kilcormack,*
> *Spurred up the rocks with a warning cry,*
> *"Arm! Arm!" he cried, "for I've come to lead you,*
> *For Ireland's freedom we fight or die.*

Just then Mickeen Muldoon rushed in, shouting, "Stop the singing! Stop the singing and stay quiet for the present. There are two peelers on patrol at the end of the boreen and if they hear ye singing rebel songs they will come up for sure and we will all be in trouble". With Fenian blood coursing through his veins – his forebears for generations back were involved in the fight for freedom and one of them paid the supreme penalty – to be asked to stop singing a rebel song just because two peelers were parading the road was to Tom Redden like a red rag to a bull and he went berserk.

"Who are they to tell us what we should or shouldn't sing," he shouted. "Let them come," up he continued, "and we'll give them a reception they will never forget."

"Here! Here!" responded the men around him. "Let them come and we'll take them on."

When some men suggested going down to attack them, Seán Fada counseled caution.

"If we do anything to antagonize them fellows now, Dan McGurk will be the sufferer and that's one thing we don't want to happen, sure it isn't?" he said.

An emphatic "No" was the response from all present.

"That's better," said Seán Fada and, moving over to Paddy the Lad, he asked him to go down to the road and discreetly check if the peelers were still around.

The Lad obliged and when he was gone Seán said, "The Lad will handle them boyos all right. He'll cajole them with plenty of lies and yarns the likes of which they never heard before".

"And that's for sure," said the Briar.

The incident could have turned very nasty only for the way Seán Fada handled it because, at that time, the peelers of the Royal Irish Constabulary were a hated force, and indeed many of the young, and not so young, men at the housewarming were drilling several nights each week, imbued with an intense desire to play their part in freeing their country from foreign rule. When calm was returned, someone shouted, "Come on, Redden, finish your song!" Tom responded immediately and it was plain to see that he was still smarting from the perceived insult of been told to stop singing his rebel song. The musicians commenced playing again and, on the spot, a young fellow in his twenties nicknamed Timmy the Duck, whose father was known as Danno the Drake, went down on his grug on the floor and gave an exhibition of the monkey dance to the acclaim of the audience.

There was a call from the crowd for Dan and Maggie to give a dancing exhibition and Dan, in fine form after a few drinks, hopped out on the floor and said, "Come on, Mag, we'll do a slip jig". Maggie changed her shoes and the band struck up a jig and the pair started and the crowd moved back in a half circle. They danced for at least fifteen minutes at a hectic pace like true professionals and the onlookers, stunned into silence by their elegance, were amazed at their stamina and grace. When they finished Dan hugged Maggie and kissed her to tumultuous applause. There were shouts of "More" from the crowd, but Maggie said she would have to get her wind back. Seán Fada called for a four-hand reel and immediately there was a rush for partners.

Paddy Joe Mike gave a few tips to the bodhrán and the musicians played Miss McLeod's reel followed as usual by the sets and hornpipe. The girls danced again with arms outstretched in order to keep the nailed boots off their toes and the boys knocked such sparks off the flag floor that some wag remarked that "you could light your pipe from them". In the meantime, Mary Kate, helped by a number of women, was serving tea in one of the bedrooms. As she predicted, there was plenty of food, including currant loaves, buns, scones and pies as well as plain bread. There was also plenty of homemade butter and home-produced blackberry jam, rhubarb jam and apple jam. As all the food was homemade, the usual comments were made by the women to the amusement of Maggie, who listened to the banter as Mary Kate had told her. Paddy the Lad returned and reported that there was no peeler to be seen, he assumed they must have returned to barracks. That news eased a certain amount of tension which Seán Fada and a few others felt. As master of ceremonies, Seán Fada was kept busy giving out the drink, making sure that everyone was well treated, especially the musicians.

The night moved on and the entertainment consisted of recitations, songs and non-stop music. Dan and Maggie were called upon several times to dance, and the more they danced the more they enjoyed themselves. Maggie's earlier inhibitions about the housewarming were dispelled. She now felt she was among friends and let herself go. For the McGurks it was a night they would always remember fondly. And there was also some romance in the air among the younger generation, but it was nipped in the bud! Big Peg McFadden spotted her daughter, Sally, making for the door with her shawl neatly folded under her arm, closely followed by Mick Seán's son, Micko. But they didn't get far as

Peg pounced like a cat on a mouse and threw poor Micko out of her way. In a vice-like grip with her big agricultural hands, she caught her daughter by the neck and shouted, "Where do you think you are going, me lady?" The poor girl was mortified and while Big Peg was giving her daughter a dressing down, Micko ducked out the door and ran all the way home across the fields. Paddy the Lad remarked, "He'll have nightmares tonight".

At about three o'clock in the morning most of the revellers started to leave until only the musicians, Tom and Rebecca Redden Seán Fada and Mary Kate were left. Maggie and Mary Kate made tea for the remaining guests after which the musicians went home, having been suitably thanked by Dan and Maggie. The Reddens had to wait for their son to collect them and they also offered to give Mary Kate a lift home as they passed her house. Seán Fada planned to go home across the fields. In the meantime Rebecca Redden was chatting with the two McGurk girls, asking them were they working and when they told her they were working for a farmer, milking cows and feeding calves and looking after poultry, she called her husband and told him about the girls. Tom was very interested in them and asked how long were they hired for. They said they had employment until Christmas.

"Well," said Tom, "two of my girls are leaving at Christmas and the job is yours if you care to take it."

The McGurk girls were overjoyed and said, "Oh, thanks, Mr Redden. We'll take it of course, we'd love to be near home". Dan and Maggie were also delighted. They were a close-knit family and they couldn't believe their luck to have their daughters near them.

Tom Óg didn't arrive with the pony and trap for the Reddens until five o'clock in the morning. He explained that he was held up as the sow they had put into the back kitchen had started to farrow and he had to stay with her.

"Had she a big litter?" asked Tom.

"She had, she had seventeen," answered Tom Óg.

"Seventeen," said Tom as if amazed. "We'll have a couple of pets so. She never has that many teats."

Tom and Rebecca left immediately, taking Mary Kate with them, after having been thanked by Dan and Maggie for all their kindness. Seán Fada was the last to leave, after Dan thanked him for all he had done for them, the getting of the house and now the housewarming. Seán replied, "You're very welcome. Don't mention it, it cost me nothing". And then he added, "Now

Dan, the honeymoon is over. From today on it is back to reality but we will do the best we can for you always".

"I know that," said Dan with a sincere handshake.

Settling In

On the second morning after the housewarming, the McGurk family were up and about early. As Seán Fada had said, the honeymoon was over and the serious business of living had to carry on. Dan was out checking the goats and found that one of them had given birth to a lovely kid during the night. The new arrival was already frisking around in a playful mood, brimful of health. Coming in after his stroll, Dan had his breakfast, which consisted of the leftovers from the party. His appetite wasn't great, as the effects of the celebrations were still taking their toll. Dan was not a man used to staying idle, so he said to Maggie that he was thinking of turning a bit of ground and setting a handful of sceallans.

"That's not a bad idea," said Maggie, "and as soon you start turning bawn I'll start cutting the seed."

"Right-o," said Dan, "I'll start this minute, it might help clear my head."

He went out the back door and got his spade from inside the ducks' house. After sharpening it to the best of his ability with a coarse stone, he put it over his shoulder and proceeded to the very top corner of the plot of ground where there was an angle patch. Here he commenced turning bawn in preparation for setting the spuds. In the meantime Maggie went out to the pit and brought in a butt of spuds and commenced cutting the seed. Cutting seed That's because shewas usually done by women - for some reason they seemed to be more adept at it than men. It was a very responsible job, because if it wasn't properly done it could result in a lot of failures, thereby diminishing the return from the crop, and the whole year's work could be in vain.

Maggie sat on a big chair near the dresser with a bag apron around her. She commenced cutting the spuds for seed and filling a sack with the sceallans, which was another name for the cut seed. She was happy in her work, smiling to herself at times when the events of the housewarming crossed her mind. She felt she was making great progress and so she was, as she was an expert in the field of seed cutting. Suddenly there was knock on the door and Maggie called out, "Come in". The door opened and in walked the Briar. Taken aback by what Maggie was doing, he didn't say God bless, hello or how are you, only "Can you cut seed?"

"Don't you see me cutting them?" retorted Maggie.

"I see you all right," said the Briar, "but I saw a woman cutting them for myself last year and I had an amount of failures."

"That's because she didn't know her job," said Maggie.

"I know that too, but look at what it cost me to find out," grumbled the Briar.

Maggie put her hand into the bag, took out a spud and lifted it up between her thumb and forefinger and said to the Briar, "Do you see that spud?"

"I do," he said, "what about it?"

"The thing about it is, that I can make four seeds from that one spud and I never have a failure," Maggie said proudly.

"Says you!" muttered the Briar.

"Says me, then," said Maggie, oozing confidence and she thereupon cut the spud in four parts, not all of equal size.

Handing them to the Briar she said, "Examine those and you will see that each one of them has a strong eye so you can be sure each one of them will throw up a stalk, and a strong stalk at that". The Briar looked at them closely and said, "I have to admit that I think you're right".

The Briar then changed the subject.

"Where's Dan?" he asked.

"Turning bawn," answered Maggie.

"For who?" asked the Briar.

"For himself of course, do you want him?" said Maggie.

"Ah well, yes and no," answered the Briar, to which Maggie enquired, "Which of them is it?"

"Well, I suppose I can ask you," said the Briar, "I have a goat, could I bring her down to the puck?"

"You can of course," replied Maggie warmly, "when do you want to bring her?"

"Oh, that will be up to the goat," answered the Briar and he continued, "by the way, is there any chance that you'd cut the seed for me? I'll give you two shillings for the day."

After a moment's thought Maggie said, "I will, no problem and no failures either. When do want them cut?" The Briar said he'd let her know, bid her good day and left.

A short time later she stopped cutting, threw off the bag apron, and started to prepare the dinner by putting spuds into the pot and hanging it on the crane to boil. Gathering up more of the leftovers from the big night, she wasn't long preparing the meal and when she had it ready, she stood outside the back door to call Dan by putting two fingers to her mouth and squeezing her lips around them. She gave a whistle that would wake the dead. Dan responded with a whistle of the same intensity and shortly arrived for dinner. Still kind of crawsick after the mighty craic of two nights before, he looked at his dinner plate and then looked at Maggie and said, "Half that would do me. A drop of the bottle would be a better healer". In fairness to Maggie she took the cue and, rummaging in the press under the dresser, she returned to the table with a cup which, to Dan's delight, contained a respectable drop of the cratur. Downing it with relish he asked Maggie how she managed to have that drop of poitín in the house without his knowing it. Maggie gave a look at him with laughing eyes and retorted, "That's why 'twas there, because you didn't know about it". Somehow, it seemed to give Dan an appetite and he turned his attention to the dinner and soon had the plate empty.

As Maggie was pouring a cup of tay, Dan remarked that he'd had a visit from Tom Redden.

"Oh my goodness, is there something wrong?" Maggie asked in a worried tone.

"Not at all," replied Dan, "he was in great form. You'd never guess what he wanted."

"How would I know what he wanted," said Maggie, "maybe he wants to cut seed."

"Guess again," laughed Dan. "Maybe he wants the girls to come working to him sooner," she said.

"No, there wasn't a mention of the girls, 'tis something he wants to give us," said Dan.

"Give us!" exclaimed Maggie, "what would he want to give us now, hasn't he given us a lot already?"

"He has, but guess again anyway," taunted Dan.

Rather angrily Maggie exclaimed, "Will you stop the messing and tell me what he is giving us".

"Two pet banbhs," said Dan.

"Two banbhs," repeated Maggie.

"That's right, two pet banbhs. Will you take them?" asked Dan.

"Will I take them?" she asked in surprise.

"'Tis you that will have to mind them," Dan answered.

"I'll mind them," said Maggie emphatically, "I often minded pet banbhs before. I minded them for the very first farmer I worked for and for several farmers afterwards during my years in service."

Scratching his head, Dan wondered out loud where they would put them. "Where will we put them, only where pet banbhs were always put, inside in a box near the fire in the kitchen – the heat is great for them," Maggie replied confidently.

"What will we feed them with though?" asked Dan.

"Plenty of goats' milk for a start," replied Maggie, "I'll put a nipple on a bottle, or maybe on two bottles, for fear they fight over the one bottle, even little banbhs can be jealous you know," she chuckled.

"Well, I can't believe it – you have it all sorted out in a few minutes," said Dan, "will I tell him to bring them on so? He'll be calling to me again on his way home."

"Do, of course," Maggie said enthusiastically, "we never before had a pig of our own so this is our chance."

And so it transpired that later that evening Tom Óg Redden arrived at the slate house in a horse and cart carrying a square wooden box covered with a sack. Dan and himself lifted the box out of the cart and took it into the kitchen. When the sacking was stripped off, Maggie and Dan stood enthralled, looking at the two pets. Maggie was the first to speak.

"Well, thank you and thank you again. They're two beauties! And the blessing of God on ye all and on all yer pigs and banbhs and everything ye have and that all yer sows will always have big litters," she said.

Taking up one of the pets, she cradled it in her arms and stroked its head. Then she upbraided Dan saying, "Wouldn't you take up the other little cratur and rub him. Anyhow Tom Óg will want his box".

"I'm not taking the box at all, ye can keep it," said Tom Óg.

"Oh, the blessing of God again on you," prayed Maggie, "that's another problem solved. That box will do them until they are ready to go out."

"Out where?" asked Dan.

"Well now, that's another day's work, you'll have to build a bothán for them," warned Maggie.

"That's more than a day's work, but we'll cross that bridge when we come to it," replied Dan.

"That bridge isn't very far away so you'd better be looking out for bits and pieces to build it," counseled Maggie.

Tom Óg came to the rescue to calm their fears and anxieties. "Yerra, don't be worrying about that now, we have plenty of straw over in a rick so you can have all you want of it to thatch it and wouldn't five or six horse loads of stones from the Stoaner Kelly's quarry up the road build a nice sized cabin," he said.

"True for you," said Dan, "as I said, we'll manage that too when the time comes."

Tom Óg soon took his leave and shortly had his horse in a lively trot on the road home. Needless to say there was no more seed cut or bawn turned for the remainder of that evening, as the pair continued to fuss over the two pets. Maggie ordered Dan to milk the goats immediately and shouted after him to bring in the milk while it was hot as the banbhs would do better on hot milk than cold. Dan obliged and so began Maggie's feeding ritual with her two bottles fitted with nipples. Her system certainly worked as the two pets thrived and in a few weeks the box was getting too small for them. In the meantime, several of their new neighbours called to see the pets, including Mary Kate and the Briar. Paddy the Lad and Seán Fada arrived one evening and they drew down Dan's big problem - a little bothán to fatten the pigs. Seán Fada was very forthcoming and drew a plan in the ashes on the hearth with the handle of the kitchen brush. He detailed the size and shape it should take and, pushing the fire aside, he even mapped out a nice little square yard in front of it where they could exercise. A discussion ensued and continued for the most of an hour until Maggie said, "If ye don't put back the fire ye'll get no tay".

So engrossed were they in their discussion that none of them seemed to hear her, or if they did they just ignored her. Anyway, who could be bothered with tay with the planning of the construction of a big project, like a bothán, swirling in their minds. Seán Fada declared that it would be better to make the bothán bigger rather than smaller as, who knew, but they might have four banbhs by next year. Soon the decision was made to build a twelve foot square in an inney shape up against the eastern gable end of the slate house where it would be possible to get good height into the bothán, and height was very important for air space according to Seán Fada. The next problem was material. Dan said that he noticed an old clochán of stones like the remains of an old house above where he was turning bawn. Even though it was getting dusk they decided to go and have a look. Sure enough, there seemed to be a quantity of stone there all right, and when Dan gave the place a fuller investigation the next day and cleared the overgrowth of briars and bushes, he was satisfied that he would get enough stones to build the narrow walls as suggested by Seán Fada. The plan was to then support them on the outside with a sod wall and this, with a thatched roof of straw, would make it a very warm little piggery indeed and heat was vital for the fattening pig.

The next day Dan organised Paudeen and Donal and put them digging out the stones while he himself commenced drawing them down with his donkey. By eight o'clock that evening he had a lot of stones brought down and felt that another day would give him an ample supply. As he was about to stop drawing, Seán Fada called in to see how things were going and was surprised at the amount of stone Dan had procured. Furthermore, they were all nice building stones and were obviously from a demolished house.

"So much the better," said Seán Fada, "it will make our job easier."

He had already indicated to Dan that he would give him a hand building the bothán. Seán suggested that they would start the following day and put in the foundations and have one of the boys continue drawing the stones. Thus commenced the construction of the bothán and within a week of long hours they had it built and thatched with golden straw from Tom Redden's rick. It was completed with a lovely floor of flags from the Stoner Kelly's quarry and a door in two parts so that the top part could be opened in warm weather. Then it was finally ready for the pets.

However, Maggie decreed that the pets weren't ready for it – yet. But before a week was out she changed her mind, or at least the pets changed it for her. They started jumping out over the side of the box and soon were upsetting the cock and the hens and the turkey in the coop. The cock voiced his disapproval with an ear-splitting crowing every time they went grunting near the coop, and the turkey stuck her long neck out through the lathes of her section and did her best to peck them whenever they came near. Maggie had a full-time job trying to keep the pigs in their box, even covering it with an old sack, but all to no avail, as their little razor-sharp teeth could rip it open in minutes. They had got the taste of freedom and they wanted more of it. So the only solution was to put a big bed of straw in the bothán and shift them out there. Once ensconced in their new home, their frolicsome antics were a sight to behold. Soon again peace reigned supreme in the poultry kingdom of the kitchen.

Being so well taken care of by Dan and Maggie, the pigs continued to thrive and in six months they were two fine hefty specimen. Several of the neighbours would call from time to time to look at them and compare their progress with their own pigs – a custom that was usual at the time. Paddy the Lad would call now and again, as would the Briar and Seán Fada. Tom Redden called a few times and was delighted with their progress and the great care the animals were receiving from Dan and Maggie. This was a great omen for the McGurks and if Redden had pets to give away again, they would probably get first choice because at the time the criteria used by farmers giving pets away was that they would be well treated.

One day Seán Fada arrived, and himself, Dan and Maggie went to inspect the pigs to see if they were ready for the market.

"What weight do you think they are?" asked Dan.

Seán, in deep concentration, was feeling their backs with his thumb and exerting fair pressure in the process. Eventually he answered: "They are as solid as iron. They must be two and a quarter hundredweight."

They were still discussing weight when the Lad looked in over the half-door.

"Come in," said Seán, "I have given my verdict, now, what weight would you call them?"

The Lad walked around the pigs, then thumbed their backs and looked at them back and front again, before finally saying: "I'd call them well over two hundredweight, they're as hard as rocks. What did you call them?"

"I was saying two and a quarter," said Seán, "they are two fine pigs."

Always a man to throw a spanner in the works, the Lad then turned to Dan and said, "What a fine tub of bacon would be in one of them. I suppose ye'll kill one for yourselves?"

"I suppose we will," said Dan, "twould be a first for us to have a pig in the tub."

"What?" shouted Maggie in a roar that frightened even the two pigs, "what are ye saying about killing my pets? I'm surprised at you, Dan."

"Yerra, calm down, Maggie," advised Dan. "Sure there would be nothing wrong with wan of them in the tub."

Maggie was livid.

"I'll tell you one thing, Dan, if you want to kill one of them poor craturs, you'll will have to kill me first," she said.

Then she turned on the Lad.

"What brought you here today trying to put bad thoughts into Dan's head? What do you think we are, cannibals, is it, that we'd ate our little pets? 'Tis no wonder you're called 'the Lad'."

That outburst didn't knock a feather out of the Lad, he was well used to abuse for all his pranks. The tension eased and in a short time, Maggie, realizing that the Lad was just having her on, went over to him and said she was sorry.

"Apology accepted," he replied jocosely.

She then said she was gong in to put the kettle on and told himself and Seán to be sure to come in for tay.

"Right," said the Lad, "we'll be in after you."

Ever the joker, he shouted after her, "Can we kill one of them now so!" She just looked around and, with a smile, proceeded in home.

A few days later Seán Fada helped Dan load the two pigs on to the Briar's jennet and accompanied him to the market where they sold the pigs for eight pounds and nine shillings for the pair. Dan was so delighted with the good price that Seán Fada talked him into buying two banbhs for twenty-five shillings. He said it was important to "keep the seed" and the new purchases would help Maggie to forget the pets and start anew. And so it did, as they were a complete surprise to her. Remarking that she had felt the place very quiet since her pets were gone, she quickly prepared mess for the newcomers. She was back in business!

"God bless Tom Redden who started us off," she said.

Soon Dan had the spuds sat along with a hundred of cabbage plants. The goats were kidding, the hens were laying and the eggs paying for the groceries. Dan and the two boys got the odd day's work locally and, even though they had some moments of nostalgia about the fishing, the family felt they had really settled in.

Postscript

During that time when Ireland was under foreign rule, most of the Great Houses were built, some of which still stand today. It has also to be remembered that by that era, many of our churches and monasteries had been sacked and destroyed. Bishops and priests were forced into hiding, and many of them were arrested and executed. Yet, young men still studied for the priesthood with many studying in European seminaries. Returning incognito to Ireland after ordination and taking a cover job as a disguise, they took up duty in various parishes. But, the informer, accepting 'blood money', made the identity of some of them known to the authorities. This resulted in many of them, some only in their mid- to late twenties, being executed.

Yet, generation after generation, the people seemed to have responded well to the constraints they were under and held on to as much of their culture as they could, including their religion, their dance and their music, although throughout most of the country, their language was lost.

But their will to fight for their freedom was never broken, never lost. As a result, the cream of Ireland's fighting men died in combat. But over all the years of conflict, there were others to take their place until, finally, the breakthrough came and Ireland was a nation once again.

Unfortunately, freedom didn't signal immediate prosperity for the hard-pressed farming community or indeed the nation as a whole. On the contrary, the unbelievable happened and a bloody civil war broke out, where brother fought brother and former fighting colleagues, who had fought the invader together, now found themselves on opposing sides. This resulted in more executions, this time of Irishmen by Irishmen. As if this wasn't enough for the hard-pressed people to bear, there followed a disastrous economic war which slowed the process of recovery for many years.

But hopes were high for better times ahead and, in time, albeit a long time, the better days arrived. Long may they last!